THE UNFORGOTTEN

Also by Patrice Chaplin

HARRIET HUNTER
HAVING IT AWAY
THE SIESTA
FROM THE BALCONY (*a play*)

The Unforgotten

Patrice Chaplin

Harmony Books/New York

We hereby acknowledge the use of
excerpts from "The Four Quartets" by T. S. Eliot

Published by Harmony Books, a division of Crown Publishers, Inc.,
One Park Avenue, New York, New York 10016 and simultaneously in
Canada by General Publishing Company Limited

HARMONY and colophon are trademarks of Crown Publishers, Inc.

Manufactured in the United States of America

Library of Congress Cataloging on Publication Data

Chaplin, Patrice.
The unforgotten.

I. Title.
PR6053.H348U5   1984   823'.914   83-26489
ISBN 0-517-55284-1

10   9   8   7   6   5   4   3   2   1

First Edition

THE UNFORGOTTEN

CHAPTER · 1

THE LONG ROPE SWING HUNG FROM THE BIRCH TREE AT THE end of the garden. Swinging high, free, Victoria could see across the meadow as far as the Oxford colleges. The glorious day brought out the roses, so many of them—she hadn't expected there would be so many. Yet oddly, the air was full of the smell of the little, sharp wild flowers from the meadow. Perhaps because the rose garden had not yet come into its own.

Swinging accentuated her happiness as she watched Gerry. He was forty-seven but seemed so much younger. He loved youth and the fact, she, Victoria, was twenty-two, pleased him. His grandchild stayed close, holding his leg as he cut thornless dog roses and made a garland for her hair. By the barn, his son James and daughter-in-law Lilly, just arrived from America, held hands beneath fruit trees loaded with blossom. The sunlight made every nondescript thing important. Even the trash cans had glamour. Gerry looked at Victoria briefly and smiled, a little private smile—he was remembering the night.

Victoria whizzed through the scented air and could just see the porch of the rundown church in the village. Last night Gerry had said, "You make me feel . . ."

"What?"

"Something I thought I'd lost for good. Happiness."

The weekend before, Gerry and Victoria had stayed two days in Palermos, in northern Spain, on their way back from

Barcelona. Holiday trade was so bad the waiters stayed in the doorway till all hours, flicking napkins aggressively. If a sun-dulled tourist was unwise enough to hesitate by the menu board, they crept up, napkins swinging.

"Sangria, the best on the coast." The doubtful diner would be swatted into the dark, empty interior.

Palermos was an odd, defeated place, but they enjoyed it. Sufficient in themselves, they could be happy anywhere. They ate in a restaurant *típico* away from the tourist traps. The food was plentiful and fresh, the salad the best she'd ever had. Huge firm tomatoes, crisp lettuce, fresh asparagus, olives, garlic, covered in heavy olive oil. Afterward they went back to the beach and lay on the bleached, apple-crumble sand. The Spanish sat out of danger in the shade of the wall. Only foreigners took the "bad sun" of the early afternoon.

Now, how she wanted him. She thought about the way he took off her clothes, biting her neck, her breasts. The more she got, the more she wanted. She longed—no, ached for him. Some days she thought about nothing else.

Swinging high above the trees, she watched as Gerry encouraged his granddaughter to feel the petals of a splendid yellow rose. Then he showed her the simple white ones by the fence.

"Dog rose." Little Ruth said it distinctly, and Gerry was pleased. The child loved the syllables and went on enjoying the words.

Gerry took hold of people in a sensuous, giving way. It was his pleasure touching them that was so compelling. Victoria was pleased for him and them. Happiness made her generous.

When the swing reached its highest point, she could hear music. She thought it was coming from the church. Because Gerry was mature, grown-up, he knew about constancy.

He'd protect their happiness as he would her. The music was louder. Did the church have a piano? That was new.

From the swing she could see the entire garden. It was always such a happy garden, even in winter. It was during the cold weather she'd first known he loved her. Now she could feel his love in the rhythm of the swing. But the swing was never used. Whose was it? It couldn't be the grand-child's. She'd never thought about it before. James's swing? It was too elegant for a schoolboy. Suddenly she knew with a funny kind of certainty that it had been made for the first wife. It had about it, a sort of delight.

And that took all the brightness out of the day.

As the swing slowed she could no longer hear music. The wife had been dark and voluptuous and worn a scarlet dress. Roses played their part. She used to be given a pink bud before each concert. Who had told Victoria that? Certainly he had not told her. New buds belonged to that fresh unspoiled time, the best of Gerry's life. Victoria knew about the glorious success, the pianist's, then Gerry's, and some-where among it the disease that shriveled her body. Some-how he'd got through the stunned vacuum of her dying.

Victoria got off the swing and trailed toward the house. She thought it must have been her sister Mary who'd told her about the first wife. She'd never thought much about it. She'd been too happy.

The tenderness as Gerry bent to share the child's crows of pretty astonishment made Victoria thoughtful. She'd never touched one of her family except in a national emergency.

*   *   *

At midday, the family gathered for a drink and she would have spoken as she normally did, about her friends, her journalism, her greedy mother, but there was no place for her. The conversation was academic and critical; she felt excluded. What did she talk about usually? Suddenly she couldn't remember. It used to please Gerry. He said she was young. No, new! She had a childlike delight. She was the one to share good things with. With her, he'd become himself again, a new self, ready for fun. "You're so free, Victoria. Carefree. You always have a lovely time."

Midday. That was when the black feeling began, an edge framing her thoughts, unmistakable as a migraine headache. Everyone else was having a good time. Was it because she saw Gerry loving the others? Or because he seemed to forget her? She felt the others ignored her although they spoke from time to time.

You must be looking forward to it. You must be so happy. They meant the wedding.

During their last day in Palermos, the weather had changed. Between one minute and the next, the sky blackened, the beach became menacing, depressing. Sunbathers covered themselves with towels and stood up as though frightened. The boats came in all together, swiftly. A sun umbrella was upturned in the violent wind that raced from one end of the beach to the other. Just one gust. A warning. They ran without dressing toward the hotel. The street was empty and cold.

"You get very dramatic weather in this area," Gerry said.

* * *

Blackness, sudden cold. It was here in the garden yet it wasn't climatic, this time.

The family made some attempt to include her at lunch.

"Gerry says you write rather well. Didn't you once model?"

"I've done rather a lot of things." All of a sudden, she felt ashamed of that as though the difficulty of her early life diminished her. The others were all too successful for her. James, a recent Rhodes Scholar, seemed to excel at everything, even marriage. Lilly looked sexually satiated to the point of indolence. She had creamy skin, faultless hormones.

Her dark, fine hair frothed to her shoulders.

"You used to have a white rose by the wall," said Lilly. She wore a silk dress, with nothing underneath. Gerry had mentioned teaching her at UCLA, the university in California. Lilly had known James since they were children. But there were a lot of gaps in the relationship Gerry hadn't bothered to fill in.

"Yes, you did. Small greenish-white petals. Oh, years ago."

"The Chinese climber, you mean?" Gerry's voice was unexpectedly curt.

"It was so beautiful, Gerry. One day it was there. Then it wasn't there." Her large, bright eyes filled with tears. It was the first soft thing Victoria had seen her do.

"The frost got it," said Gerry, suddenly.

"Come on. It was summer."

"Then you muddled it up with something else."

Was the following silence a trifle tense? Victoria saw James take notice. He tried to catch his wife's eye. It wouldn't be caught.

"It was when I first came here to Crowsley, to play. Just before—just—"

Gerry cleared his throat and turned to his son. "Your mother was particularly fond of tea roses. I don't suppose you remember." His hands shook slightly. "I never had any luck with them. Hybrid teas are much easier."

"They've a good constitution," said James, feeding him safe lines quickly.

But Lilly clung to the lost white climbing rose and wanted answers. "It had such an unforgettable fragrance. How could it just die off?"

James kicked her under the table and the knives and forks rattled. Lilly tried to keep the effect of the kick out of her face.

"Why don't you just plant another one, Gerry?" Victoria

suggested mildly. She could see the tension had nothing to do with roses.

"Oh, they're rare," said Gerry smoothly. "You don't see many around."

His voice was soft and distinct. Was everything about him unique because she loved him? There was no affectation, not even any American influence, in spite of the years he'd spent there. It was classless and seductive.

"Hybrid teas are so common," said Lilly. "You ought to see the roses we grow."

Gerry gave his son the first portion of veal. "I didn't know you grew roses. You never liked them."

"Lilly means her father. It's his house and his roses we're talking about."

"In Boston?"

James hesitated. "Atlantic City."

"I didn't know you went there," said Gerry.

Victoria was too quiet. She should join in. "You must be tired," she said, eventually, to Lilly.

"Tired? Why?" Lilly acted as if she were suggesting there was something wrong with her.

"Jet lag."

Lilly refused to admit it existed. She seemed to think unhealthy conditions would put her at a disadvantage. Victoria could see Lilly made it her daily business never to be at a disadvantage. There was something wrong about her. Everything was so expensive. Victoria's sister Mary, who knew about these things, would call it insecurity.

After the veal, the talk turned to Charles Dickens's influence on Henry James. Victoria managed one round of that conversation, then the seas of scholarship closed over her.

* * *

The first time Victoria saw Gerry, he was standing with a rangy brunette in the lobby of a West End movie theater. It was a charity event, an invitation-only Francis Ford Coppola retrospective with speeches by movie-world celebrities. The proceeds would help fund a new film school. Victoria, temporary critic for her local Surrey newspaper, had not been invited. Her sister Mary had used influence to get the ticket. The first film was *The Godfather, Part One.* The atmosphere in the lobby was tough and intimidating. Then she saw him, standing by the Royal Circle banister. He had streaked hair and powerful, farseeing eyes. He looked distinguished, unapproachable. She stalked through the privileged crowd and joined him on the carpeted stairs. Was he an actor? A movie star? She tried to place him. The brunette tried to place her. Victoria could only stare. She longed for him to turn full face, to smile, to reveal himself. She wanted to hear him speak. He stood his ground as self-contained as a cat, saying nothing. When at last he turned toward her he was almost familiar. She felt she knew him. Provoked by her girlish interest, he looked at her. So did the woman.

During the intervening months before she saw him again, she'd looked at passing faces in the street, faces in newspapers, in restaurants, on trains. The excitement had not left her. She'd held on to the longing. The moments spent almost in his company had created an effect as solid as that of an actual affair.

Surprisingly, there were no resemblances. The streaked hair and air of distinction that pinpointed him in public places, the strongly colored compelling eyes, were not duplicated.

She wasn't looking for anything the morning she went into the Oxford coffee shop. Still temporary critic of her local newspaper, she'd gone to Oxford to cover the film festival. Her application for a permanent position on a London magazine had been turned down. Her mother was insisting she accompany her to some royal entertainment. Her first lover, Alexander Galsworthy, had married again. This was not one of her better days.

She joined the self-service line for black coffee, her hair disheveled. He was in another line quietly buying coffee beans. He turned toward her. Things had shrunk in his face. Ordinariness had found a place. How memory had let her down! His hair was shorter, duller. How she'd anticipated the moment of coming together. But if he saw her, she meant nothing to him. He was about to pass. Her arm lifted unquestioningly and touched him.

"Hello," said her mouth, following rules of its own. "You're the man in the movie theater."

He didn't disagree. At least the eyes were the same.

"I wondered if I'd see you again."

He was looking at her kindly, but his voice was cool as he asked, "Do you live in Oxford then?" No shock of recognition.

"I'm writing about the festival."

"Oh yes," as though she'd already told him her job.

"You don't approve of it?"

"I suppose the boat race is worse."

A dangerous pause. He might go. They both spoke at once.

"You should go to Magdalen College," he said. His eyes took in everything about her without staring at anything in particular. "They're having a séance in Oscar Wilde's old rooms. It might be something to write about."

"Will you come?" Choice had nothing to do with the suggestion. "I don't want to lose you again." She was breathless. "Will you show me where Magdalen College is?" she asked.

He hesitated. "All right. Come on."

It had been hard to admit to herself that the second meeting was a disappointment. She'd believed the moment of attraction in the lobby was predestined, permanent. How could it be forgotten? There had been conversation, although none of it involved speech. She'd been eternally, irrevocably locked in love to that man. Yet he behaved as though he hadn't given her another thought.

He drove her to a friend's room in college and made love to her. She wasn't allowed near Crowsley, his home in the nearby village. She was surprised by what she said to him. Not one of her disclosures followed the blueprint of her fantasies.

"What college are you at?" he'd asked. "Come on— you're a student, aren't you?"

"I told you what I do."

When she asked him later about the London theater and *The Godfather,* he always laughed. It became a joke, for him.

* * *

Now, thirteen months later, she waited to marry him. They would leave immediately for UCLA where he'd lecture for two terms.

"Will you carry roses?" Lilly asked. Victoria didn't hear her at first. "In your bouquet. Gerry particularly likes roses."

"Yes. Well then, yes."

"We could get them from the garden. I could arrange your bouquet."

The child Ruth grabbed at Victoria. She thought Ruth wanted to hold her hand but it was the ring she wanted, the diamond engagement ring. Victoria tried to be friendly and asked about Boston. The child didn't speak. She wanted the ring.

Gerry suggested a walk in Witham Woods, then tea by the river. But first he wanted to let them see Victoria walk a tightrope in the garden. "She used to do it in Paris." He wanted to show her off. Victoria loved dancing, balancing, cartwheels, anything physical and skillful, but she didn't feel like doing it today. "She can do somersaults on the swing."

"Yes, I saw her," said Lilly, and that was the end of that.

The child decided to make perfume. Gerry half filled a milk bottle with water and pushed in a few pink petals. She watched them float. But little Ruth wanted proper perfume bottles, bigger flowers. Then she could be like her mother, Lilly. She seemed to believe the key to the advantages of womanhood was cosmetic. Victoria remembered believing that, too. Gerry knelt beside the little girl, kissed the golden curls. The child was unimpressed. She wanted *things*. Losing interest in Gerry, the child slapped her hands over Victoria's eyes, roughly. It was a game, perhaps.

"Do you want to play hide-and-seek?" Victoria tried to sound gentle. One small hand went away and fluttered softly on Victoria's fingers like an insect.

"I expect you play that in Boston?" The fluttering stopped, there was a pause, then sharp pain. Victoria felt as though she'd been stung. Tiny nails scraped at her finger.

"Stop that, Ruth!" She grabbed at the childish hand still pressed against her left eye. It was sticky with sweets and smelled of rose petals. It seemed small and innocent. She held it, waiting for the dark dots to clear from her eyes. Then the child screamed unnervingly. Victoria let go.

"She's such a tease," said James.

Victoria looked at her hand. The scratches had almost drawn blood. Her ring was gone. The little girl rushed off into the rose garden, squealing with delight.

"She's got my ring, Gerry."

"Well, go and get it." He sounded almost irritable.

The child was not to be seen. The rose garden was still.

"If you lose the ring your grandfather will be cross, Ruth," Victoria called after her.

She crept toward the lovely yellow bushes, the perfect

hiding place, but the child was behind her. Her thrilled screech was piercing. She held back a huge stiff brier, inviting Victoria to come and get her, the perfect ambush.

"Let the roses go or you'll get scratched." Victoria's tone was no longer placating. "Give me the ring and I'll give you some perfume." As she moved toward her, the child let the brier swing back hard into Victoria's face. She cried out. The creeper's arms tangled in her hair. As she tried to lift them away, a huge thorn lodged in her hand like a tooth. Gerry was there beside her in seconds.

He pulled it out swiftly. "It's nothing."

They both looked at the scratch. The small tear was hardly visible. "She's naughty, Gerry. That child." Then the blood seeped up, far too much. It trickled over her hand, spilled onto the flowers.

"Come on. It's deeper than I thought."

He half carried her into the house and held her hand under cold water in the bathroom. He was soothing, utterly reliable. Nothing, not even death's agony, would take away his calm, steady attention and care. He seemed to absorb the other person's shock so that nothing felt as bad when he was there. He took an adhesive bandage, some cotton balls and antiseptic from the cupboard over the sink. His movements were unhurried and reassuring. But then he was used to dealing with medical emergencies. Hadn't he nursed his wife? She'd forgotten that.

Gerry turned the tap off. The cut looked pale and innocent. He reached for the medication and the blood started again.

"It's too fast. Jesus!"

"Lift up your arm." He pressed a point in the wrist and held her hand above her head.

"It will stop, won't it?" she asked, frightened.

He laughed. "It's nothing."

James brought her a cup of tea. "I've put plenty of sugar in." Gerry dismissed it with a shrug. He brought her hand down and pressed the cut, hard. She wouldn't look. Then he applied the bandage. She held on to him. Their bodies were always ready for pleasure, whatever the circumstances.

He was already somewhat excited but pushed her away. She pulled his hair and put her hand on his cock. "Not while they're in the kitchen," he advised.

She unzipped his trousers and got hold of it. He made some small resistance. "When they go to bed," he promised. She told him how big it was and how it made her feel. She lifted up one leg and wrapped it around him hungrily. She pushed her tongue deep into his mouth, grabbed his buttocks, pushed him against her, into her.

"Don't play," he said.

She got hold of his cock and said all the things he liked. As it got hard she pushed her black underpants to one side and rubbed it against her.

"But it's all wet," she said; "you must."

She eased herself onto it and made him fuck her hard against the sink, all her movements rough and greedy. The coldness of the porcelain against her hot body pleased her.

"Make me come," she said.

He knew all about that, all the touches and expressions she liked. He tore her dress, getting at her breasts. Still aware of the others, he tried to stop her making sounds as she came. Then he didn't care and lost himself in his own pleasure. He bent her back over the bathroom sink, fucking her hard, out of control.

"Oh, hurt me as you come," she begged him. "Dig your nails in, anything."

He wanted to do it in other positions but came too soon. For minutes afterward, he held on to her, very tight, breathing fast.

"It hurts," she said.

"It's because you came hard."

"My hand. The thorn."

"I love it with you. It's never been that good. Never. It's—"
Then he stopped.

"What?"

He disengaged himself, not without anxiety.

"What is it?"

"It's never been like that with anyone. At least not for a
long time."

He kept his hands on her and looked thoughtful. Then he
stepped back and straightened her dress. She thought he
loved her because she was like a naughty little girl.

CHAPTER · 2

SHE DREAMED ABOUT THE ROSE GARDEN. SHE SAW IT RE-
flected in the back door. As always the flowers looked beautiful,
inviting, but as she got nearer, she saw they were covered in greenfly
and mildew. Some of them, the bigger blooms, were wet and rotting.
Cobwebs hung between the bushes.

"It's a graveyard," she said aloud, and the back door slammed shut
and smashed. She woke up, covered in sweat.

After she had showered, she went into the kitchen in
search of something to eat. Colin was scrubbing the stove.
Since the death of Ruth, Gerry's wife, Colin had looked after
him. After six months of visiting Crowsley, Victoria was
allowed to discover that Ruth had been Colin's sister.

Colin was a professional stage actor, and his one-man
performance had made him a cult figure in the sixties. He
described his stint in Gerry's kitchen as being "between
shows." His face was an oval, neat and full of craft like a
playing card. The jack of spades with black guileless eyes,
female skin.

When he saw Victoria, he managed his everyday smile of
goodwill but his eyes did not join in. Gerry had made love to
her again in the night, and Colin had no doubt overheard
even the subtler moments.

"For lunch there's cucumber soup, honey, then some
veal." His accent was mostly American these days.

"Can I help?"

"But baby, it's all done."

"Isn't everything in this house?" she whispered.

Before Victoria, women had not been invited to Crowsley. Gerry's sexual relationships after his wife's death were secret and short-lived. A procession of mistresses passed through his rooms in college and hotels in London. He told Victoria she was the girl he'd been waiting for.

This morning Gerry didn't go to college and played with his grandchild. Victoria watched them from the kitchen window. Gerry sat with her in the garden and drew pictures of perfume bottles. The big crinkly one was eau de cologne, the tiny green one, expensive French perfume. He added lipstick, a powder compact, a cardboard box of rouge, a fat jar of face cream. The child held the drawing as though it were a passport to a better world. Then she squealed as Gerry swung her high into the air.

"Why don't you rest, honey?" suggested Colin. "You must be tired."

He knew she'd just gotten up. She ignored all that and went to the window and watched the excitement with the child.

"How long are they here for?"

"They seem to have come for the wedding."

"But that's three months away." She was taken aback. Perhaps Colin was just being provocative. As Gerry lifted the child to see the higher roses, they both watched him. Like a movie star, he captured the scene. Even the flowers were on his side.

"Isn't there something I can do, Colin?"

"Not now. I've got to get everything looking its best. The television people are coming to interview us and—"

"Us?" She was horrified.

"Well, Gerry. You'd better find your ring. I've never heard of a fiancée losing her ring. We've looked everywhere. It's not in the rose garden. Now will you get out of my kitchen, please!"

She supposed he wanted to put on one of the homemade beauty masks he thought no one knew about.

The sitting room was soft and dark with enduring furnishings. It was always full of flowers. There were elegant mirrors belonging to Gerry's mother and gloomy, greenish paintings of horses. Everything blended. Even the grand piano was subdued. It was always kept closed and she'd never heard it played. Crowsley was a peaceful place, easy to live in. It was dim and airy with occasional patches of sunlight. It was a kind house. But today she did not feel comfortable. She took her reviewing work into the meadow but watched the family through the bushes.

Gerry kissed Lilly and gave her a rose. "My lovely Lilly. A real Jamesian heroine."

Lilly responded with pleasure. Gerry's son James was smiling. It was all right with him. Their enjoyment in each other was so practiced, so harmonious, it was like a regional dance.

Physical intimacy had not been a requirement in Victoria's home. As far as she knew, nobody touched except in anger. Greetings and farewells were ghastly occasions. She'd always smudge her mother's full makeup. The long, much admired eyelashes would be revealed as false. Her mother believed the adolescent girl had done it on purpose. So did the psychiatrist neighbor, Walter Guinea, always alert for clients. The occasions aroused in Victoria a scalding fury.

At first her love affair with Gerry had changed her life. She was so captivated, so chemically changed by love, she felt she could do anything, that all her problems had been solved. All she wanted was to be with him at all times, to feel him, watch him, arouse his passion. Then one day, a month ago, he showed Victoria a barrier. He liked to do things alone. Gardening, walking and reading were some of them. He liked to spend time at Crowsley on his own. He couldn't help her with her relationship with her mother. Neither could he choose her a permanent job. Marrying him would not answer all the questions. She was still Victoria Brooke, temporary journalist, and she had to be responsible for herself.

* * *

At the lunch table, James tried to despise Dickens for his father's benefit. "He was all fragments, details, rotten architecture but wonderful gargoyles."

"Your father said that, darling," Lilly corrected, softly.

Gerry laughed. "Orwell, actually."

Then Colin laughed, not so kindly. Lilly stared at him without friendliness and said, "You don't understand. Even mistakes. So why laugh? Is it just your way of being clever?"

"It beats yours, honey," whispered Colin, venomously. "At least I don't bore people to death."

Victoria wondered what in their previous relationship accounted for such bitterness. No one else seemed to take any notice.

"I remember Professor Ricks said *Hard Times* and *The Europeans* were moral fables. At least he was consistent about that," said James.

Gerry looked irritated at the reference to his old lecturer's faults.

"Henry James dismissed Dickens's influence but would *The Europeans* have been written without *Hard Times*?" asked Lilly.

"Oh, my! Look who's been to school," said Colin softly.

Victoria giggled.

"He was a great entertainer," said James. "Dickens, I mean. But I wouldn't use 'moral fable' to describe any of his work. Would you?"

For a moment, Victoria thought he was asking her. Before confusion set in, Gerry replied neatly.

17

"Henry James didn't think so. He was disillusioned with the English," Gerry told his son. "He had once believed they offered the ideal way of life."

"A lot of Americans have been fooled." Lilly sounded personal.

"At that time there was considerable confusion between American and European viewpoints," said Gerry.

There's considerable confusion around this table, too, thought Victoria.

Before dessert there was a brief disturbance. The child was not in her bed. She was out in the garden killing things.

When they were settled again, Lilly remarked, with mock surprise, "You're not wearing your ring."

"How can I? When it's lost."

"It'll turn up," said Gerry, too casually.

"It'll turn up when Ruth decides it should," Victoria said sharply. James shifted awkwardly.

"It happened yesterday," said Lilly. "How can she remember where she put it? She's three, for godsake!"

* * *

After lunch, there was another outburst of family loving. Victoria tried to see a positive side. She was privileged to see real, sensual, uninhibited love. She did try to join in, at least to say something, but Lilly always got there first. She was very funny about Boston. At one point, Gerry put his arms over her shoulders and the American girl grasped them, her face bright pink. She held them against her breasts, the action undeniably sexual. Victoria poured another drink and wished she could go home. Then she remembered, this was home. James once again raked the garden looking for the ring.

Oxford dons came to tea. They seemed high on egotism, low on entertainment. Gerry encouraged his son to talk about the latest developments in his own field, microchip technology. However admirable the advances, they had little charm for the dons. They were more concerned with who took Gerry's place when he lectured in California.

"I'm more on the commercial side. I do a selling job really," said James.

"Selling, my ass!" Gerry was proud of his son. "He's already an executive, and just graduated from the university, too."

"James must have married young," commented one of the guests, desperate to change the subject.

Gerry was offended by the suggestion that his son's precocious position had something to do with marrying Lilly. This was possibly the truth. Victoria's sister Mary had heard reference to the advantageous marriage at New York dinner parties.

"Isn't your father a movie producer?" the inquisitive guest asked Lilly.

"You must be thinking of my brother." Her brother was a well-known Italian-American movie star and she didn't like talking about it.

"So what does your father do?"

"He's a technician."

Colin choked. One of his cutting laughs had gone badly wrong. Everyone turned around. "Sorry. I've got that nervous thing in my throat."

"Well, stop working so hard, Col," advised Gerry. "You do too much."

Colin went back to the kitchen. He was never absent from his territory for too long.

After a time the dons noticed Victoria. One said to her, "You must be so happy." By the end of the day this had deteriorated to "You should be so happy."

She was glad when the child, plump and rosy with love, lifted her baby's shovel and bashed a rose. The falling red petals reminded Victoria of a wedding, a love-match ceremony in a small country church, strong on passion, low on protocol. Before dying, the petals gave off a gasp of fragrance.

CHAPTER · 3

SOMEONE WAS LISTENING. WAS IT COLIN? SOMEONE ON THE other side of the wall? Or Lilly just outside the open window? She tried to tell Gerry but he was only interested in his own pleasure and her response to what he was doing.

"Come on. Look at me. Go on, let me see you. Do what you like doing. Come on."

"Gerry, there's someone in the room."

He thought that was part of her fantasy. "Go on. It's all for you."

She was so drawn to him she was almost blind with excitement, but something held her back. She told him the bed made too much noise, so he finished it off holding her against the wall.

"Go on, dig your nails in as I come." He was obviously mad about her body. Because it was young?

"Gerry, there was someone listening."

"Who cares?"

"It was Lilly."

"They're in the barn asleep."

"Will you be faithful to me?" she asked. He turned and smiled at her, his eyes completely beautiful and revealing, unlike any eyes she'd seen before. Even in the movies.

"Of course."

This was such a happy moment she wanted to gather it to her, hold it for the future.

"Why 'of course'?"

"I suppose I'm a faithful creature."

"Were you with your first wife?"

There was a sharp intake of breath, but he spoke normally. "I was completely faithful to her." He paused. "You can call her by her name, can't you?"

"Who?"

"You know who."

Neither one of them seemed inclined to mention her name.

She knew nothing about Ruth except she'd come from nowhere, played the piano beautifully, got cancer, and died young.

She tried a change of subject. "What exactly will I do in America?"

The decision to marry had happened quite suddenly three weeks ago. She believed it was prompted by a sexually ecstatic weekend at the sea. He'd said he was happy for the first time in ten years and wanted to repay her. Then her mother got involved and insisted on a society wedding.

"I can't be a journalist, can I? What about the green card?"

"I think you should study. You can do a course at UCLA." He didn't think much of her writing.

"And when we come back here?"

"Well—something temporary until you find what you want to do. You're young. You've got time."

"Why don't I just stay here and look after you?" He laughed, a small one.

"You don't like people around all the time, do you, Gerry?"

He shook his head. "I think it's because I've been alone so much. I wasn't always like this." He caressed her so tenderly she wanted to cry.

She sat up and could see the garden. The roses were

luxurious and large like a cluster of three-quarter moons. A mist rose off them like damp pollen. She'd never seen that before.

"Perhaps I could get something on a local paper here."

He lay on his back and read galley proofs of a colleague's book.

"How long are they staying for?"

"James is doing some research here."

"I feel left out."

"I hadn't noticed. They like you very much. Surely they've told you that."

"Well, all Americans say that. I don't fit in. And you sort of disappear into them."

He wasn't listening. He went on with the book, peacefully.

"When did Lilly first come here?"

"I think she was eleven."

"She's very clever."

He looked as though he could say something about that but thought better of it. "When she was a girl she went to live with the dean of UCLA—Willy Vass. You'll meet him. We had an exchange system. I lived in his house and taught for six months in L.A. and he came here. Lilly started coming over for holidays. She was company for James. Took his mind off his mother's illness."

"How did she get on with your wife?"

The question surprised him. "All right, I suppose."

"Why did she stay with Willy Vass? What was wrong with her own home?"

"I'm sure I've told you about Lilly. Her father wanted her to acquire education." The "acquire" sounded odd. "He was rather keen on that sort of thing."

"What does he do?"

"He's a businessman in Boston."

"She said he's a technician."

"Well then, a technician. If you know, why ask?" He tried to go on reading.

"She's very beautiful."

There were some nights when she could do anything with him. This wasn't one of them. She said, "I wonder what she's like in bed?"

"Why? Do you fancy her?" His tone was taunting. "What's the matter with you?"

"The matter?"

"All these questions. You're not usually like this." His hands reached inside her thighs. "They're so plump and strong, aren't they? Is that from playing basketball?" He moved his hand to her pale, flat stomach.

She got out of bed and went to the window where there should be more air. She felt breathless, on the edge of something. He lay still, watching her.

"Why did you call Lilly a Jamesian heroine? What does that mean?"

"She exemplifies all the advantages of the American girl. Free, emancipated, she has her own code of honor."

"But she's Italian."

"Of Italian origin." He folded the proofs regretfully and prepared to sleep. She tried to tell him about that Sunday, the bitter blackness that stayed at the edge of her thinking threatening to take over. His memory of that day was so different from hers. He recalled being pleased to see his son and going for walks with his granddaughter. Everyone had loved Victoria. Hadn't they said so?

"What was all that about a white rose? Lilly went on about a white climbing rose."

He looked up defensively. "What do you want to know about that for? It was years ago."

"What did happen to it?"

"The frost got it." His tone discouraged any more questions.

Gerry turned sensuously onto his back and threw off the covering sheet. His tongue moved slowly along his top lip. She watched it and forgot the family. He pulled her on top of him. It was much better this time.

*   *   *

When she woke up the light was still on. His arms were tight around her, his face in her hair. All was not well. At first she had trouble breathing. Then she realized she felt sick and was trembling. It was the sweet scent. It hung in the room, stagnant, unmoving.

"Has someone spilled perfume in here?" she asked aloud.

He didn't wake immediately. She bent forward, almost stifled. It was coming from the rose garden, a solid anesthetic presence. She started coughing. "Can't you smell it, Gerry? The perfume?"

"It's the roses, that's all. Go to sleep."

"Open the windows."

"They are open."

Gasping, she sat up and tried to drink some water. He patted her back. "Just breathe deeply from the bottom of your lungs. Let it out slowly. Breathe again." He stopped her panic. When she could breathe properly she remained sitting up.

"The roses seem a bit dramatic, Gerry."

"Do they?" He spoke absently.

"What are they called?" She tried to sound normal.

"Superstar. And there's some Japanese. The ones with the big pink flowers."

"They're not pink tonight." She felt cold.

"There's an Iceberg."

"Why do they glow like that?"

25

He shrugged and wouldn't look. "The air, I expect. It's nearly midsummer."

She drank more water. "Who planted all those roses?"

"I did."

"Why?"

"For my wife. My first wife," he corrected, quickly. "When she was so ill I used to carry her out there in the evening. She could still enjoy the flowers. In the end she could only lie here, of course. But I used to open the window and the scent came into the room. She liked that."

"How long is it since she died?"

"Fourteen years, eleven and a half months."

His voice was expressionless. He cheered up a bit with his next comment. "The rose is a symbol of elegance, perfection and love. It can't do you any harm."

" 'What's in a name? A rose by any other name would smell as sweet.' " She remembered that from school. He held her, cradled her protectively. The cloying, nauseous smell became overpowering as soon as she lay down. She thought it odd, how little they talked about Gerry's first wife. He'd described her once; that was enough—as far as he was concerned.

Suddenly she started choking. She broke out of Gerry's arms, rushed into the bathroom and drank water. She held her head under the tap. Terrified now, she ran from the house in her nightgown. It was only when she reached the main road that she could breathe. There were no roses there.

* * *

They all said it was an allergy and she must stay in bed. The windows were shut and Colin brought her tray after tray of medication and gentle broth. She didn't take the antihistamine tablets. She'd be surprised if what she'd suffered from was rose fever. For a while, Gerry sat with her and

26

talked about America, what he liked, what she'd like. Telling her about it seemed to freshen it up for him.

After lunch he decided to read to her. He believed being read to was soothing when you were ill. Effortlessly, you followed the person's voice. It took your mind away from— he nearly said "pain." She supposed he'd read to Ruth.

In the afternoon, she lay in bed listening to him playing with the child. "Ring a ring of roses, all fall down." There was a distant sound of a transistor radio, bat and ball, birds, the murmur of voices. Is this how Ruth felt? Lying there hour after hour? Desperate to get better. Lying there almost awake, getting to know the secret signs in the molded ceiling, longing to be a wife again in all ways, and he dealing with her approaching death in his study or down in the rose garden, pruning things.

She could hear Lilly's voice strident, coarse. "But James and I are right on top of the roses. No, we did not get affected. How do you mean, 'looks' different?"

"Not so loud," said Gerry.

"Yeah, they started up the lawn like something from *Macbeth*. These upper-class girls are always neurotic. It's overbreeding."

"Be quiet!" His tone had the effect of a slap.

*   *   *

When Victoria ran away to Paris at seventeen, she modeled for the well-known artist, Alex Galsworthy. They very quickly became lovers. He liked to live a poor bohemian sort of life, although he was successful and rich enough to do anything. He despised the upper classes but had a habit of marrying them.

Alex wanted to change her. He wanted to burn away all those values and ideas she'd mindlessly absorbed from her socially ambitious, power-crazed mother. He wanted Victoria to live in the moment and be brave enough to ignore

27

tomorrow. Then all her energy would be spent on the present and she would be so much more alive.

After she'd fallen in love with him and seen he was not the stuff relationships were made of, she ran away again, to secretarial school. She thought she wanted security. Then she tried modeling, then journalism. She made the mistake of thinking being temporary was living spontaneously. Also, she could never find what she wanted to do. She had no interest in roses, but she remembered roses came into that time.

Alex painted what he called "the roses in her cheeks." He said roses would be important to her later on.

* * *

In the later afternoon, Gerry found the ring. The child had put it on her doll.

CHAPTER · 4

THE NEXT DAY SHE WENT BACK TO HER MOTHER'S HOUSE IN stockbroker country, Surrey, and started some preparations for the wedding. At least in her mother's company there was no chance of being threatened by displays of love.

She needed to hold on to a clear, attractive picture of Gerry, but the rose garden kept interfering with her vision.

It had been laid out to resemble a T. S. Eliot poem. At least that's what Gerry's colleague Professor Gully had said. She never knew when he was joking, which made friendship difficult. And she had never read the poem. But it was true that there was a pond in the middle, full of fallen leaves and brackish water in which nothing lived except the occasional beam of reflected sunlight.

She concentrated her attention on Gerry. His gray-blue eyes were candid, clear, his facial expressions, eloquent. A lot of soft brown hair streaked with gray fell naturally into a good shape no hairdresser could improve. It flopped boyishly over one eye. All on its own it swept back in a wide curve at each side and came to rest neatly, low on his neck. His cheekbones were high and he had a sensual, precise mouth. It was his eyes, the strength of their gaze that people remembered.

Gerry's magnetic presence identified him anywhere. Movie stars in the flesh did not have it; they were invariably a disappointment. She'd found that out going to her sister Mary's Chelsea cocktail parties. Gerry had the sturdy body of a peasant and the hands of an artist. He was the first person you saw when you came into a room. Without ever speaking to him you felt assured he would not let you down. The only drawback was that such a man would have a lot of admirers. He had.

The charismatic quality was not hereditary. His son James had no magnetism. He was precise and distrusted charm. He sometimes managed a polished social manner that wore off after half an hour. His high-powered job obsessed him night and day, and holidays were agony. Victoria found out from Colin that running a microchip empire was too much for him. "He'd need to be at least thirty-five to do something like that. After all, there's nothing extraordinary about James. He's clever but he's not his father."

Victoria's mother broke into her reverie. She shouted up the stairs. Something about quarreling with Gerry.

To begin with, Victoria had kept her family hidden. She didn't think Gerry would be able to cope, not with Mother, her withering vowel sounds, secondhand court gossip and the never-ending obsession with their relatives, the Bonham-Hays. His charm disarmed Mother at first. He'd likened her life to some setting in a classical novel, Victoria couldn't remember which. He made a habit of that—putting life into literature. It seemed to make it safe.

Victoria had got rid of her boarding school accent. Classless, apolitical, she thought of herself as an individual, not an inconsequential member of a well-known family. She'd decided not to react to her background; that was as bad as accepting it. She wanted to select what worked for her and reject the rest. Choice, rather than mindless reaction. There might even come a time when some aspects of Mother would be acceptable.

She was not the favorite of the two girls. Even in marriage, she'd failed. Her sister Mary had got hold of a minor aristocrat. Victoria wasn't dramatically beautiful the way

Mary was. But she had style that other girls said was French and tried to copy. She was healthy, relaxed and moved as though she liked being in her body.

The competitive atmosphere at home had never suited her. Before his death, her father, a corporation lawyer in the city, had been single-mindedly seeking inroads into the wealth of Saudi Arabia. Her mother had shown no consideration for his heart or blood pressure. Almost rich, he died of jet lag.

Now that he was gone, Mother had to live through someone else. Victoria was not a good choice but Mother was doing her best. She'd been set on the wedding taking place at St. Margaret's Westminster, but Victoria refused and threatened to run away. Mother believed her and settled for St. Margaret's Haslemere and a marquee reception at the country estate of her brother-in-law, Earl Bonham-Hay. A thousand guests were invited. Mother had already lured photographers from the glossy magazines. The bridesmaids were to be dressed by the latest fashion favorite in Knightsbridge. The wedding dress, a triumph in raw silk, was being altered.

And now Gerry had called Mother during a relaxed tutorial in college and said he did not want a big wedding, but something simple in his local church. He said he hated fuss. He let lines from a Yeats poem speak for him, but Mother was no wiser. She couldn't see why an illustrious don, influential in America, should want to drag her younger daughter into an anonymous country church.

"Perhaps he's ashamed of me," Victoria said provocatively.

"And that word 'modest' he's so fond of. I find that particularly offensive. He did better for the first Mrs. de Santos."

Victoria laughed secretly as Mother reminded Gerry of her family tree stretching, often illegitimately, to a royal bed in the thirteenth century. Her rich speech became cloyed as her sugar levels rose. Listing her ancestors gave her the same pleasure as gluttony.

But Victoria also wondered at Gerry's decision. Why this local church? She had never seen him in it.

Mother scrapped with Gerry by phone throughout the afternoon. There was no room for Victoria's contribution. There was always chaos around her; she was worn out by other people's dramas.

Victoria invited her friend Sylvia, a nurse, over to the house and offered her the role of maid of honor.

"The engagement was quick, Vee. And now the wedding is quick. The usual reason? Or is he a spontaneous sort of person?"

"The engagement is for my mother. He decided he wanted to get married, so why wait?"

"Have a drink, Vee. It'll stop the wedding day nerves."

"Brandy? Whiskey? What do you want? I am not nervous."

"I never drink spirits during the day." Sylvia was outraged. Like many out-of-control drinkers she had some impeccable self-deceiving habits.

"A little white wine if anything."

Sylvia was very fair with light hair, gold skin and a beautiful face. Her body was big and boyish. She had the same slanted eyes as her famous novelist father, Dan Jago. The eyes were assessing and intelligent and never deteriorated, however much drinking there was. She looked like him. He had a good time; she had a very bad time. Her mother had got out early, married a titled person and lived in a château in France. One of her many analysts had described Sylvia satisfactorily: Out of the outrageous sexual chaos of her childhood, she'd hung on to two ideas. However bad a situation, drinking soothed it. If you couldn't afford that, there was sex, though the oblivion was shorter. She'd delib-

erately constructed the most normal identity she could. Her
father found her so boring nowadays, he wouldn't let her in
the house, unless he was ill.

"I saw an article about Gerry in the *Guardian*. Do you
think you will go to America?"

Victoria started packing some clothes and books to be
taken to Crowsley. "I expect so. Gerry's a visiting professor
at UCLA."

"I liked his photograph. You can tell he's a good lover."

"You sure get a lot from a photograph, Syl. You'll have to
meet him." Even the promise sounded empty.

"Your old boyfriend Galsworthy would have enjoyed all
this," said Sylvia.

"All what?"

"The big wedding. He loves the aristocracy. Or does he
hate it? He spends most of his time in the gutter—how can
one tell? It's quite a switch. Alex Galsworthy and the don.
Has he got your engagement ring yet?"

Victoria nodded. The question brought something else to
mind.

"If you get scratched by a thorn would there be a lot of
blood?"

"The thing about blood is it always looks like more than it
is. A thimbleful makes such a mess you think you're bleeding to death."

"Don't give me all that professional crap, Syl. I'm talking
about blood rushing out from a minuscule wound." She
decided not to tell her about the suffocation in the night.
That would be dismissed as an allergy.

"What sort of ring? You're not wearing it."

"Silver with a single diamond." Victoria's mind was not
on the ring.

"The simpler the better for the big things. You don't need
a lot of show."

It seemed that Sylvia had seen so many human beings in

trouble at the hospital that off-duty she saw only well people everywhere.

* * *

The postcard arrived with the next batch of engagement congratulations. Victoria's name and address were typed on the cheap, brown envelope. The card was postmarked 1915. It was addressed to Alice Murray in South London and bore a penciled love message from a James Hamilton serving in the trenches.

"What's this to do with me? I don't collect them." She flicked the card onto the pile of correspondence.

Mother, breathless and overweight from too much eating, accosted her on the stairs. "What do you think the Iranians are going to do next? It could mean war."

"I don't know anything about it," said Victoria, as though the Iranian mess were her fault.

"You don't know anything about it?" Her mother sucked noisily on a peppermint. "You don't seem to know even the alarming facts." Mother's eyes popped dangerously.

Victoria wasn't deceived. Outrage abroad meant unresolved distress about something nearer home. Her mother didn't care about the world beyond Haslemere. Victoria supposed she hadn't won the battle with Gerry.

"What does Gerry say?"

Victoria shrugged.

"Whatever does he find to talk to you about?"

"I'm all right when I'm screwing," she replied venomously. "Don't worry. He hasn't got around to my vertical inadequacies yet."

"Your father would have something to say about it if he were alive." She meant the Iranian crisis; Victoria's disgusting outbursts were not allowed to register and therefore did not exist. "And when are you going to let the nurse meet Gerry? She's been back over a month."

"His original lover's impulse to get to know everyone around me has been sadly discouraged."

"By whom?"

"You! I don't think it's fair to unload other difficult people on him. Sylvia likes to drink, she likes to screw. She makes no secret of either. She particularly likes doing both with an older man. She'll go through Gerry's Oxford community like a rat up a drain. I think it's better to wait till I've married him."

Mother unwrapped another peppermint eagerly. "You're scared he'll take a fancy to her, you mean?"

* * *

In the evening Sylvia helped sort through the childhood things that would have no place in the new life at Crowsley. Victoria refused to throw much away and packed her movie albums and toys in a tea chest under the stairs. She wasn't sure about doing away with the past.

Sylvia picked up the old postcard from James to Alice.

> Dear Alice,
>   I write you these few lines to let you know that I got your letter all right and I am glad you're well at home. Tell Lil I've had no word from my pal yet. If you can, will you send me some cigarettes as we can't get any up here? Think of me.
> >   From your loving sweetheart,
> >   James Hamilton

"Who sent it?"

Victoria didn't know.

"I didn't realize they used to write in pencil."

The card, a brown-and-white war photograph, had a title in French: *"La Reprise du Village."* A French village was on fire and soldiers with bayonets approached the enemy lurk-

35

ing farther up in a doorway. Sky full of hell. Dead and wounded lying there together in the street. On the back a triangle was stamped in pink with a number: "Passed by Censor. Aug. 29, 1915." There was no postage stamp.

Two more had come by special delivery. No sender's name. They, too, were addressed to Alice Murray in South London. There was a tinted one of a girl with crimped hair wearing a diaphanous gown. She carried a bunch of artificial flowers and her smile was winsome.

> Dear Alice,
>   A line as promised. We are not coming back till Sat afternoon so I will see you Sat evening. Hope you are well. Kindest regards to your mother.
>   From your sincere friends,
>   Will and Flo

> Dear Alice,
>   Just a P.C. to let you know I got your letter all right. I am glad to hear that you are all well. No word from my pal so I'll write to his father. Tell Lil I expect she'll hear before I do.
>   Love,
>   James Hamilton

Mother laboriously climbed the winding stairs to the attic. Victoria could hear her gasping breath and hid the wine.

"She's far too fat," Sylvia whispered. "How long was I in Africa? Five months? She's put on thirty pounds. It's bad for her heart."

"She doesn't really want to live now that he's dead. She never expected he'd be the first to go. She did what she could to be first. All that eating. But death ignored her and now she's just fat."

Mother sank back against the headboard of the narrow bed and revived herself with a mouthful of peppermints.

"You don't have to do these stairs, Mummy. Why don't you ring and I'll come down."

"Doesn't like fuss?" she began abruptly. His life's nothing else. All these presentations and ceremonies. He's always being awarded something or other. He wouldn't insult me to my face. But I know the Latin for megalomaniac, however sweetly it's put. Does he think I'm uneducated?"

"Don't be paranoid, Mummy. You misheard. He never speaks Latin."

"Why these sudden impulses?" Really she resented Gerry knowing so many influential people and not sharing them. "Is he going through menopause, do you suppose?" She looked at Sylvia. "Late forties? If it's glandular I can only sympathize. I know all about glands."

Sylvia snorted contemptuously. The Honorable Mrs. Brooke's weight hadn't got there by itself.

Mother dropped a cheap brown envelope onto the bed. Three more First World War postcards had arrived. Victoria had read two of them. Glimpses into someone else's ecstatically happy love affair was the last thing she wanted now.

"Who will give you away?"

Victoria wouldn't answer. Mother kept pecking at her silence with shrill questions. In the end she turned to Sylvia. "She's not like her sister. Mary's bright, thank God."

Mother looked at photographs Victoria had taken of Crowsley and couldn't see much to disapprove of. The first Mrs. de Santos had taste.

"I must have his mother's list of the guests she intends to invite. The invitations should have gone off. They're always sent at least fourteen weeks before the day. I've told you that, Vee. Why did he want this marriage in such a rush? This sort of thing takes months."

"He doesn't want this sort of thing, Mother."

"Didn't you have any idea you were going to marry him? You could have told me. And has he given you the engagement ring at least?"

Victoria nodded.

Her mother leaned forward greedily. "How much?"

"About six hundred." She sighed.

"Well, why aren't you wearing it?"

"Because I'm doing chores, as you can see."

"Let's have a look at it then."

Victoria took it out of its deep blue, satin-lined box, and Sylvia and Mother oohed and aahed, making much the same response women do over new babies.

Mother said, "I'll be glad when all this is over."

CHAPTER · 5

SHE WAITED UNTIL LILLY WAS HAVING A BATH AND COLIN WAS slaving in the kitchen before confronting Gerry. He was sitting with James by the grand piano looking at a scrapbook of his old tutor, Professor Gilbert Ricks.

"How about your final-year students? How will they do?" asked James.

"All right. As you know, I don't believe in exams but I know how to pass them. I never told you about Ricks—"

Victoria cut in abruptly. "We're supposed to go to church next Sunday."

The scrapbook snapped shut.

"For the reading of the banns. And the hymns. We have to decide what we want."

"Short ones."

" 'Baking tins, barbecue, bread knife, cutting board . . .' " She read quickly from the wedding-gift list. "Well?"

"Well?" he echoed.

"The wedding-gift list."

He laughed. "I thought you were reading a concrete poem."

James took the list. " 'Deep freeze, spit, microwave.' This wedding business is worse than Christmas. What's wrong with a registry office?"

"Victoria's mother."

Somewhere in the house the child wasn't getting what she wanted. Gerry reopened the scrapbook.

"These days it's fashionable to say Ricks couldn't deal with students on a personal basis."

The screaming child was carried in to Gerry. He soothed her and petted her and she quieted down. With him, she could be anything she wanted to be. Naughty, willful, greedy, sleepless—his caring would encompass the bad behavior. But the child was never bad with him. That was the thing about being loved: It made you good.

"Gerry, I have to talk to you about the church. My mother—"

"If she's so eager for a fashionable charade let her remarry; she's only doing it to impress the Bonham-Hays. Her whole life is devoted to getting the better of her sister. You'll have to stand up to her, Vee. For once in your life you'll have to."

"Well, let's not do it. Who gives a shit!"

She made an untidy exit.

Every room was occupied except the bedroom. The quilt was cold and slippery and didn't warm up. The furniture looked as though it had been in the same position for years. She didn't think she'd ever be at ease in this room again. She didn't like the wallpaper. She sensed hostility. If inanimate objects were capable of negative sentiments, the ones in that room were working overtime.

Colin carried in the gift list. "You left it behind, honey. The baby's chewed the edges. I'm looking through it, but we've got everything. All Ruth's stuff just lasts and lasts."

He realized he'd possibly said the wrong thing. "But you decide. I mean you're the bride. Garden shears—now I'm in favor there. I'll need to get to work in the rose garden. Since he met you he's just let it go."

Colin pretended to like her. When other people were present he overpraised her, placated her, waited on her. He treated her like a huge enemy he hadn't yet found the means to destroy. But his eyes challenged her with the past.

"By the way, Colin, what was Gerry like with your sister?"

"Like?" He was angry.

He pretended something dangerous was happening in the kitchen. Victoria followed him. "What sort of person was he then?"

"Well, he just adored her. What else can anyone say? But then he was different in those days."

*   *   *

Gerry came to bed as the sun came up. "What will happen to Colin?" she asked.

He feigned puzzlement.

"When we're married?"

"Just because we're getting married doesn't mean he has to change his life. After all, you don't want to work in the kitchen."

"I'd be very happy looking after you."

"But you'll have a job. And what about when we're in the States? Someone will have to look after the dogs."

She didn't argue because he'd started stroking and kissing her body. When he did that she'd give in to him about anything.

*   *   *

The roses were planted in triangular beds and soft double lines to provide a walk. The entrance to the garden was through a spindly wooden arch made crooked by the weight of a thousand healthy blooms. A space in the middle was dotted with boxtrees. The never-used, brown-edged pool was off to one side, gleaming and smooth in the sun, like a sheet of buttergold paper. There were wrought-iron benches at the intersection of the three paths, subsiding gently in the moist, dark soil. Old-fashioned lantern lamps, broken and filled with ivy, stood beside them.

At the end of the garden, the flowers reached a crescendo

of color and energy and swarmed up and over the trembling trellis, beyond which briers, gorse and other pushy shrubs waited to gain admittance. Gerry's friend Professor Gully had said, "The roses are alert, as if they are being looked at."

Victoria picked up people's atmosphere and mood. If an argument were taking place in another street, even though it had nothing to do with her, she'd be affected, distressed. It made living with her mother a tricky business. "Victoria's too sensitive. That's her trouble." Her family had condemned her since childhood.

And now, in the rose garden, she was picking up sadness. Sadness and longing.

In the house Gerry was talking to James about Zen Buddhism. Once again she'd been excluded. Her slight education at a fashionable girls' school had not prepared her for marriage to an Oxford don.

She wandered listlessly back into the house. She had no place there. Last Sunday's blackness, no more than a splinter in the sunlight, had changed all that.

He found her in the bedroom. "What are you doing?"

"The reviews," she lied.

"Why don't you join us?"

"How can I? I don't know what you're talking about."

"I'll help you. Would you like that? If I gave you some books to read—"

"Yes. I want to understand the things you like."

"Oh, you are sweet, Vee. Don't worry. I'll help you. I want you to grow up and be responsible for yourself."

"What a bore for you. Having to go over all the old stuff."

"On the contrary. It'll freshen it up for me."

"I know you're not looking forward to the wedding."

"No, I'm not."

"Then why not run away with me? Let's go to Scotland."

"Because I want to marry you properly."

42

"You could have said all this before."

"I didn't feel it before."

"What's wrong?"

"It's just—I suppose I am irritated, Vee. All the drama. And now I've got to go to church. As soon as the vicar decides I'm an agnostic I've had it. And your mother. Excavating all my relatives. Flying them from the Bahamas. Why can't she leave them alone?"

"If you don't want it, say so and we won't have it. My mother's a bully and the only way to deal with one is to stand your ground and resist each and every attack."

"So I've noticed." He laughed, then held out his hand. She refused to look at him. "But I want you to have a nice day."

"You're lucky it's not St. Margaret's Westminster. That's where my sister was married."

She watched his reflection in the mirror. He moved restlessly as though trying to extricate himself. From the wedding? Her mother? Her?

"What sort of wedding did your other wife have?"

"Not at St. Margaret's, you can be sure of that."

"Yet you went into a church for her."

"I had less reason to be disillusioned with God in those days."

She stayed at the window and he opened a book. She was full of half-understood grievances.

All of a sudden he did not want a big wedding. Was it because of all the useless activity it involved or because that ceremony belonged to the dead first wife and could not be repeated? He was gently amused by her and tolerant of her lack of intellectual development. But then, she possessed the one thing he did not have: youth.

"Your mother called, Vee. She's on about some old postcards."

* * *

Victoria took the latest postcards to Guy's Hospital where Sylvia was introducing a new medical student to Emergency. She observed her for a while from the reception area.

"You clamp here and here, then stitch." Sylvia smiled reassuringly at the patient. "All right, Mr. Bird?"

The student spoke softly across the many shallow wounds. "You've got eyes just like your father's. I saw his latest book jacket."

"Take blood pressure first. The swabs are kept here."

"Do you see much of your father?"

"No. Do you?" she said tartly.

"Of course not. I've never met him. He's so famous and—"

"If you want to pick him up don't pick me up. He picks up all right on his own."

The student laughed. "You are a tease, Nurse Jago."

A drunk in the next cubicle was vomiting.

"Pay attention to what I'm showing you. I don't know why they send second years down here. They're all crazy. At least you didn't faint."

"I nearly did. When I saw you."

Then Sylvia was called away to Reception. Sylvia always lived up to her perfect, starched uniform. However wild the night before, no trace was allowed to show the following day.

"You've just ruined this evening's entertainment."

"How?" said Victoria.

"That student over there was poised to take me out."

Victoria eyed him suspiciously. Sylvia laughed. "When did I say I didn't like them young?"

"I wanted to show you these. No sender's name."

Sylvia took Victoria into the nurses' lounge and sat in the corner to avoid the sun. The first card showed a bombarded sector of Paris reduced to rubble. A soldier stood alone in the middle of the chaos, his back to the camera. The back was eloquent. A caption could not have said more.

> Dear Alice,
>
> Thank you for the cigarettes. Tell Lil I got a letter from my pal's father and he was killed at Serbia three weeks ago. I had a letter from my cousin in the Dardanelles and he is all right again. I think this is all at present.
>
> From James,
with love

"He must have been used to death," said Victoria. She felt personally involved as though she'd just received the bad news. Sylvia did, too. She was no more adept at passing on bad news to friends and relatives than James Hamilton.

"He was at the front. He must have got the worst of it. I wonder who he was. And who's Alice? What happened to them?"

The postcard was dated April 20, 1916. The pencil was smudged.

> Dear Alice,
>
> I write these few lines to say that nothing could ever be so good as those sweet hours in Jordans Wood. I didn't know happiness like that existed. I want you to understand. I've had pleasure but never happiness like that. And so unexpected. I know all this longing will in the end be made up to us. You'll see.
>
> Love, all love,
James

For perhaps a second, Victoria could see the sunlight in the woods, the golden air made unforgettable by the fragrance of wild flowers. Their happiness, limited by departure, threatened by death. But gloriously unexpected. She understood that during the exquisite interlude, everything was so lovely that even the future was attracted. All James Hamilton had to do was stay alive.

Victoria's throat was tight with unshed tears. She wanted more cards so that she could be reassured James and Alice did get together in the end. The love wedding in the simple country church belonged to them. As Sylvia said, the big things should be simple. They put the cards back in the envelope.

"They don't write postcards like that anymore," said Victoria.

"He didn't send it to her house, that card. Another address in South London. They didn't do *that* in those days. Or they weren't supposed to. He was educated, James Hamilton. I wonder who's sending them to you."

" 'I didn't know happiness like that existed.' " Victoria couldn't get the message out of her mind. No one had ever said that to her. Alice had made her lover marvelously happy. How many people did that?

"It's not a joke, is it?" asked Sylvia.

"Perhaps. To the sender." Victoria sounded dispirited.

"Who?" mouthed Sylvia in good emergency-nurse style.

"Lilly's sending them, of course."

* * *

The Haslemere restaurant was full and as they waited at the bar, Sylvia drank her evening quota and picked up two businessmen new to the area.

"Why is Lilly sending them?" asked Sylvia.

"Because she's decided I'm cold. She sends two, sometimes three, every post."

"I wouldn't have thought you were cold," said Sylvia. "I mean, that isn't a problem, is it? It wasn't with Alex Galsworthy surely? Anyway, what's it to do with her what

you do in bed? It's a lousy thing to do. Send things anonymously."

"It's too perfect, that's what's wrong."

"What is?"

"All that loving."

"Well, don't knock it. Enjoy it."

"People aren't used to things being perfect. It makes you
jumpy. You wonder when the bomb's going off. They
weren't like that—James and Alice in the postcards."

"There wasn't time for much to go wrong. Anyway, that
was different."

"In what way?" asked Victoria sharply.

"Well—it just happened. It was obviously a lovely, life-
shattering surprise." Victoria had never heard her friend
talk like that before.

She took a postcard out of her bag. Two scarlet roses
glistened with dew. Beside them was a verse in gold.

"Roses were big then, too." She read the message on the
back. " 'I will never forget anything about you, Alice. There
is no one like you. I shall remember every little thing about
you for always.' "

Sylvia made no comment.

"In what way is James's affair with Alice different? Passionate, you mean?" Victoria asked.

"Well—a real love affair."

Victoria was silent. Was hers a real love affair? Did Gerry
feel, "There's no one like you"? Would he "remember every
little thing about her for always"? She wanted to call and ask
him. But Colin would answer and the rosebud child would
be awakened. Colin would act surprised. "It's after ten,
ducky. Where's the fire?"

"Challenge Lilly," Sylvia said.

"Oh, I will."

"What does Gerry say? Does he think it's Lilly?"

"I haven't told him."

"Why on earth not?"

She shrugged. She felt somehow that the anonymous arrival of the cards put her in a bad light.

"What's wrong with you, Vee?"

"Nothing I know of."

"You're different. Is everything all right? I mean with Gerry?"

"Yes, it's perfect. I told you."

But she wondered all the same. Who is Gerry? Underneath all the charm?

His life had changed little since her arrival. He filled his time from the moment he got up at six, mostly with private activities: running, meditation, writing, reading. He spent hours walking the dogs. He liked cooking, arranging flowers, mending clocks and lamps. He always spent some time in the garden. He was available to his students whenever they needed him. He was kind, even motherly. His life was simple, ordered, and he chose frugality. The dressing up and going out was for Victoria's benefit. Left alone, he always had a good day. It was never frustrating or insufficient. She was surprised he could feel so good on so little. He purposely tried to achieve balance. Even with her. When she first asked him if he loved her, he had said, "More than you realize."

"A lot? A little?"

"Enough."

He seemed very different from the ambitious young pupil of Gilbert Ricks or the passionate adoring husband of the first Mrs. de Santos.

CHAPTER · 6

OUT IN THE GARDEN, LILLY WAS SITTING HUNCHED ON A chair. She seemed to be in pain. Victoria watched her pull a clump of roses toward her, bury her face in the petals and inhale deeply. She used the mask of flowers like an anesthetic during labor. How Victoria's father would have approved of her. A real woman with her provocative breasts and sharp, breathless laugh.

Victoria crept up as though she was an enemy. Lilly's voice, though, was pleasant as she greeted her. Rising on some floral high, she was prepared to be friendly. They'd seen everything that was to be seen about each other within the first minute of meeting.

"Thank you for the postcards."

Lilly let go of the roses, and they swung back into place, efficiently.

"The First World War postcards."

Lilly's expression showed only innocence as she shook her head. "I've never sent you any cards."

They looked at each other without friendliness.

"Well?" said Lilly.

"Well what?"

"Why ask me?"

"I keep getting postcards. I've had over fifty. No sender's name."

"It's a chain letter. We get them in the States. Someone's put your name on an old-postcard chain. They have postage-stamp chains, photographs, money—"

"But would they all come from the same part of London? N.W. 5?"

"Well, wait and see if they come from anywhere else."

Gerry, followed by his son, walked close by in another part of the garden. She could hear their words quite clearly.

"Did she really walk a tightrope?" asked James.

"In Paris. In a nightclub in Pigalle. She took her clothes off as she walked the rope and met a black girl in the middle," Gerry replied.

Lilly's large brown eyes were full on Victoria's face.

"I put a rope up between the trees," said Gerry. "But she wouldn't take her clothes off."

"She doesn't do everything you want then," said James suggestively.

Lilly went on staring. Her eyes were old and assessing, not without cruelty.

Victoria was embarrassed. "It was only a temporary job. I had to do it for money. I don't suppose I did it twenty times."

"Well, it certainly made an impression on Gerry."

"I'd love to have seen her on a tightrope," said Gerry, wistfully.

"I'm on one right here, don't worry," said Victoria.

Lilly smiled, amused. Victoria knew she didn't like her.

Gerry described Victoria's mother eating forbidden sweets. "There was telltale sherbet all over her blouse and her chin." The men laughed. Meanwhile Lilly and Victoria were stranded in each other's company.

"We'll pick the roses for your bouquet just before you set off for the church."

"It's a lovely idea, Lilly, but my mother is having the flowers done professionally." She realized her tone was not unlike her mother's.

Lilly stared without warmth. "What school did you go to?"

Victoria named the fashionable private school patronized by royalty.

"And what was that like?"

Victoria shrugged. A difficult silence followed and they both heard the end of Gerry's anecdote.

"Victoria tried to say her mother was senile to explain the eccentric behavior. 'A bit early for that,' I replied. 'Well, I can't help it,' she said. 'We go off early in this family. Better make the most of me while you can.' And I do," he said softly. "How I do! I never thought I could be happy again."

Lilly shivered.

"Is she really only twenty-two?" James asked.

"She's just a kid but she's been around."

Colin, dressed in a sharp-shouldered suit, walked between Lilly and Victoria. He tried to hitch up a stream of yellow roses.

"Gerry's just let it go," said Lilly. "It's a shame. He always kept it just as it was—well, the way—" she sighed.

"Wait till Softdrinks comes out here," said Colin. "He'll make him get down to it."

Lilly looked uneasy.

"Who's Softdrinks?" said Victoria.

"A businessman in America. Gerry's friend."

"What's his name?"

"Oh, he's never mentioned by name. He's too . . ." Colin paused. "Famous."

Gerry had never mentioned Softdrinks to her. "Do you know him?" Victoria asked Lilly.

The woman hesitated. "No."

Victoria did not miss Colin's amused glance.

"Once met, never forgotten. That's Softdrinks," said Colin. "He won't even go to the local shop without a bodyguard. He has crumpled-up newspaper all around his bed. You can never be too careful. It's a brutal world."

"I like your jacket," said Lilly, trying to change the subject.

"There are people who say he's CIA, but we all know he's Mafia."

Lilly turned around for Gerry. He came toward her. He didn't smile or even touch her. He was just there—for her.

"Still, they're both the same thing these days," said Colin, and the roses pricked his hands. They bled normally.

"Change the subject, Col," said Gerry. "After all, Vee hasn't even met him."

"When's he coming here?" asked Victoria.

"He isn't." Gerry was reassuring, as always.

"He's very tough for all his religion," Colin continued. "Gerry and I were with him in the States and he got his young partner to cozy up to a real Chicago baddie. He wanted to get his new vitaminized squash into the Vegas casinos. The young man—"

Gerry grabbed him from behind and covered his mouth. Colin's work-reddened hands were still bleeding. Thorns scratched at his arm. "Are you going to be good?" asked Gerry playfully.

"Be careful," said Lilly scathingly. "You'll smudge his makeup."

"Gerry, let go," Colin said immediately. "You can't say he's not a syndicate man. He used to wash the Chicago money in New York. He lives through Gerry. Even fucks by proxy. He has an identity problem; even his shrink says so. On good days he thinks he's Gerry. On bad days he thinks he's his mother."

Then he looked at Lilly. He'd get around to her later, in private.

Lilly turned to Gerry and said softly, "Do you remember Sicily? Our holiday there?"

Colin burst into tears.

At first they hoped he was laughing. Then Gerry started gently toward him. Colin, muttering savagely, dodged his outstretched arms and made off across the meadow. Gerry followed. For a while the others stayed silent.

"The sun's gone in," said Lilly cheerfully.

"It's a funny summer altogether," said James.

"You can say that again. I only mentioned that holiday in Sicily because the weather's so nice. Surely it's nothing to cry about."

"Why did you go to Sicily?" said Victoria.

"Why not?" she answered rudely. "My grandmother lives there. That's why."

"Let's go in," said Victoria. "I'll make some tea."

As Victoria talked to her mother on Gerry's bedroom extension, she faced the window. The light was just right to provide a clear reflection. She saw what seemed to be a white wing. She turned. In reality it was a simple folded paper on the bedside table. It stuck out at a jaunty angle from behind Gerry's bedtime book. If she hadn't seen it in the reflection she probably would not have seen it at all. Thinking it was a note that had got accidentally pushed out of sight, she picked it up.

> My love,
>   The shame makes me mute before you. I have to face the real motive for that which did you harm. It was all ill-done. All of it. Think well of me.

For once, Gerry had taken trouble with his handwriting. She put the paper back where she'd found it, went and stood in the sun. She still felt cold.

* * *

Colin and Lilly talked about Crowsley in the old days. There was no place for Victoria. The black feeling was there again. The need to let something out was imperative. She sat very still, swallowing back distress. Then Gerry came into the kitchen and everything was transformed. He brought calm and good humor. Some days he was so soothing there was something almost medicinal about him. He checked off ten items on the gift list and telephoned his mother for the names of her guests. He wanted to please, to make up for his churlish behavior about the ceremony. "Of course I want to marry you. You deserve the best and you'll get it." That was his message to her. She didn't mention the other one, the written one. The next time she went into the bedroom it was gone.

Gerry was smiling at Victoria. She knew with her he could think about his youth without pain. It was back in place, nourishing the present, not painfully detached. He'd absorbed love from her. Every neglected, lonely piece of his body had had its share. His eyes lingered. Secretly, behind the others' backs, he caressed her body, and the black feeling started to lift. He whispered an invitation and she agreed.

There were five people in the kitchen. James sat at the table reading a newspaper. The child stood beside him eating her father's cake. Lilly was making tea at the stove. Gerry stood with Victoria by the back door.

Victoria saw them all reflected in the glass. And then she saw something else. At first she thought it was a trick of the light.

"We'll make love as soon as they start putting the baby to bed," Gerry whispered.

Victoria turned now toward the room, but what she had seen in the glass was still there.

The figure was dark against the light, quite at home.

Victoria looked away quickly. Lilly was going on about Boston. The figure was there at the table. She didn't have to look to know that.

"I want to undress you and . . ." Gerry whispered the rest of the sexual program.

She broke away from him and ran. She ran across the grass but could not get away from that image in the kitchen. The family and the extra person sort of fitted in, a darkish, slim figure, made conveniently anonymous because of the light. The others seemed to have known it was there. They had acknowledged its presence, given it space. She ran into the rose garden, Gerry right behind her.

The sky swung forward and her body banged against the black earth he was so proud of. She lay jarred, looking up at the bushes. He picked her up.

"Why did you run away like that?"

"There seemed to be more people. One more."

"Oh, is that all. I thought you were getting prudish."

"One more person, Gerry."

"You saw yourself reflected in the back door."

"No."

"A trick of the light. It's the time of year. Colin coming in."

"No." But she wanted to believe it. She clung to him and wanted to lose herself in the way she could always get pleasure. She kept thinking about Gerry. She'd think about anything to keep the other thought out. Six people, not five.

*   *   *

They ate dinner in the garden and throughout the meal Gerry discussed plans for their marriage. He thrilled Victoria with his warm, slow smiles. There was a resonance to his voice that she loved. It made it different from any other voice. Lilly hung on to his every word, too. The level of female excitement was high. Colin was included in that category.

The inside of the house was ordinary. Everything was doing its best to suggest nothing was wrong. There was no extra person. What she'd seen in the kitchen should be forgotten. Some chemical mistake during that charged afternoon had revealed the invisible. The calm of the sitting room promised it would never happen again.

Victoria's engagement photograph on the piano had been joined by a new picture of the grandchild. James's schoolboy butterfly collection had been moved to the packed bookshelves. An official-looking photograph of Gerry's father hung in the hall. There were three photographs of Professor Gilbert Ricks at various stages of his embittered life, with lines of poetry written by hand beneath the last.

> What might have been and what has been
> Point to one end, which is always present.
> Footfalls echo in the memory
> Down the passage which we did not take
> Towards the door we never opened
> Into the rose-garden.

Lines from T. S. Eliot. She read them again. This was the poem that had made such an impression on Gerry that he'd planted the garden. Another picture of Gilbert Ricks hung over their bed.

* * *

She ran a bath and Gerry got in with her. "What's all this about postcards? Lilly said something about it."

"I keep getting sent some."

"How nice."

"Anonymously. That's not so nice."

"What—dirty ones, you mean?"

"Shiny old-fashioned ones."

"How lovely."

She asked him questions about his past. She half suspected a jealous rival. Their engagement had been announced ten days ago in the national press. Was there a student with a crush on him? A hundred, both sexes. She didn't feel she could show him the cards, but she described a couple. He didn't remember any from either war. He'd never heard of Alice Murray or James Hamilton.

When he got into bed he was still in a good mood. But when she touched him, moved her hand slowly across his thighs, he lay motionless, not feeling anything. He just wasn't there for her.

* * *

Four o'clock in the morning. All was not well. She heard the living room clock strike, then the tinkling one in the study. She had had the rose-garden dream with a new variation: The roses had looked beautiful but as she got nearer, they were covered with greenfly and mildew. The bigger ones were wet and rotting. Diseased patches fell off in chunks and plopped to the ground. Cobwebs swung between the bushes like old wedding veils hung out to dry. And the rope swing, not hanging as it should, was swinging wildly, to and fro, empty, dangerous, not a happy sight, as though someone had just leaped from it in full flight. She realized, of course, she'd always known, that the rose garden was a graveyard. Somewhere quite near was the sepulcher in which the first wife lay. She asked a gardener where it was. She thought he was Professor Ricks. He pointed the way. It wasn't hidden at all but right among them, where they least expected it.

"Of course, it's the house."

Gerry was awake, stroking her face.

"I don't like the garden, Gerry. I don't feel well."

"Why not? Flowers are healing. Colors make healing changes in your body if you can absorb them." He told her that color was important. She fell asleep before she understood why. It had to do with vibrations.

Her dream led her straight back to the rose garden. She could even feel the wet, black earth.

CHAPTER · 7

WHEN VICTORIA GOT BACK FROM DELIVERING HER LATEST reviews, Gerry was entertaining his Oxford colleagues. Professor Gully's wild, tightly frizzed hair hung in lumps like Brillo pads gone mad. Colin was watching it cautiously. He said he'd never seen anything like it. "But then lecturing is one profession where a hairstyle doesn't count against you."

Gerry trimmed the boxtrees and told malicious stories innocently and the professors laughed fit to burst. Lilly stood close to Gerry as he worked. She looked at him with such sexual appetite that for a moment it seemed she was going to grab him. She thought better of it and sat down by her husband, out of trouble.

Victoria knew that Lilly was in love with Gerry. She was sure James knew too, but he didn't want to think about it. They all wanted to maintain the status quo. Nothing must change. Even Victoria's wedding must be kept to a minimum.

Professor Gully got the conversation back to the controversial Gilbert Ricks. "You surpassed him in every way, Gerry."

"Because he was not an Establishment figure. I was," said Gerry. "He didn't manage the required kowtow. I'd learned to do it without losing face. My father spent most of his life with the Chinese.

"The recognition Joyce has now is in part thanks to him. The same goes for Eliot. He championed them when no one so much as read them." Gerry sighed. "How I envy him."

"But he denounced you in his lectures." Professor Gully was starting to enjoy himself. "You were number one on his enemy list." A dust like dry soap lifted off the Brillo pads. It was all the excitement.

"Oh, forget it," said James. "He's dead."

Left out, Victoria decided to walk in the sun.

The roses looked too red. Full of color and juice. It reminded her of her menstrual period. She walked through the arch toward the red enemy. "Towards the door we never opened/Into the rose-garden." She knew the T. S. Eliot poem by heart. Everything was still; even the convivial sounds from the house were hushed.

> What might have been and what has been
> Point to one end, which is always present.

She felt the approach of the unseen presence.

> Footfalls echo in the memory
> Down the passage which we did not take
> Towards . . .

She expected panic would send her scurrying to Gerry, but her feet were solidly pressed against the dark, beneficial earth he had personally tended. The roses looked as though they were about to bleed. Panic had been replaced by a wish to understand. What was the presence? The past? Its unforgettable incidents? Or was it an intruder? Whatever it was it did not wish her well. Bushes rustled as though touched. The worst that could happen was death. You had to die sometime.

Then she saw Lilly behind her, picking some buds.

"Glorious, aren't they?" She sounded normal. "Superstar—did they name it after Gerry, I wonder?"

"Do you notice anything?"

"Like what?"

"A lowering of the atmosphere?"

"Oh, that's just Oxford. There's real humidity here. It doesn't suit a lot of people."

Just the weather then. Not that bad. She remembered the first time she'd been shown into the garden. She'd felt something even then.

Victoria went back to the group. The dons rose to acknowledge her. Gerry said, "Education should be set against the social environment." They all sat down again.

Later she went to get Professor Gully's coat. She hesitated before pushing open the bedroom door. The French lace curtains moved a little but only with the breeze. Hardly breathing, she stayed near the door. She felt the room was occupied or had just been. She was the interloper. She hoped it was some nervous thing.

Gerry helped Professor Gully into his dusty, food-stained jacket. Shyly the untidy man shook hands with the family. Gerry walked with him to the gate, holding his arm. He'd picked him a bunch of roses, packed up some cake. He talked to him kindly about the forthcoming summer holidays. The professor's eternal problem, loneliness, seemed worse in the bright days. Gerry watched him cycle shakily toward the main road.

When all the dons had left, Lilly sat on Gerry's lap, her silk skirt high above her knees. The glow of her thighs filled the room. Victoria went into the bedroom.

Gerry followed her. She pretended to be writing movie reviews. He kissed her on the back of the neck.

She could hear Lilly laughing in the kitchen. Sometimes the noise she made was crude, jarring. She had a rough side that all the society parties and education couldn't hide, like her passion for her father-in-law.

"Do you think our relationship is passionate?" she asked.
He didn't answer.

"Well, what about romantic?"

"It's companionable with erotic interludes." He kissed
her. "I love being with you."

"Do you long for me?"

"Well, of course not. I'm with you. I'm not pursuing you.
We're not separate at all, are we? I feel we're in it together,
which is very nice."

"It's not intense?"

"It's harmonious."

She swallowed back a rather large amount of disappointment.

"What did Lilly do before she was married?"

"She was a student at UCLA. You know that."

"I mean sexually."

"Why all the questions? You know I don't like that." He
tried to sound casual.

"Why not?"

"Most of the time there are no answers. Just more questions. I'll answer that question but my answer will only lead
to another."

"Fun for your students," she said angrily. "Well, how
about this one? Answer this and there won't be any need for
another question."

She was about to bring the whole thing, the wedding,
America, down on her head. For a moment she was scared.
How would Alice handle this? The definitive question was
not about Lilly. It was about the earlier woman, his wife. But
the question could not be asked. Instead she said, "Are you
happy with me?"

"Happy? Happy?"

"Well, that's what everyone wants."

"You make it sound so simple."

"Shall I dress it up then in some scene from a classical novel? That's what you find acceptable. You liken everything to one of those lousy dead plots."

"Oh, Victoria. That's a showstopper." He laughed. "What about you? Everything comes out of a movie."

She burst out laughing. Still laughing, they reached for each other and fell across the bed. He kissed her breasts, his hands moving over her in the way she loved. She was, as always, drawn toward him in spite of her doubts. She could not resist. It was delicious, every teasing sexual thing he did to her. They made love too well.

Afterward she looked up roses in a book about flowers and mythology. Were they malevolent? Had they ever killed anybody? The book didn't say anything about that.

Roses had played a significant part in the Black Death. It was believed their fragrance purified the air and so protected people from the disease. "Ring around the rosie" originated at that time and was recited as a purifying ritual. A passage about air purification had been underlined in pencil. On the flyleaf of the book she read, "To my husband, Gerry, with all my heart I love you. May '63." She was getting used to other people's love correspondence.

She went back to the bedroom and reread the postcards. South London, 1915, was a world she could believe in.

Suddenly she knew Gerry was capable of great, intense love. He could be consumed by passion, made electric by the physical presence of the person he wanted. She knew all this. She also knew he did not feel that for her. He was marvelous in bed, of course, because it was something he needed and felt confident about. The happiness she made him feel was not the happiness of the postcards. Youth by proxy, an end to loneliness, a new domestic coziness. But could he feel as James Hamilton had once? " 'I will remember every little thing about you for always. . . . I didn't know happiness like that existed.' " Gerry had experienced ecstasy, she was sure of that, but he didn't expect to touch those high notes again.

When Gerry asked to see the postcards again, she wasn't eager to show them. If he read them, he would see, as she did, that their relationship was ordinary in comparison. Victoria was ashamed because he did not seem to feel as intensely about her. She thought, in some way, that it was her fault. "They're in Haslemere," she lied.

*　　*　　*

By the time they got to the town, the gray weather had turned electric with approaching thunder and didn't suit anyone. Victoria hadn't wanted to come but she wouldn't be alone in that house anymore. They sat down together at a coffee shop.

Gerry had gone onto his biannual diet, eating six pounds of grapes and three heads of lettuce a day. He drank only mineral water. The diet lasted seven days and he felt lousy during six of them. He explained the benefit of cleaning out the body. "Accumulation of waste leads to tiredness and a breakdown in health. Being well is my responsibility, not a doctor's—or God's. You can choose whether or not to allow sickness into your body."

James had trouble with that one. He was remembering his mother.

"I see no benefit in living like a fag rabbit." Lilly felt faddish health care was something you kept to yourself, like impotence.

Gerry changed the subject deftly. "Tell them again about the tightrope-walking in Paris, Vee. Go on."

She told them how she'd changed the date of birth on her passport so she could get a job in a high-paying nightclub. "You had to be nineteen. The police said I was under age. They said I'd tampered with the date. I said it had got wet. How? It fell in the sea. Then how come only the date was affected? They took me into custody. Then I escaped." She left out Alex Galsworthy's part in it. She'd done it for him, all of it.

Victoria's love of fun was infectious, and Gerry looked much better. He watched her enjoying a cream bun. She told him about the customers' sexual requirements and the money they offered.

"These upper-class girls will do anything," said Lilly.

"Yes," said Gerry eagerly. He winked at Victoria and laughed, enjoying himself. Then he shivered.

"Don't tell me you're getting a cold now," said Lilly.

"Someone just walked over my grave." He turned back to Victoria. "Do you remember this place?"

"Of course. Do you remember that morning in the theater lobby?"

"Of course not." He laughed.

"Oh, come on. Who was that woman? The dark one?"

He shook his head. "I was never at a movie theater in London in the morning with a dark woman. I've tried to tell you."

Victoria felt disturbed. "But when I said hello a year later, you said you were."

"I didn't say I was or I wasn't."

"Well, why didn't you say we'd never met?"

"Because I thought it was your way of picking me up. I liked the look of you. Who am I to disagree about a theater lobby?"

"Oh Gerry, stop kidding me."

On the way home she knew why he had refused to admit he was the man in the theater. The brunette was somebody's wife.

CHAPTER · 8

As Victoria tried on the restyled Chinese silk wedding dress in Knightsbridge, she thought about Colin. When I'm away from him I know he dislikes me. But when I go into the kitchen and ask for a drink, his response is friendly. She wished urgently that someone would offer him another show so she could take her rightful place in the kitchen, looking after her husband.

"We've put Chinese embroidery around the waist as well as the hem. How's Mary? She is so beautiful. Think twice before you get rid of the rose chain. Roses are effective."

"I know that."

She walked through Piccadilly to Fortnum's restaurant and looked for Gerry. In every stranger, she looked for him. With surprise she realized that her old habit of seeking Mr. Right had not gone away. She looked for the hair, its soft thickness, the way it swept back in a curve at each side. Every slim, middle-aged man of medium height, dressed darkly, was Gerry until she got close. She had the uncanny feeling he was everywhere.

* * *

On the way to the restaurant to meet Victoria, Sylvia had driven to Alice's original home in South London. It had been replaced by a shopping complex. Now Victoria handed her the latest cards.

> Dear Alice,
> My time is altered today to a late shift at 407

Branch so shall not be done early enough to go to the first house of anywhere. So I will have to put it off. Hope your mother is better. Love to all.

> From your sincere friend,
> George

It was dated 1916.

There was a black shiny one dated 1917 with ALICE printed across the front in white capitals filled with photographs of girls' faces.

Dear Alice,
    Just a card to let you know I arrived safely after six hours riding. It was very unpleasant facing cold wind all the way.

> George

"Who's this George?" said Sylvia.

"Lilly said it's a chain letter."

"I don't think so. Would all the senders come from North West five?"

Southend, 1916.
Dear Mum,
    Arrived safely at 1:45. The weather is V.G. I'm going to look for a room. Will write later.

> With love,
> Alice

"Seven kisses! She didn't know what to say," said Sylvia, pointing to another card. "None of them did except James."

A winsome girl with crimped, fair, tinted hair sat in front of a mountain backdrop. She carried artificial flowers in one hand and tried to balance herself on a bridge with the other, making the most of her curves as she did so. The models hadn't yet learned to smile for the camera and the result was more a leer from a horror movie.

"There's one from James."

> Dear Alice,
>   I've been thinking about the first time I met you at Charles's party. I starcd at you but didn't know how to talk to you. You were so earthy and natural, so life-loving. My friend Beth was jealous. She stood beside me. Do you remember? I'm dying to make love—

There was no room on the card to finish the message.

"Well, he was still alive in May 1916," said Sylvia.

A black-and-white mat card showed a French church reduced to rubble. The pulpit stood alone among heaps of plaster and hanging beams. Three plaster angels hung dangerously above a doorway almost swallowed by falling masonry. A penciled message on the back had been rubbed out. Did this card inform Alice of the death of James Hamilton? Is that why it was rubbed out?

Sylvia had the same idea. "They used cards instead of phones in those days. James used a postcard to tell Alice about his pal dying. Perhaps Charles wrote to her, 'Dear Alice, I'm afraid my pal James Hamilton got it in France. I'm sure he'd want me to let you know.' I can't bear him to be dead. He was so alive, wasn't he? And attractive?"

"I thought you weren't sentimental," said Victoria.

"Those days were different. It was all right then."

For once Sylvia was soft and vulnerable. She couldn't allow it for herself but it was all right for Alice. "I looked in the phone book. There are Murrays in South London, but they don't know of an Alice. I can't help feeling he did die, yet the wartime cards from her friends were quite cheerful." Sylvia picked one up.

Dear Alice,
   Just a card to let you know I am having a gay time
which you would have if you were here.

Best love,
Lil

After the war the cards showed British vacation spots. The
messages were about the weather. No mention of war. No
mention of James.

Many cards showed women with waved hair, arch smiles,
wispy dresses decorated with cloth flowers. The messages
were written in indelible pencil turning pink. One or two
were in faded brown ink, the handwriting spindly. James
alone had a voice. The card about Jordans Wood and
James's unexpected happiness was unforgettable.

"They really had a love affair, didn't they? In comparison, my wedding seems almost dull."

"Perhaps that's what the sender wants you to feel. They're
not sent in friendship, Vee."

The continuing arrival of the cards troubled Victoria. But
it was her own yearning for a time that was gone that
preoccupied her more than the identity and purpose of the
sender.

"So how's Crowsley?" Sylvia asked.

"Fine."

"And Gerry?"

"Marvelous."

"You're not thinking of chucking your wedding, are
you?"

Victoria was affronted. "Of course not. I've only got
eleven weeks left." She made it sound like a prison sentence.
But every social occasion that involved her mother brought
out the very worst in her. Penal adjectives were not unusual.
Eleven weeks and one day.

"Vee, listen to me. You don't have to do it. Maybe he is not Mr. Right and Mr. Right is still to come. I know after seeing him in that movie theater you decided he was Mr. Right and—"

"Reason didn't come into it. I wanted to go to him. We were like two halves coming together. All my lonely, separated feelings vanished. It was like coming home. This is where I belong."

"It's a bit hazardous putting all your eggs in one basket."

"As you've never tried, how do you know?"

She apologized immediately but Sylvia ignored it.

"There's a right road and a wrong road," Victoria insisted.

"Did you screw the religious instructor at school? Is that where all this comes from?" Sylvia asked.

"Seeing Gerry was finding the right road at last but I still had to wait a year before I saw him again. I've been in so many dark lanes and cul-de-sacs. Such a waste of time."

It was too much for Sylvia. But then Victoria had always been old-fashioned.

Victoria wanted to talk about the sixth person in the kitchen. Was it a trick of the light? Her own fatigue? Had other people experienced similar distortions? She tried to describe the threatening atmosphere, the black sunlight.

"Have you heard of it before?"

Sylvia, fresh from the emergency room, had heard of everything.

"Well, what caused it?"

"The sun."

"The son?" Victoria was flabbergasted. "What has he got to do with me?"

"Sitting in the sun. If you overdo it you get chilled and feel a bit funny. Especially if you've been drinking. I know."

Victoria was disgusted. She could see why so many people

had no use for hospitals. "I've never known anything like it. It started the Sunday they arrived from Boston."

"It was Sunday and Sundays, like Christmas, are special." Sylvia added quietly, "For neurotics."

"It's the rose garden. It stinks of depression. I can't get it out of my mind. I even dream about it."

"You're trying to disown your feelings. Have you talked to Walter Guinea?"

"The shrink next door? Really, Syl!" She was disappointed.

"Let's try and find Alice, and then we'll know who's sending the cards," Sylvia suggested.

"She's dead. If she isn't she's too old to be bothered."

Victoria took out one of the cards dated 1916: " 'I've just been thinking about the first time I saw you, Alice. Through the gloom I could just make you out. You wore a yellow dress. Even at that distance I loved the way you smiled. I'm dying to hold you.' "

Victoria sat holding the card. "Does Gerry still feel that about me?"

* * *

The sweetest moments were when he held his granddaughter. The child knew all about getting attention. When she wasn't, her mother, Lilly, was. Then a student arrived with a domestic problem. Really, he was in love with Gerry and upset because he was leaving for America. Victoria expected Gerry to suggest a siesta when the others were out in Witham Woods, hoping that that was one side of love only she could provide. But Gerry wanted to go to Oxford. He said something about a bookshop closing. She held him tenderly, but if he was affected, he was keeping it to himself.

She phoned Sylvia urgently and arranged to meet her.

Seated together at a pub, Victoria tried to express her fears to Sylvia.

"He keeps touching them. He keeps on with the child. She captivates him. He loves everybody. No, everybody loves him. The thing is, they're all in love with each other. Lilly, James, the rosebud child, Gerry. I could never respond on that scale." She stopped, out of breath.

"Why don't you just join in?" Sylvia appeared disappointed. When Victoria had said something was wrong, she'd expected something else.

"I can only be a spectator. That's what they want me to be."

"My, you sound bitter." She held Victoria's hand. "Come on. Why aren't you laughing? Don't tell me you're taking rivals seriously. You *have* changed."

"Everything started after that Sunday. That's when he wanted everything reduced. The modest wedding. Everything small. No fuss." The black Sunday reminded her of something half learned, half remembered. Something she'd seen or read, it eluded her.

"And of course *she* would have joined in."

"Who?"

"The first wife. You remember one of the Alice cards? The one from her friend Lil in 1910. A beggar girl stood barefoot in the snow looking into a fancy restaurant. A couple sat by the window. He was elegant, she was beautiful. The table was loaded with food. They were enjoying themselves. They weren't looking at the poor girl outside but they were aware of her. Her exclusion, her hunger made their enjoyment greater. So you see, they need me there. My presence heightens their love games. There's nothing like a character left out in the cold to enrich a scene. And on top of everything I have the cards. Why on the eve of marriage should an anonymous sender present a bouquet of somebody else's romance, one more heady than my own?"

"If they make love to each other that much, perhaps

there's something wrong. Perhaps they're hiding something," Sylvia suggested.

"Do you think so?" Victoria sounded almost pleased.

"It's not English."

"What do you think is wrong?"

"I'm not there so how should I know?"

Victoria said something about inviting her the following
week.

"Cheer up. I think it's the child that's upset you. Nobody
steals scenes the way they do. You're the bride and you
expect a bit of attention. Anyone would feel the same."

Victoria felt a little better. Then she remembered Sylvia
was a professional at cheering people up.

"You know, I don't feel safe anymore."

"Well, you'll feel safe after you're married."

"Oh, I don't know. I'm just a visitor in his life, really."

"Perhaps he's in here," said Sylvia suddenly.

"Who?"

"Mr. Right."

Victoria looked around at the meek stockbrokers on a
showy night out on expense accounts with imported London
naughties. "You wouldn't even get Mr. Wrong in this
place."

Sylvia ordered another bottle of wine.

"I could be anyone at Crowsley. A passerby, an *au pair*. I
vow at the next meal they'll notice me and listen to what I
say. But as soon as conversation starts, I'm struck dumb."

"Make a statement. Anything. What did you talk about
with Alex?"

"Talk?" She almost laughed. "We used to quarrel, I
remember that. You know, Gerry and I have never had a
fight."

"If you want fights try staying with my father. His latest
award hasn't done him any good at all. He's drinking so

much he goes to bed on all fours."

"We don't have quarrels because Gerry doesn't want them. He controls everything."

* * *

There was certainly tension at the Scrabble table and it had nothing to do with winning a game. Lilly's laugh was slightly out of control. James was too quiet. Had he noticed the way she'd got hold of his father? Twice Lilly had grasped Gerry's hand and pushed it down out of sight into her lap.

"I can still come each year?" Lilly's question had nothing to do with traveling.

"But of course," said Gerry, calmly. He lifted his hands into sight and concentrated on the game. Lilly made several more claims on Gerry for the future. She did it in public so she had witnesses. The bride was not to change anything.

Victoria reeled with the complexities of his relationships. Every mealtime introduced a new admirer, either in the house or in the States. The ocean didn't make them any less of a threat; he liked admiration and didn't care where it came from. From the bedroom window she'd seen him take his prize student into the rose garden. Every small movement, each facial expression was designed to tantalize. Seen through glass it was especially noticeable.

He has to have everyone in love with him. And I thought I'd outgrown movie stars years ago.

Colin spelled "slut" and "tart." He couldn't quite manage "gangster."

Lilly turned to Victoria and spoke confidentially. "I used to have such a crush on Gerry."

Why put it in the past? Victoria wondered.

"When he came to L.A. I spent my life trying to see him undressed. I hung around—"

"That's enough." James patted her without affection.

"That bathroom, the bedroom. And when I saw it, it was so big!"

Victoria looked embarrassed, so Lilly assured her it was all in the past. "I was just a girl."

"Why don't you stop chattering, Lilly," Gerry advised. "It's not as though you're winning." He sounded as if he meant other things.

"They say size isn't important, but I disagree. It's important to me. Mind you, he was always fascinated with America. He called us the Opportunity Market."

"What? Americans?" asked Victoria.

"My family."

"Why?"

"Because we have all that money."

Victoria turned to Gerry. "I didn't know you were interested in money."

"Come on, Vee, it's your turn," said James.

Lilly laughed harshly. "But he's fascinated by money. The making of it. You should hear him with my father. But it was different in those days. I mean he wanted it for Ruth. He wanted to give her everything."

Victoria's jealousy smoldered and she thought of the postcards. Were they sent out of jealousy?

"Your daughter's too pale, Lilly," Gerry said. "It's that New York air."

"But she's hardly in New York," protested Lilly. "We live in Boston, remember?"

"James works in New York a lot, doesn't he?"

She had to agree.

"He's away too much. That's what I meant."

Victoria could see he'd have preferred to blame the appalling air pollution. The absent father was second choice.

"And she's three and doesn't yet speak."

Gerry's tone was not friendly. Lilly gave him her loveliest

smile. She bent over to give him a view down the front of her dress. She could do what she wanted with him because she had beautiful breasts.

He couldn't quite look away from her so he got up and put on a record of Mozart, loudly. It was the first time Victoria had heard music in that house.

*   *   *

The next morning Lilly was up early and offered to bring Victoria some coffee. Gerry was out running. "I'm sorry about last night. I was drunk."

"How long are you staying?"

"Well, Gerry wants us to be at the wedding."

"But that's weeks away." Victoria was appalled.

"It's Ruthie he wants."

"Why?"

"Because she looks just like—" She pulled back from the precipice. "Gerry's mother."

Victoria recognized her folly. She'd seen Gerry's mother.

"In some lights," continued Lilly, uncertainly.

"What was Ruth like?"

"How can I remember? It was years ago."

Victoria was going to ask if she'd slept with Gerry but Lilly would only say no and asking would put Victoria in an inferior position.

"Thank you for saying sorry, Lilly. Gerry told me all about your relationship anyway."

"I bet he did not," she retorted swiftly.

"I can assure you he did."

"Then he has changed." She got up and wrapped the silk dressing gown securely around her, keeping her precious body out of the unpleasantness. "He never says anything to anyone."

"Why don't you leave him alone and go away?"

It had all gone too far for Lilly. She didn't mind trouble,

but she couldn't bear to be in disgrace with Gerry. She tried for a friendlier tone.

"It's all in the past. I never think about it normally. It's just being in this house that reminds me." Her mouth opened, then closed decisively.

"I'll talk to Gerry when he gets back," said Victoria.

"This house was so sexual. I used to lie in bed and masturbate like mad because he was with her. He did it all the time. The things she used to like. She used to make him come over her face. I watched it through the door. He tied her legs to—" She stopped and rubbed her arms. "I feel funny. It's her room, that's why."

She ran out into the sun.

CHAPTER · 9

THE POSTCARDS COMFORTED HER. LONDON, 1915, WAS STILL A world that made sense. On her twenty-first birthday, Alice's mother had given her a shiny deluxe card showing a huge red rose.

> Good Health, much Wealth and Happiness,
> Be yours through all the years,
> And many a friend be near
> To make life sweet and dear.

Nothing from James.

She didn't bother asking Colin anymore if she could have a share in running the house. She watched him rolling pastry for a meat pie. The flour accentuated the redness of his hands. She asked him why he didn't use hand cream.

"Hand cream, honey?" As though a cosmetic prop was unthinkable. He waited for Gerry to arrive fully in the kitchen before continuing. "Hand cream would not touch the problem. I've worked my hands to the bone looking after—well, things here."

Gerry opened the wine and left the kitchen. He did not like guilt.

"All his clothes are hand-laundered; his vegetables are fresh and scraped."

The suffering hands would keep him there forever.

"Why don't you go back on stage? You're always talking about it."

"Haven't I wanted to. But who would have looked after him?"

"Don't you ever go out and see people?"

He clattered two biscuit tins and made a lot of emptying out a package of ginger snaps. She thought, he's scared to even leave the house because I'll get in the kitchen and take his place.

"Were you here as much when your sister was ill?"

"I was on stage, honey, but I helped out."

"Did they talk about his work?" Suddenly, she had to know about that first, loving marriage, all the hurting truth.

"Well, of course, he could talk to her. She was educated."

There was a burning, incomprehensible expression in his eyes. He busied himself among the biscuit tins until it was gone.

"But I shouldn't be telling you all this. He wouldn't like it. He doesn't like being reminded of the happy times."

She grabbed two biscuit tins and shoved them angrily in the broom cupboard.

Amused, Colin rescued the tins. "Food goes in the food cupboard. At least it does in my house."

She bowed out into the sunshine. Lilly was sorting out her child's clothes. James and Professor Gully played croquet. Gerry amused the child. Everyone had their place, their tasks. Victoria wandered disconsolately through the rooms.

*   *   *

At Haslemere, Mother was trying to impress her family history on a small Swiss pastrycook as he decorated the cake. His hands started to shake. He tried to tell her to go away, but his English was poor. At the same time, Victoria talked to the regular chef about Mother's eating habits. She asked him to trim down the portions. He said it had nothing to do with him; he just did his job. He was sulking because someone else had been brought in to do the cake. He was soft and plump and when he smiled his eyes disappeared in a nest of wrinkles. Yet he was hardly forty. The crinkled eyes were supposed to make him look well-disposed and happy when he'd run out of being well-disposed and happy long ago. She supposed living with Mother had something to do with that.

While Victoria had been at Oxford, the Honorable Mrs. Brooke had sneaked in some embellishments. A full orchestra for the reception. A professional opera singer to join the choir in two Schubert songs while the couple signed the register in the vestry. New words had been added to the ceremony, but her mother couldn't remember them. " 'With my body I thee cherish.' Something like that. Cherish or adore. Your sister talked to the minister. They leave it out of services nowadays. I can't think why. Mary thought it would be a nice touch. It makes the whole thing physical. I thought you'd be the one to appreciate that."

Victoria let it pass. "I thought you were going to tone things down."

"He didn't skimp on the first Mrs. de Santos. Mary met some people who knew her. A journalist and his wife. The Kingsley-Roes. You're leaving everything to the last minute. What are you hanging around in Oxford for?"

Victoria could hardly say she felt insecure about a rose garden. Mother flounced over to the mirror and impulsively tried on a very small, square hat with tall feathers. It looked like two quill pens in an old-fashioned inkstand and should have been fun but Victoria was in no mood for laughter.

"I'm giving a supper so Gerry can get to know the Bonham-Hays."

"You can't wear that hat."

"What does he like to talk about?"

"Gilbert Ricks."

"I don't think I know him. Have we had him here?"

"He's dead. Gerry talks about American writers."

"What's wrong with English ones?"

"I don't know. Whatever the reason, he does well out of Americans." She felt that wherever he was, Gerry was thinking of her. Some days she felt he was inside her, a jack-in-the-box ready to leap out and illuminate all the dreary times. How she loved him.

"What on earth do you find to talk about? I understand his set is rather intellectual."

"If you don't have a vast vocabulary, it is possible to get across what you want to say with an expressive face and a pair of hands," Victoria retorted.

"You're always trying for worlds you can't enter."

"Meaning what?"

"You know what I mean." Mother turned away with her bitter little smile and tried on another hat.

Now Victoria was depressed. Even on everyday stuff she could only go one round of the conversation. Then Gerry lost her in the five-syllable labyrinth.

"I hate those fucking roses," she muttered.

"Sylvia doesn't give you cocaine, does she?" Mother asked calmly.

Victoria knew she was being quarrelsome and didn't answer.

"She takes all kinds of things, so I hear. And I hear plenty, don't you worry. I expect she gets it from the hospital. A sniff of this, a nibble of that."

"That's not nice." Victoria imitated Mother's distorted vowel sounds.

"She ought to get hold of herself or go back to Africa. They wouldn't notice it there. She's taken to drink, of course. Always at someone else's expense."

"She was always being dragged off to famous psychiatrists when she was a child. It made her think there was something wrong with her," Victoria commented.

"What did they say?" Mother was genuinely interested.

"Her father's too well known. She feels she can't compete with his audience for his attention. Sex comes into it, too. Remember that? S-E-X?" She was getting her own back.

"I can't stand him, I must say. He'd make anyone sick."

* * *

Mother got to Sylvia before she could be shown the latest postcards. Her huge girth was blocking the stairs. Sylvia had to help her down the last flight and scolded her for overeating.

"I eat all right. It's glands." She was always defensive. "You should know that, being a nurse." When they got into the parlor, with its magnificent fireplace, Mother opened a new bottle of port. "Can I offer you a glass, Sylvia?"

"I never drink during the day."

"You make up for it in the evening, so I hear. Well, I do. Medicinal reasons."

Sylvia admired the fireplace. Like the Honorable Mrs. Brooke, it had royal connections.

"You've been chosen as Victoria's maid of honor. Do you know your duties?"

"Well—to give her confidence."

"We'll all be doing that. We're already doing that. Temporary groom's assistant. Temporary journalist. She's always temporary. Temporary wife? What do you think? I must say I don't get a permanent feeling about this either."

This wedding might be her last crack at the Bonham-Hays.

"I want you to go with the florist to Crowsley and make sure she gets the best roses. Why not? He's got that huge rose garden. And get enough. Make sure she's not intimidated. Take charge of her wedding dress at the reception. I want her to change into the Yves Saint Laurent traveling suit.

Encourage that, Sylvia, will you? She has other ideas."

Victoria rescued her friend and took her up to the attic.

"Christ, I'm wrecked," Sylvia said. "Three stiffs today. They waited till I came on duty to die. Had to lay them out myself. We're short-staffed again."

Victoria flipped half a dozen postcards into Sylvia's lap, "Here's one she never sent."

> Dear James,
>   For the wall of your hut. Remember this place? You could put an X, we were here. And another and another. A lovely day so I'm off. Will write you where later. Maybe!!
>
>   Much love darling,
>   Alice

The card showed a deserted cliff in Hastings.

> Dear Alice,
>   On Tuesday my two cousins will be in London and would like you to spend some time helping to entertain them. As only you can! I will see you before they come. I'll tell you what they like . . . Guess!
>
>   Love,
>   Lil

"What did James and Alice have that we haven't?" said Victoria.

"Illusions."

Victoria shook her head.

"They were sentimental."

"No."

"Poor?"

"Fun. They had fun."

"Isn't Gerry fun?"

"I know everything about Alice was lighthearted and enjoyable. I know she looked forward to things. I think about her quite a lot actually. She cheers me up. It's very important when you're around someone like Gerry to keep your own identity. Or at least to keep something of your own. Otherwise you get sucked into his excitements and moods. You can be ecstatic with him, but you can also be stranded. So I keep Alice."

"I think he's the man for you. You've always been looking for an identity. You thought being a secretary was the answer. Then it was horses."

"I can't find what I want to do," Victoria explained simply.

"Maybe not, but at least he offers you a firm place in his life. He's well established. With him you'll get the attention you can't get on your own."

"To do something, you have to really want to do it. Passionately. Otherwise leave it alone. Alex taught me that. I wonder what he'd make of Crowsley. He hates intellectuals, and he'd hate Lilly, too. That's one response we'd have in common," Victoria said.

"I've been going through the hospital records looking for Alice. If she's alive she'd be attending an outpatients' clinic at the very least," Sylvia said.

"Since when has going to the hospital been a sign of longevity?"

"If she's still alive I'll find her," Sylvia said passionately.

"Why?"

"I want to know what she's got to do with you."

Sylvia went to ask Mother if Alice Murray had ever worked for her as a nanny or a cook. Mother was in no mood for chitchat about the past.

"Victoria's asked me. My mother had a lot of staff. How can I remember with all this going on? And tell her to take that tea chest of old things with her. I don't want it here— it'll mean she'll be coming back."

"If you can't recall an Alice Murray do you remember a James Hamilton? He served in the First War."

"If the don wanted an informal wedding he should have said so at the beginning. Thank God she didn't marry the painter. Think of the chaos that would have been."

"It wouldn't have lasted with him," said Sylvia.

"Nor will this," said Mother defiantly. She powdered her face with a huge pink puff and rang the bell for tea. "It's a big wedding or no wedding at all. He's just being cheap, doesn't want to pay his share." Mother shooed her out. She didn't want Sylvia to watch her eating.

Victoria stuffed a trash bag with out-of-date shoes. She was confused about what to throw away. Sylvia suggested the entire lot. "Make Crowsley a new start. I spoke to my father about Gerry. He remembers the first wife. He's surprised Gerry's marrying again. Ten years after she died Gerry said to my father, 'I thought at the time I wouldn't get over it. I know now I will never get over it.' My father said you should talk about roses if you get stuck. They're safe."

"Not when I'm around," Victoria whispered.

Victoria's sister Mary, long-limbed and elegant, came in and pretended to put on makeup. Sylvia couldn't stand her and left. Mary eyed Victoria suspiciously. She wasn't her idea of a bride.

Another trash bag waited shapelessly in the middle of the attic. Victoria picked up an evening dress that was too expensive to throw away, so she started a pile for charity.

"What do you talk about at Crowsley? It's all a bit over one's head, isn't it?" said Mary.

"I can't think of a thing. I just make faces. Before I go back I ought to get into practice. I'll read two pages of the dictionary each night. Well, that's what they do. You're not born with words like *curlicue* and *atavism*."

"Atavism? Is that the new tranquilizer?"

Victoria found a clock given to her by an aunt years ago. She tried to wind it up. Not knowing what to do with it, she put it on the narrow mantelpiece. It settled precariously on its broken feet like a lopsided bird, timeless, useless.

"Try and seem a bit grateful, Vee. Mummy's put a lot into it." Mary was beautiful, solvent, established, loved. Everything was easy for her, always had been. She was born that way.

When she'd gone, Victoria sat among her unsorted possessions. Late-afternoon sun appeared around a corner of the window, and soon the attic was a blaze of light and the objects took on a new and mournful character. The sun showed their scars, their dustiness. She sat still, nearly bursting with sadness. Finding Mr. Right had not changed anything.

The sunlight trailed out of the room and down the side of the house. It almost reached the wall next door. The clock, her aunt's gift for Christmas all those years ago, reminded her of long-lost treasures. A *Little Gray Rabbit* book, a Victorian doll with cracked china cheeks; the smell of Vicks in the nursery, haunting sunlight that belonged to childhood. It did not have the same radiance now.

CHAPTER · 10

VICTORIA DID TAKE RESPONSIBILITY FOR HER ACTIONS, AS Gerry had suggested, but not in the way he would have liked. She left a summer dance in a nearby village and walked across the fields to Crowsley.

First she asked Colin if he was sending the cards. He was depressed and his skin was steeped in massage oil.

"Why should I send anything? If I had something to say I'd say it to your face." He started mixing a wet, white paste. It was either a facial or tomorrow's pudding. "He's quite transformed that little girl. She'll miss him if she has to go back to America."

"What do you mean *if?*"

"He'll try and keep her. He wants her to go to Bedales. He'll get James a job here if he has to."

Victoria thought he might be saying this to upset her and tried not to rise to the bait. "Well, since he's going to America—"

"America!" he scoffed. "Between you and me, playtime with baby is what he wants."

"Did he tell you this, Colin?"

He began to whip the batter and didn't answer. Victoria realized she was unique. She was possibly the only person in the whole world Colin had power over. How had she let something like that happen?

"Now, look here. Fuck off, Colin. I want you out. So fuck off with this chapped-hands suffering shit. Take your mud-pack and get out."

"That's no way for a don's wife to speak. You won't get Gerry if you haven't by now. Taking over the cooking won't make any difference."

She rushed crazily into the bedroom, calling over her shoulder, "He's mine, you bastard!" Ironically she looked into Gilbert Ricks's somber eyes as he waited above the bed. Rage took her out into the barn. Colin followed anxiously, still carrying the whisk dripping with his concoction.

The barn had been divided to make two bedrooms and a bathroom. In earlier days it was James's playroom and his old things were stored there. So were Ruth's, Victoria suspected. They certainly weren't in the house. Lilly's silk clothes were draped suggestively about. Her brown-skinned cigarette butts spread across floors and surfaces like a plague of insects. Then Victoria saw the end of the metal chest poking from under the bed. She calmed down. "R.H." Ruth Holt in gilt on the lid. She pulled it out with difficulty. "Why is it locked?"

"That's always kept locked."

"What's in it?"

"His documents, I should think."

"I shouldn't. His documents are all over his desk, as you well know."

"I've got to go out," Colin said nervously. "Stay and watch TV or take a bath. Use my bath oil; it's very soothing."

He spoke as though she were a difficult guest he didn't know what to do with. She knew she looked bad. Uncontrollable attacks on Gerry's cook could hardly be passed off as wedding nerves.

The chest would be full of Ruth's things. Photographs, letters, diaries. Victoria kicked it. She was sick to death of the past.

"I'd forget about all that." Colin swallowed with difficulty. "Gerry must think an awful lot of you. No one else has been able to get him into church. Not even at Christmas."

Too much from the past, all of it, too much. "Open this chest!" She grasped his diet-thin arm and frightened him. He blurted out something about a key. She propelled him outside and into the house. He chose Gerry's bedroom and made a pretense of searching.

"He must have it on him, Victoria." She tore down the photograph of Gilbert Ricks, huge above the bed. Colin rushed out for some Scotch tape. Then she saw she was behaving like her mother and quieted down.

She found Colin in the study. He jumped away from her.

"I want you to leave. It's nothing personal." She was herself again.

Colin burst into tears. He was so agitated he'd forgotten to blot off the oil from his face. Music could be heard faintly. He left the house and ran across the meadow in the direction of the dance.

She tried to open the chest with James's penknife, but all she succeeded in doing was scratching the lock. She crossed the lawn to the kitchen to look for a chisel. She opened the broom closet to get a hammer and heard sounds coming from the bedroom. A cry. It sounded like pleasure. So Gerry had somehow sneaked in the front door with a woman. A woman's voice, light and excited, "Go on, oh, go on. Now!" Rustlings of sheets as they changed position. A bedspring. Then a whisper. "Oh, Ruthie." Then nothing.

Terrified, she left the house. It wasn't in her head. Yet it wasn't real. It had been real once.

* * *

She tried to speak to Sylvia, but she was out with her father's literary agent, Richard Holly. In their absence the famous author, ignored, had gotten hopelessly drunk. Victoria took the last train to Haslemere.

Mother was reading *The Glorious Empire* and chewing grayish milk chocolates supplied by the new Swiss pastry-cook. A half-finished box of candied fruits waited beside her. Victoria had to talk to someone. She watched her mother eating.

"Colin wants to stay on after we're married. Gerry wants him to."

"Well, that's a relief. He's a better cook than you'll ever be. Gerry's no fool."

"But he's gay."

"Well, there's nothing to worry about then, is there?"

"There's everything to worry about."

Mother, busy reading and eating, didn't pay any more attention. Victoria tried to take the candied fruits away.

"You're killing yourself, Mummy." She couldn't talk to her mother. If she hadn't been able to for twenty-two years, there was no reason why she should start now. She'd have to find the solution within herself.

As she went to the door, Mother said, "You're not thinking of chucking your wedding, are you?"

Victoria turned angrily.

"Well, you chucked everything else."

Victoria went up to the attic and opened the mail. Only two more Alice cards.

> Dear Alice,
>   Just a line to let you know we are having lovely weather, sunshine every day. Plenty of swimming. Leave for home Sat. morning.
>
>   Love to all,
>   Lil and Mick

Well, marriage must have quieted her down. Who is sending them? She felt desperate. Somebody from the past—

the past is the clue. That's what the cards represent. So many have roses on them.

She got Sylvia on the phone and described the noises at Crowsley. Sylvia lost patience. "I don't think you have enough to do. These reviews are hardly time-consuming. There should be more to the day than Harrod's and little lunches with old school friends."

"There would be if I could just get in that kitchen. And don't give me the poor-little-rich-girl routine."

"Get in the kitchen? But you don't even like kitchens. I talked to my analyst about Crowsley. He said it's all about exclusion, being left out. Gerry's a specialist at it."

Victoria could see that sometimes analysts had a point.

"I'm going through the hospital records looking for Alice," Sylvia said.

"Don't bother. The cards are coming from beyond the grave."

She went into the garden. How simple it was compared with Crowsley. High on weeds, low on atmosphere. The night was cold, and although it was after midnight she could hear the psychiatrist Walter Guinea watering things next door in the dark. She leaned over the wall and saw he was not watering anything. He was spraying weed killer liberally along the fence, keeping his territory protected from the chaos next door. He did it late at night so he wouldn't offend the Honorable Mrs. Brooke.

Victoria asked Dr. Guinea what made Oxfordshire roses glow in the night. Could their perfume be toxic? He looked at her as though she were a loony and didn't answer. Then he straightened up and wished he hadn't. The Brooke family weeds, tough and stringy, were ready to invade. The sight of their sappy stalks would give him another sleepless night. Victoria described the ghostly noises in the house.

He sighed. "Victoria, I have enough of this sort of thing all day."

"I'm serious."

"Isn't every patient?"

She told him about the first wife dying. "And now the house is haunted."

He put down the weed killer and lit a cigarette. "You remember when you were in your teens saying good-bye to your mother? Every time you kissed her you messed up her makeup. It was extraordinary, the mess you made. Some people would say it was uncanny. You see, deeply repressed fury in an active, volatile person causes all sorts of manifestations. But it wasn't caused by the supernatural but adolescent fury. You were being sent away to boarding school, leaving Mother with all the benefits of cosmetics to win Father."

"Oh, look. I don't know about all that." She felt quite sick. That kind of talk never did her any good.

"You could say unexplained manifestations suggest the presence of poltergeists or spirits. I say it's transferred rage."

"Rage?" she whispered.

"What you describe happening at Crowsley is the powerful transference of rage."

"Rage?" she repeated. "Yet I've never even seen him angry. Gerry de Santos doesn't want to marry me. Is that what you're trying to say?"

"How can I say? He's not talking over the fence, you are. What are your problems?

"People get angry when their loved one is taken away. Sometimes it comes out as depression," he continued.

"Oh, he's never depressed. Anyway, it was fifteen years ago."

"I can't help that. What you describe to me is not

supernatural. There are no ghosts—only in people's minds. Anyway, I won't have this psychiatry over the fence. Your family is always popping up borrowing the proverbial cup of sugar. Then they try and get treatment. That's sick for a start."

"Is it? It saves a hell of a lot of money."

She went off laughing. Walter was no good. She could ask better questions herself.

CHAPTER · 11

AT NOON THE NEXT DAY, VICTORIA WALKED INTO THE KITCHEN at Crowsley expecting some reprisal for her dramatic behavior. But in her absence there had been a bigger and better crisis. Lilly had quarreled with Gerry about the future of her child, and Lilly could outdo Victoria on bad behavior any day. By the time Victoria came back the anger had hardened to hurting silence. But it wasn't allowed to exist in front of an outsider. They all put on a love show, a short one.

Victoria squatted in the sun between the coal bin and open back door as Lilly appealed to Colin in the kitchen.

"What does he mean he doesn't want her educated in the States? What's wrong with that? I was. What's all this about a frigging private school? He says there's something wrong because she can't speak. But that's what he likes, for crissakes. He adores her because she's passive and can't ask anything."

"I don't want to get in it, Lilly."

"But you are in it. Try and be a man. Just once in your life. What does he mean she can't speak? She calls me Lilly. She says 'Hi,' 'dog rose,' 'dog.' "

"That's not a lot for three years."

"What do you know, you stupid faggot!" She left the kitchen, tripped over Victoria, then slammed the back door.

Gerry looked out of the study window. "Watch that door, Lilly."

"For a leftist you're very concerned with property."

"Yes. I am." He was polite.

"So I've noticed." She laughed, a menacing sound. "And you're not sending it to Bedales."

"The child is going to be properly educated and I'm going to see to it. She's part of me and she'll get everything I can give her." All charm, all persuasion was gone. He sounded blunt, even threatening as the hot possessiveness gushed. Then it was over and he was magnetic again.

Victoria discovered the child was his weakness. He couldn't handle his feeling for her at all. "We'll put her name down. It's what James's mother would have wanted." Then he saw Victoria outside. "Have you talked to your mother about toning down the wedding?"

"Yes," she lied.

Lilly tapped her high heels impatiently. The fight for her was not over. Gerry went back to his work.

"Where'd you get all those silk clothes?" asked Victoria, walking toward the barn with Lilly.

"They were Ruth's, of course. He gave them to me. Gerry."

"Why?"

"Well, he must think they suit me. I had to get them restyled, but the silk's expensive so it's worth it."

"There are so many."

"He liked it so much. He liked fucking her in silk. He was turned on by it. He used to make her keep her silk panties on and he'd rub—" She sighed. "It's just an idea of his, keeping my baby."

"Keeping her?"

"Forget it." Lilly sounded fierce. "It's just the kid looks like his wife and he's never gotten over her."

Even the insects croaked alarm. The birds signaled danger, dismay. The animal world filled the silence; the humans couldn't. Lilly paled significantly, leaving her tan stranded like a layer of makeup. Victoria twisted the Crowsley door key around and around in her fingers.

"For crissakes, don't let on I said that," said Lilly raucously. "I don't want to cause any trouble."

Gerry brought Victoria a drink in the bedroom. "It's this royal wedding. It's getting on your nerves. You mustn't take it out on Colin."

Firmly, she said, "He must go."

"Well, let's leave it for now. We'll be in America nearly a year. Are you still getting those postcards?"

She nodded.

"Why don't you show them to me?" He was persuasive, gentle.

She showed him one.

> Dear Alice,
>   Many happy returns. Excuse card. Thanks for sweater.
>
>   Love,
>   Lil

A coy, tinted photograph showed a simpering girl and a sexually interested soldier sitting by a millstream. At first Gerry thought the soldier's hand was up her long skirt, but it was only the way she was sitting and her smug look. The verse amused him.

> On the Banks of Allen Water
> When the sweet Spring time did fall,
> Was the miller's lovely daughter, fairest
>   of them all.
> For his bride a soldier sought her, a
>   winning tongue had he!
> On the banks of Allen Water, none so
>   gay as he.

He stopped laughing and winced. Someone else walking over his grave? Or the same person? It only happened when he was lighthearted.

"It's a fun present. Have you any more?"

"Not on me," she lied.

"But this isn't to Alice Murray," said Gerry. "This is to Mrs. George Hunter."

"Oh God," said Victoria.

"What?"

"She didn't marry James Hamilton."

She got out a set of three strangely tinted cards entitled "Hope on Brave Heart." In the first, a woman sat at a table. She seemed to be waiting for news. Was this how Alice had waited for news of James? James Hamilton, lost in war?

She pushed her head into Gerry's thighs and longed for him to really get hold of her. She sensed he wanted to but he kept his hands to himself. He said he was worried about the child. She might wander in. He was worried the pollen-filled air would affect her if she breathed too hard with excitement. She had to agree with one thing. He was worried.

"You did talk to your mother, then?"

She nodded.

"Would you believe that dressing the bridesmaids alone is costing her over six hundred. The flowers for the reception . . . It isn't fair, is it?"

"No."

"So let's do it quietly. Save her the trouble. A registry office takes five minutes and costs ten pounds."

She thought of her mother's reaction to this impulse. Fat Mummy had moments of physical violence. But it wasn't that that frightened her. It was seeing her mother cry because she, Victoria, had upset her. Mummy out of control, gasping for breath. The ambulance on its way and Walter Guinea at the door with a handful of pills. Then Victoria would be sent away again until Mummy was well enough to have her back. They had never wanted her, the aunts. It was the guilt, the insecurity she was afraid of.

"What did you say and what did she say? About reducing it?"

"Well . . ." Her mouth was dry. She wasn't a child now and tried to speak. "She was busy." The house had been riddled with tension. Her mother, wearing piles of makeup, always a bad sign, had gone from room to room talking to herself. Victoria had only to enter the house when she was in that condition to be churned up, frightened. It had nothing to do with common sense or maturity. It was a chemical change that happened as soon as Mother was spotted.

"Come on, what did you say to her?" He knew she'd said nothing.

She would have felt helpless standing in front of her mother suggesting reducing things. She felt no better than she had when she was six. Gerry might not understand that. Even on good days Victoria had to make some sort of effort to resist her mother. Just to survive. "Mummy's health, Gerry. And everything's too far gone. All the preparations. She'd crack up."

"She's got rather a lot out of you one way and another, hasn't she? At least her crack-ups have." He sounded unfriendly. He called the dogs and set off across the meadow.

She didn't want to stay in the room so she left the house through the window. Colin was in the kitchen and she was in no mood to see him.

The depression waited where the garden sloped. It was as dense as fog. James was writing letters in the barn. Was he conscious of the atmosphere? If there was something wrong he'd be the one to ask. He was deliberately unfanciful. These days especially, he wanted to reduce everything to common sense. But she could not ask one of the family because they were part of it, the thing that was wrong. James saw her from out the window and beckoned.

"I've got you something. I got it in London." He handed her an album full of photographs of movie stars through the window. Then he joined her outside in the garden.

She realized then that he liked her. Also, it was the first time they'd had a chance to talk together. Genuinely pleased, she kissed him. "You are an angel."

"There are no angels, Victoria, you can be sure of that." It was said lightly but with unmistakable bitterness.

"I used to believe that at the point of death you changed into an angel or tried to," she said. "To see someone die is a real test of faith because there is no guarantee they go on. If when the person fell to the ground an angel rose up, wings flapping, you'd be reassured. I'd like to have seen it, if only once."

"It wouldn't be right," James replied.

"Why not?"

"If it's that good, everyone would be doing it."

"What?" Victoria asked.

"Dying." He laughed.

"Why do you say there are no angels?"

"You're the same person when you pass into the spirit world. Just because you go through the process of dying doesn't mean you become a saint. I've seen enough of death."

Lines of wash flapped in the wind. "I wish Colin would stop all this," James added.

"He's obsessed," Victoria said.

"Only since you've been here. He's just insecure."

"Your father wants him to stay."

"He looked after Dad when my mother died. He can't just kick him out."

"It must have been hard being brought up without a

mother." She didn't suppose it was. In some cases, her own in particular, it might even be preferable. But she wanted to introduce the subject of Ruth Holt.

"Gerry was father and mother to me. He did everything right, more than right." He didn't say any more. He put his things away and suggested they have tea.

"When you say you're the same when you go into the spirit world, you're contradicting the popular idea. You're supposed to be automatically bathed in light and goodness—" Victoria began.

"If there is a spirit world, you mean." Lilly had been in earshot all the time. The rose garden had hidden her. "I believe in God the same as the next person. But dead people existing in another place and recognizable? Forget it." She spat. "And as for God! If He's so marvelous, let Him show Himself." She viciously kicked a grouping of garden gnomes and sent them scattering. She'd bought them for Gerry the previous day. He said they were vulgar and refused to have them on his land. In the end Lilly had made her daughter arrange them by the pond.

James watched his wife saunter voluptuously toward the house. The silk emphasized the various delights of her body. His expression was thoughtful. These days Lilly made him cautious.

"Who told you about a spirit world, James?" Victoria asked.

"My father, of course."

"I was under the impression he was against religion."

"Against man-made church trappings, that's all."

"So he thinks people go on?"

James hesitated. "Well, yes."

"It must have been terrible to see his wife die."

"Oh, he was marvelous." All at once he started remembering. He described her dying, more for himself than for

Victoria. "She kept spitting blood. It took her ages to die. She coughed up dark muck, then blood. The blood was terrible. I thought it would never stop. I didn't think so much could come out of such a small, wasted person. It was so colorful, the dying. I can never forget the colors. Then the noise began, the terrible sighing—"

"But why were you there, James?"

"I think he forgot all about me. I came into the room because I heard her choke. I stood between the door and the bed, terrified. I didn't know what to do. He rushed in and jumped onto the bed and crouched over her, supporting her."

"Wasn't he scared?"

"Quite calm. He held her, talked to her gently. He helped her to die. Then he brought her out to the rose garden. I'm sure he did. He always says I imagined that." James stopped abruptly. There was a lot about his mother's death he wouldn't recall, in front of her. She could see he had to fight back unwelcome confidences.

"I remember when your mother died. It was on the news. Our housekeeper cried. Your mother was very popular. The housekeeper read somewhere that they gave her porridge twice a day to try and bring her weight up. Haven't you got any of her programs or anything?"

"Colin has. Dozens. People wrote to my father consoling—" He didn't want to talk anymore and led her toward the house. She sat by the back door while he made tea.

"She gave concerts all over the world?"

"That's right," said James.

"Did you go with her?"

"No."

"But Gerry did?"

"Of course not. He had his teaching."

"She must have been away a lot."

"Quite a lot, yes."

"Quite a lot, yes." It had a funny echo. The rose garden took it up, kept it going, teasing, tormenting. The rose garden, the graveyard, and nearby, in full view, her resting-place, the house.

"I read that roses were significant during the plague."

"Yes, the plague." James didn't like the conversation. His voice lacked energy. "Like people at that time, my father believed if he could only protect the air around her, she'd be saved. That's why he planted that." He waved a hand at the rose garden and a thousand blooms nodded back.

"What a strange thing to believe."

"Oh, he was desperate. He couldn't accept that she was sick. It couldn't come from her, someone so young, so lovely. I think he really believed her illness came out of the earth."

"What a funny thing to think."

"That's why the air was so vital. If he could only change it. As a last resort he clung to that. He told her it wasn't cancer but some malevolent exhalation of the earth. That's what they said the plague was. He had to believe that. He was so stunned, poor man."

"What did she think?"

"Oh, she was a realist. And she wasn't altogether sur-prised she'd—" He stopped. Whatever it was that had not surprised the pianist would not come from him.

"Did she suffer much?"

"Oh, she was wretched. There were some afternoons when I got back from school. There'd be this stillness. It seemed the whole house was waiting for her to die. I never knew if she was breathing or not. I think my father should tell you all this." He hurried off to rescue his daughter who was busy drowning the new gromes. The back door slammed shut and the glass shattered.

101

Gerry was furious. "Of course it was the wind. I've said time after time that it must be hooked, not left swinging."

"But there was no wind," said James.

He didn't bother with that. It was Colin he was cross with.

Victoria didn't say anything. It was almost as real as the dream.

CHAPTER · 12

"The postcards have stopped. Nothing for three days."

"What was the last one?" said Sylvia.

Victoria reached into a shopping bag.

> Dear Alice,
> Had a bad journey. Missed the train too. I waited
> for you till the last minute, then—

"Who wrote that? Not James. Too boring."

There were tired pink roses on the table, gone brown at the edges like old lettuce. The lunch, Sylvia's idea, was an extravagant attempt to have a good time.

The roses reminded Victoria of the stifling Oxford nights, symptoms of something wrong. Wrong? No. Dangerous.

The day after the glass was replaced in the back door, something had gone wrong. Gerry was walking toward the kitchen to get some lemonade for Lilly. Before he reached the back door, he stopped. Victoria could see he'd had a shock. Did Colin's mudpack look that bad? She ran up to him; he was still pale. Instead of speaking to her, he looked behind him, then back at the door. Was it a reflection he'd seen?

"Are you ill, Gerry?"

He looked at her, surprised she was there, surprised she existed. He shook his head to clear it and went into the kitchen.

"So we shall never know what happened to James Hamilton." Sylvia was disappointed.

"There was one from a church in Chester showing a lot of new graves. It was sent to Mrs. G. Hunter. 'I think this card will interest you, Alice.' No signature."

"Chester? Is that where James Hamilton is buried?"

> My Dear A,
>   I shall be outside the pictures at eight and I hope to see you. Excuse P.C. but it is all I have at present. Hope to see you tomorrow.
>
>   Love from G

"Who is this G?" said Sylvia.

"George Hunter, she married him."

The card showed Britannia Pier, Great Yarmouth. The sand was full of people in long skirts and suits, all wearing hats. Stalls sold tea, coffee, cocoa, and English ices.

Sylvia was upset that Alice had married George. Was James so soon forgotten?

"I spent half the night being seduced by Father's agent, Richard Holly. I vowed I wouldn't do it again but he's so insistent. There comes a point where it's easier to give in than to keep saying no."

"No."

"What do you mean, no?" she snapped. "I suppose your sex life is perfect?" Her shoulders shook, her breasts were hard and round like green apples.

"It's very bad for you, for your body, to make love with someone you're not attracted to."

"I thought you were going to say if you took the wrong road you'd get the clap. You see moral qualities geographically."

"That's not right."

"There's no Mr. Right. You can take my word for that." Her eyes were hard and angry.

Victoria thought she'd been bitterly disappointed. Her father was still the most important person in her life. He'd always let her down.

"Everything in this life is contingent," Sylvia continued. "It may happen. It may not. There is no cause and effect. No rewards. No punishment. If you *are* a goody-goody, you don't get the guy on the white charger. You just get lonely. So I do whatever I feel like and as much as I can. Yes, I do as much as possible. That's important. Do what you want, Victoria. We all die. I see enough of it. The important thing is to get your share."

"Oh, drop it, Syl." Victoria didn't want to quarrel.

"I can't be at work all the time. I need a well world. You should start thinking about getting a permanent job. It'll get you off all this screwy haunting business."

"What did she look like?" asked Victoria suddenly. "He told me she had dark hair and she was voluptuous. She liked wearing silk. I think Lilly remembers her style and tries to copy it."

"You've seen a photograph, surely?"

Victoria shook her head. "She just never came into the conversation. He only mentioned her once."

"She was incredibly famous to begin with, then she just dropped out. It could be one of her fans sending the cards."

Victoria liked that idea.

A brown official war card had been left behind in the last envelope. " 'Royal North Lancs Regiment Cheering Gaily When Ordered to the Trenches,' " Victoria read aloud.

"I bet," said Sylvia.

The picture was taken from above and packed with men looking up, smiling. Their steel helmets were propped on their bayonets. They looked like a field of nodding daisies and as transitory.

That was the last card. No more were sent after that.

Sylvia, shocked that Alice had married George, searched South London. She phoned Victoria in Oxford. "I went to the last address where she was Mrs. Hunter in 'thirty-five. They'd never heard of her. The people next door thought there was an English couple there before the war. She was a nurse. No children. I think Colin's sending them. Doesn't he act?"

"Only in the kitchen."

"I'll find her. I'll advertise."

The roses reached maturity that afternoon. In some lights they looked dark red as though filled with blood.

* * *

After lunch at a professor's house in North Oxford, the older guests went swimming in the river. Teenage children, all punk, refused to take their clothes off in spite of the heat.

Gerry had accepted the invitation reluctantly. He preferred to stay at Crowsley these days. He said he had to wait for Softdrinks, who took planes on the spur of the moment. "That way nobody can bump him off," Colin added maliciously.

A lecturer from America sat on the riverbank and prepared a speech welcoming Gerry back to UCLA.

"I'd like to say a little about you, Victoria. Can I call you a member of the upper classes?"

"You could. It wouldn't signify anything."

"It would in the States," said Lilly. "Lords and ladies go down very well."

The American turned to Gerry. "Although I'm writing about you, it turns out more of a tribute to Gilbert Ricks. It's funny, that."

"Very." Gerry looked uncomfortable.

"What sort of man was he?" asked Victoria. "I can't get a clear picture. Was he married?"

"No, nothing like that," said Colin.

"He found few people to talk to," said Gerry. "Still he sometimes needed company. Like the rest of us. Genius is not exempt from that." He picked up his grandchild and walked away.

When they got home Gerry said Victoria was to go for a walk with the others to Witham Woods. He wanted to get on with his work. He made Colin go, too. "You must have exercise. Come on or you'll get fat."

When Victoria got to the bridle path she turned around. It was the last point from which she could see the house. Gerry hadn't gone into the study to attend to administrative duties after all. He was standing in the bedroom closing the curtains. She said she was cold and ran back to the house for a coat. Before she'd got inside the kitchen, she heard it, the noise of Ruth's dying. She heard it, yet she knew it wasn't happening. Scared, she backed out of the house, forgetting the coat.

The others were waiting by the old church, and Lilly remarked how run-down it looked. She opened her bag and drank from a cologne bottle containing neat Scotch. It induced a chemical friendliness toward Victoria, and she took her arm as they entered the wood.

"It's a shame you didn't know Gerry in the old days. The good things in the end worked against him. His charisma made everything too easy. Don't tell him I drink. He sees me as much better than I really am." Suddenly, genuinely warm, she said, "Something happened in each lecture. They were never tired old repeats. I wish I could give you something of the excitement. He started people thinking, acting for themselves. Oh, he was the best!"

Victoria took advantage of Lilly's friendliness. "I saw a note he'd written. To 'My love.' " She described it.

" 'Motive for that which did you harm'? Sounds a bit like

107

T. S. Eliot. Gerry's true love. But Ricks did him better."

"But what is it?"

"I expect it's a note to remind him of a lecture point."

It seemed more like a note to a lover. And there were others among his books, behind a vase of flowers, not hidden, but not deliberately noticeable.

When they got back, Gerry was in full view trimming the boxtrees but Victoria went straight into the bedroom. The bed had been used. The sheets were twisted, suggesting recent excitement. Gerry looked younger. That was the first thing she noticed. The second, he had the look of someone who'd made love well. She knew that look. Her heart, always first to register jealousy, beat its wings against her chest, fluttered at the walls of her throat. She went out into the garden. Had a girl been brought in? Some tart? The rose garden whispered persuasively. It liked all that. The wind coursing through the bushes made a sound like tiny bells.

"What is that sound?" She waited for the wind again. "Bells?"

"It's the vegetable garden over in the meadow," said Gerry. "They string up milk-bottle tops to keep the birds away."

Not across the meadow. Nearer than that. The sound came from the flowers. The rose garden was happy.

"Your mother rang, Vee. She wanted to know why you're idling away in Oxford while everyone's killing themselves on our behalf in Haslemere. Have you got the presents for the bridesmaids? You have to give them something, you know."

"I must get presents for the ushers and . . ." Funny how she could go on when her heart was breaking. She knew no woman had been brought in. There was no need.

She watched him gardening calmly. She didn't think she'd ever loved him as much. Knowing she'd never get him made her body ache. No, it was a more painful experience. A body could not register anguish. That was the soul's job.

She followed him into the house to do the thing he hated. Questions would open the whole thing up and she would find her true place, if she had one. The definitive question was not about Lilly, loving Lilly. It was about loving Ruth, his first wife. It always had been. But she did not speak. Asking these things would not give her the answer.

* * *

In the bedroom the dogs were lying low on the counter-pane. They only did that before a storm or domestic row. She looked at the sky: no sign of a storm.

The child came in dragging a large rag doll. She stopped before she got to the bed. She stood between the door and the bed and stared. At first the bedspread worried her, then the pillows. She put her hand up to her mouth and started to cry. The dogs slunk off, guiltily.

Gerry, followed by the others, rushed in. He held her, talked to her, but could not stop her crying.

"Was it the dogs?" asked Lilly.

They all looked at the innocent bed.

"Give her a piece of candy," said Colin. "Here you are, baby." But the child only stopped crying when she was taken into the sunshine.

Colin, in the kitchen, for once was doing nothing. "Do you believe in ghosts?" Victoria asked.

"Of course not. I have enough trouble with people."

* * *

Later, as she lay beside Gerry, she thought about an angel rising up from a shriveling corpse. Human beings couldn't see the transformation or, as James said, they'd all be doing it. Depending on your good deeds, you could be a small, fine angel that could pass through into heaven. If you'd been less good, you were a tough angel like a coarse bird. You flapped your wings ferociously against the barred gate but you couldn't get in. You had to go away fast and find some other place of admittance because you didn't keep the bird body for long. As you went lower, your white wings got dirty and spotted and your expression grew predatory. You ended up as a vulture of death. Then when you acknowledged your true worth, you were at last accepted into hell.

What sort of angel was Ruth? A shining one with diaphanous wings? A slender, luminous one or a tough, hopeless one? She had been musical. That helped.

"Were you at the hospital at the end?"

"Gilbert died while I was in America."

"I meant Ruth."

"She wasn't in the hospital."

"Was she in a lot of pain?"

"I've seen worse."

"Where?"

"Vietnam."

"Why aren't there any photographs of her?"

"Well, I'm sure there are. Col's probably dusting them or something or he thinks they'll upset James."

Lies. Lies.

"You decided to marry me very quickly," she said.

"Why not? I thought it would be all right. Why shouldn't I have some—companionship?" He nearly said "happiness."

"And will you? Have some companionship?"

"Yes." He said it with force and disconcerted her. "By the way, don't pay too much attention to anything Lilly says. She's inclined to see the past from a personal viewpoint."

"Doesn't everybody?"

"I'm telling you to watch her. She likes indulging the horror potential of other people's lives."

"Haven't you got a photograph of your wife then?"

"Not in bed." He lay still, not speaking, not there.

"Lilly—"

"Leave Lilly alone. She's insecure about you, that's all."

"Why?"

"I expect it's because you're—well—upper class. You've had all the advantages."

"I'd give a lot to know what they are."

Was it the perfume from the garden that made her so distressed? Her throat ached with sadness. "Colin said you're getting a job for James in Oxford so you can keep—"

"Colin said!"

The smell of the roses was so anesthetic it stopped everything, even quarrels.

CHAPTER · 13

FIRST THING NEXT MORNING SHE HEARD A CROW'S RAUCOUS, incessant cry. Indisputably, it announced doom. Ten weeks till wedding day.

Gerry had changed since his original appearance in the movie theater. A couple of lamps had gone off in his face. Was he the same man? Had she somehow done the unthinkable and gone off into a cul-de-sac with Mr. Wrong?

Although she'd begged him not to, Gerry showed Professor Gully her latest review. She felt embarrassed whenever her job was mentioned in Crowsley circles. The professor avoided saying what he really thought by calling criticism a destructive business.

"Not at all," said Gerry. "Surely the function of any critic is to raise the standards of the society he lives in."

"And how can I do that?" she asked tartly. "I can't even raise my own."

Gerry was amused by her and pulled her hair playfully. "She walked a tightrope in Paris."

"How interesting." Professor Gully's tone suggested the opposite.

"Your reviews are all right, Vee, as long as the reader doesn't want more than a glimpse of character and a summary of plot," Gerry said kindly.

"Thank you very much."

"There's more to it than that, you know."

She remembered when she'd first given him a sample of her work. She'd taken great trouble, as she wanted to please him. He'd touched the pages as though he were touching her skin. His smile seemed to lodge inside her, and she'd kept its warmth for a long time. She'd felt light and full of energy. That often happened after she'd been with him—in those days.

Lilly sauntered across to the bed and sat beside Gerry. She let her hand rest lightly on his thigh. Professor Gully left the bedroom immediately.

"When does Lilly get her treat?" Her voice tingled with appetites, all forbidden.

"And what's Lilly's treat?" He pretended she was a child, took hold of her hand and kept it out of trouble.

"Tea at Blenheim, of course. We do it every year." She behaved as though Victoria did not exist. Victoria had no argument at that point. These days she often felt insubstantial.

He sat up, away from Lilly. "I'll clear that closet out for you, Vee. Your other clothes can go in with mine. You must remember higher critical standards help—"

Lilly was irritated. "Who gives a shit what a provincial hack sheet like that prints anyway."

Gerry was shocked. "Just because she's doing it for Haslemere doesn't mean she shouldn't do it properly. I'm surprised at you."

James joined his wife on Gerry's bed.

"Who reads this little sheet?" asked Lilly.

"I like what you do," said James.

"Look, Gerry, I represent the average girl's opinion, and that's why they hired me to write for them."

"Life is ludicrous when you think about it." Lilly sounded reflective. "He started out with Gilbert Ricks and ended up with her."

"I think you should get Ruthie ready for a walk," Gerry said to Lilly.

"But, Gerry, I am not intellectual," said Victoria. She was desperate to resolve at least one thing in their life.

"You don't have to tell us, dear." Lilly left the room.

"Art should be judged by the same standards as you judge anything," said James, kindly, then left the room.

"Don't mind Lilly and James. James is worried . . ."

"About what?"

"His job." Gerry started clearing out the closet. Victoria saw his Burberry raincoat. *It was the one that the figure at the kitchen table had worn.*

"Did your wife ever wear that? The raincoat?"

"Well, yes, she did. When she was ill. She lost a lot of weight and it upset her to see her own beautiful clothes hang on her. She slipped that on, like a bathrobe." He tossed it negligently onto the pile to be thrown away. "His job's too much for him."

"What does he actually specialize in?"

"Microchip technology. He's on the development side."

"Developing what?"

He paused. "Bugs."

"Bugs? Like what you get on roses?"

"Not insects, Vee. Listening devices."

* * *

There were times when the house had an accessible atmosphere. Its doors would be open, nothing was hidden, not too much put away, as though some visitor was meant to feel at ease. She had no illusions. She was not the visitor.

Victoria knew he was avoiding her. He made excuses not to make love indoors. He was tired, there was too much work, not to mention the pressure of the wedding. He avoided her in the bedroom. No one ever pretended to sleep the way he did. She knew he was in pain. Sometimes he'd pace up and down by the window frantically like a dog in heat dying to get outside to its lover.

She tried speaking to him. She tried silence. She talked to James, any subject would do. She was surprised to hear he was not worried about his job. "It's a challenge and I'm too young. They don't—well, respect me, but they will."

Then on impulse she brought out the postcard collection and spread it across the garden table. No one showed any guilt. Gerry thought some of them were valuable. James thought they were moving. Lilly, quite entranced, read them aloud. She loved the ones from James Hamilton. She said, "Dead loves make the best loves."

Gerry shifted uncomfortably.

The postcards led to the group opening up to include her. She provided love after all. Was that why the rosebuds turned nasty? They went bad on everyone. The child got scratched, Colin broke out in a rash. But they left Gerry alone and didn't get another chance with Victoria. She knew when she was outmatched and avoided them.

In return, Gerry showed her a photograph of Ruth. He threw it casually onto the grass, in front of everyone. "Col took that. The year before she died."

"But she isn't beautiful." The relief was huge. Then she realized what she'd said. Nothing she could ever say would put that right. The others had looked away. Coldly. Gerry reached for the photograph.

There was no doubt why he adored his grandchild. She saw the expression twenty times a day. The rosebud child frowned in the same disconcerting way. The woman's eyes wouldn't quite meet the camera.

* * *

"The florist is leaving for Crowsley to look at the roses."

Victoria was instantly awake. The announcement filled her with dread. "I don't want roses, Mummy."

Mother's lungs went hysterical immediately and sounded like a pack of jackals as she tried breathing out. She was working up to a medical crisis. Victoria had to get up and give the problem of the bouquet all her attention.

"Gerry's first wife carried roses, that's why," Victoria explained. She was patient, polite. "I want something else. A seasonal mixture, I think they call it."

"Your friend Sylvia's here. She's got the clap." Mother was always alarming about people's friends so Victoria took no notice. "That bracelet's all right." She was always on the lookout for Gerry's presents. She eyed the jewels, head on one side like an aroused jackdaw. "You need something. The groom's slippery. Don't let the Bonham-Hays know."

"Where did you hear that?"

"I hear plenty. Don't you worry."

"Is Sylvia really here?"

"She's upset her father again. Some theatrical suicide attempt. She took an overdose. An underdose more like it. Ten Valiums. It wouldn't even make me doze off."

Mother rattled on. "She's a coward. Too scared to live, no guts to die. She can't make a proper job of anything."

"I think she's a brave, wild person. She used to go on all the most scary rides at carnivals. I've seen her climb trees and dive from terrifying heights."

"That shows she's suicidal. Get her out of the house and don't let her use the towels."

Victoria had had the dream again. She asked her mother about roses. "Could they be covered in a white-gray stuff?"

"What, mildew? That's a most troublesome pest. I'd be surprised if Gerry'd let his garden go like that. He's clever with roses."

There was a handwritten note from Walter Guinea. No more postcards.

"After our garden-wall talk I found this piece about hostility by Charles Rycroft: 'In some cases hostility and ambivalence have done more than induce guilt and anxiety.

They have produced the feeling that the person one loves or believes one ought to love *has actually been killed by one's hate.* The depressed person is treating internal images as though they were as real as the external figures they represent and is reacting as though the wish to kill someone was tantamount to doing so. . . .' "

Victoria showed the note to Sylvia because she thought she'd like that sort of thing. But not even psychiatrists' revelations could cheer her up today. "I've had a bad one with my father. He's banned me from the house. I've gone down the wrong road, as you would say."

"My mother says you've got the clap."

"Do you think she should still be let loose?"

"Have you tried to kill yourself?"

Sylvia sighed. "Is she drinking and taking those pills?"

"Oh, she's gone beyond the Valium zone. She's doing a lot of secret drinking. The servants say she goes crosstown twice a day to buy it. It's the slippery slope to the sanatorium again."

Mother had tried various ways of dealing with her problem of being alive. At one time she'd been very thin and taken care of her appearance. She'd bought clothes and worn makeup. Then she'd been very clean. After years of gluttony she'd taken to drink. Whatever she did, it was obsessive and upset her. She was in the wrong body on the wrong rung of society's ladder. Victoria always felt it was her fault. She hadn't been able to make her mother happy.

When Victoria said the cards had definitely stopped, Sylvia suggested going to the church in Chester to see if James Hamilton was buried there. "The way postcards played such an important part in their lives, how could the momentous occasions be left out?"

The last postcard to Alice was dated 1936 when she was Mrs. Hunter at yet another South London address. The message was restrained. Victoria knew Mrs. Hunter was no longer Miss Murray in any sense.

Sylvia observed, "There's a real feeling of loss, isn't there? Not just James disappearing. Alice's life lost its gaiety. By 1935 the sun had gone in, even on the postcards."

"After James, the good days were over," Victoria said.

Sylvia didn't like that. "Why over? Because James stopped writing in 1916? You can screw anyone, everyone, as long as you fill yourself up. Get your share. There are no penalties except not getting enough. Mr. Right? Bullshit! All your values come from your mother. Alex Galsworthy was right. You sucked them in with her milk."

Victoria shuddered.

"You think you're free. You got away from your monstrous, imperious, mad mother by running off with Alex. Now it's Gerry you're escaping to. But you're more tied to her than if you were sleeping in her lap. You carry her women's-magazine beliefs in your blood. She's so terrible, yet you can't get away from her. It's given you a real fear of commitment. That's why you're always temporary."

"I'm temporary, Sylvia, because I don't want to go down the wrong road and end up in a cul-de-sac. Several of them exist at given moments in your life. They can look very attractive at first."

"Do you really believe that?"

"I do."

"Then there's nothing I can do for you."

Sylvia sifted through the postcards. "Do you think Alice cared about right roads, cul-de-sacs? She knew what she wanted. She wanted James Hamilton."

"But she ended up with George Hunter. Even you can see the Alice of the early cards is not the same person as the Alice married to G. Hunter. She'd lost something. I've got a very definite idea of what I want, and I don't want to lose it. You want to devalue passion. You want to spread everything out until it's so thin it hardly matters. You should ask yourself why you do that."

Sylvia pointed a finger aggressively in Victoria's face. "I don't get hurt. What I do does not hurt me." Victoria did not feel like reminding her of the suicide attempt.

Mother puffed and blew her way up the stairs. "I wish you'd get on."

"Get on with what?"

She fluffed up the pillows. "Just do something. Don't stand about. Reserve a table at San Lorenzo's and take the bridesmaids to lunch."

"I've done that."

"Just get on," she shouted.

"All right, Mummy," said Victoria placatingly.

Mother heard the fear in her voice, and it didn't do her any good. "It's all too much, all of it. It always has been." She went out in a storm of violence mixed with despair.

"Do you think Valium is strong enough?" whispered Sylvia. "She says old Bonham-Hay is giving you away, after all. What's he like?"

"No humor. Well, just a touch on a good day. Imagine a bad day."

When Sylvia had gone, Victoria reread the piece from Walter Guinea. What had *hate* got to do with it? Killed by one's hate? And who was this depressed person? It was surely not Gerry de Santos.

CHAPTER · 14

GERRY OFFERED HIS SON A JOB IN OXFORD.

"But wasn't it you who said I should make a go of New York? Learn to deal with my problems by going into board meetings with a pretuned attitude. Wasn't it you who said that?"

"The job has just come up."

Victoria doubted it. The child was playing just outside the window.

"Look at her lovely rosy cheeks," said Gerry.

"They're the same in Boston." James was angry. "A directorship in New York. What my mother would have wanted. Why the switch?"

"As I see it, there's one immediate advantage. No invisible boss leaning on your operations. Just think. You can give up bugs." Gerry's voice was silky, dangerous.

"James can do what he likes," said Lilly. Colin froze. A crow started complaining, over and over.

Lilly pushed James out the door. "I'll deal with this. Now, Gerry, what exactly is your problem?"

"I don't like the air around that child." Gerry spoke with dignity.

"You're air mad. That went out with the Black Death. Everything else in your head comes from a book. Wake up, Professor, and live. If life around my father is good enough for me, it's good enough for her. You can see her on holidays, for crissakes!"

Fury made him still. It turned everything around him

glacial. Victoria felt as though she were subsiding into some polar place. Even her hands turned red. She couldn't speak.

Colin patted Lilly and whispered advice. She shoved him back against the stove. "Father, son. They have their little secrets. Better not ask them about the white climbing rose."

Gerry muttered an expletive.

"The lovely white Chinese rose that disappeared between a day and a night. Unseasonal of it, don't you think? I know what you like, Professor." Swiftly she kissed his neck, while one pale, pampered hand slid down his body, found the zipper in his trousers and reached greedily inside his underpants. She whispered crudely, her face pink with excitement. Gerry withdrew her hand and flung it back at her like some foul dishcloth. Then he rezipped his trousers. There was a slight pause, then he slapped her face, hard.

The love show was over.

Colin led the weeping temptress into the garden. The roses were fully open to the sun. Some of the petals were beginning to fall. In less than a week the rose garden would look overrich, blowsy.

"Only nine weeks." Gerry's smile was brilliant. Victoria realized he was referring to their wedding. "I'll deal with that." He indicated Lilly being comforted in the garden.

*   *   *

In the afternoon, Colin scrubbed the child's mattress. He looked less sleek. Victoria thought Gerry had been quarreling with him, too. The balance had changed. She was still an outsider but no longer a pathetic beggar girl. She was more a witness that must be impressed.

"Lilly's not an unreasonable person," Colin said, returning to the kitchen.

Victoria was used to unreasonable persons. Life with her mother had given her a good start.

"She had a drink, that's all."

Victoria didn't answer.

"And she's lively in drink."

Colin wiped his hands and faced her. "Gerry keeps telling her what's wrong with the child. He's undermining her as a mother."

"Is there something wrong with the child?"

"Only that she lives in Boston, instead of Crowsley." He poured a large glass of wine and drank it, as her mother would say, medicinally. "If you want my advice, be the way you were. It was your love of life he liked. Now you hover about like a ghost."

"There's plenty of those here. Still, he gets along better with the dead." Around Gerry, the obscure and departed became plain to see, impossible to forget. The raincoat— she'd worn the raincoat because it warmed her—made her part of the kitchen again. "And Colin, I don't want your advice. As I said, I want you out."

"*He* tells me, lady! Not you. It's his house. I want him to be happy so I'll do my best with you. If you must know, he thinks you're fabulous. I remember when he first met you in the coffee shop."

"But I met him in a theater lobby in London."

Colin was surprised.

"He was with a tall, dark woman. Do you know her?"

"What was the movie?"

"*The Godfather, Part One.*"

Colin shook his head.

"The silly thing is, he denies it."

"Oh, he's such a tease."

Victoria described the woman. Colin said she could be one of the lecturers' wives. Another drink gave him a new idea.

"You live too much on hope, Victoria."

He'd taken her by surprise. "What's wrong with that?

You take away hope and what is there? Just days to get through."

Where was the joy of her youth? She'd lost it somewhere between the rose garden and the house—the swing, dancing, skating, all the things she'd liked no longer pleased her.

"Reality—I can't pretend it's comfortable but it doesn't let you down. Life isn't meant to make you hopeful. That's not what it's for. Oh, hell. I must be getting drunk."

Colin returned the half-finished bottle to the refrigerator. "You'll be Mrs. de Santos in eight weeks and six days." He reconsidered about the wine and took a large, untidy drink.

*   *   *

Sylvia found Alice. For the first time in weeks, Victoria was unhesitatingly, gorgeously happy.

"I knew she was alive," Sylvia said. "Just as I said, she goes to a clinic. She's still in South London. I happened to see her name because she's being transferred for special drug therapy."

"What's wrong with her?"

"Cancer."

"What's she like?"

"I haven't seen her. She's eighty-two, a widow, and goes to a pain clinic Monday mornings. Get there before ten."

"Are you coming?" Victoria asked.

"I don't think so. Suddenly, I don't dare. I've got my own picture of her, you see. Her and James. The man on the white charger's okay. But someone has to clean up the shit."

*   *   *

Gerry was in the bedroom. He didn't look too cheerful. She thought she'd brighten him up by talking about Gilbert Ricks but he cut through all that with, "Don't leave your makeup lying around." He subsided into a nonspeaking state too negative to be called silence.

She sat in the sun and thought she should get another job.

123

Something permanent. Colin opened the back door, releasing the oily fog of ten boiled turnips. The door's mended glass misted. She watched it clear. She recalled the day when Gerry had stopped, shocked by something he'd glimpsed in the glass of the door. All she could see were flowers.

Gerry waited till early evening, then took her arm and led her to the car.

"We're going to Brighton for a couple of days."

"Why?"

"We were happy there."

*   *   *

His instinct was right. Happiness was sometimes reclaimable in the old places. After dinner they walked in the sand, saying little. She felt calm. Their relationship worked best when it was wordless.

There were no shadows in Brighton. He encouraged her to write seriously and devoted a great deal of the stay to her work. "What you've been doing encourages a stock response. Startle people. Make them jump a bit. You want to get your own back, don't you? Think about your mother, your beautiful, favored sister, your old husband-to-be. You've been fobbed off, Miss Brooke. Hit back."

Perhaps it was his energy as he talked that turned her around, made her eager to learn. It was quite magical, a turn-on. She didn't know how he'd done it, but that was what made it magic.

Then he chose a seat away from the crowds. He needed to define their partnership. "The thing is, I want my life to be harmonious, peaceful. You see, I've had enough of the big emotions." He breathed deeply, cleared his throat. "But I'll never let you down."

"Why do you want me?"

He had trouble answering that. Sex came into it. She certainly refreshed him and made him look again at all the worn-out subjects. "I'll give you what you need, Victoria. At least I'll try. I'll never be unfaithful to you."

"You've got nothing to be unfaithful to. You certainly aren't screwing me."

He did some more throat-clearing. Lately he seemed ill at ease in his body, couldn't breathe sufficiently. "But we're always doing it. What about just now?"

"What? Once in two weeks. Try and contain yourself." Now she could feel the bitterness, the accumulated unhappiness of the last weeks. "You still want to go on with it, Gerry?" She closed her eyes, dreading the answer.

He laughed, but his eyes weren't laughing. "But—of course."

"Is that the truth?"

"Absolutely."

Then she remembered that with these people you had to look in glass to see truth.

At midday Lilly spotted them from the pier. Gerry let her call of greeting pass. He hoped James and Lilly were some minor hallucination. Victoria had no such optimism. Sexual pleasure had made Gerry soft, and he allowed the intruders to sit down. Lilly was relieved; the home structure was safe again. Just in case, she'd brought the child.

On impulse, Victoria went into the clairvoyant's booth opposite the pier. Throughout the sitting, she could hear Lilly's laughter. Lilly certainly sounded happy now that she had Gerry to herself.

"I see a lovely garden, but when I get up close, the flowers are covered in greenfly. That means disappointment, dear."

"Is that all? I thought you were going to say something really terrible. Is the disappointment for me?"

"This belongs to someone else. Another woman. One day you'll realize." After a pause, when she could have said something else, she murmured, "One day you will be freed."

"Freed?"

"You will be lifted right out of this situation. It's not right that you're in it."

"Oh, you mean my mother's house in Haslemere?"

The woman said, "I feel you went into the garden with expectation and innocence, but the garden turned against you."

Victoria remembered the persistent dream.

"Is there anything you want to ask me?" the woman was saying.

"Well, I'm going to be married in—"

"Oh, yes. You'll be married because I hear you saying, 'I will.' So what else can that mean?"

"So you do see a wedding taking place?"

"I see a ceremony in a small country church. Rather run-down."

"No, that isn't right." The adjectives did not fit St. Margaret's Haslemere.

"That's what I get, dear. In the country. You go in through an old-fashioned gate with a porch. Made of wood. That's all I can tell you."

It sounded like the church near Crowsley.

"But I'm getting married in a big church in a country town. Is this marriage going to work? Please tell me. Will I make him happy?"

The woman said she could see nothing. Absolutely nothing.

"Well, do you see me getting a job?"

"I've told you what I've seen."

When she got outside, Victoria told Gerry about the

church. "She described a small run-down church like the one in your village."

He shrugged. "So she got the church wrong. She picks it all up from you anyway. Where do you think it comes from?"

Victoria pointed to heaven.

He laughed. "Small chance."

CHAPTER · 15

BECAUSE GERRY HAD PRUNED HIS SOCIAL LIFE, HE RARELY SAW the illustrious Kingsley-Roes. He accepted the invitation to their prestigious midsummer party because the president of UCLA would be there and he wanted Victoria to meet him. He gave her a lecture on avoiding the pitfalls of the outsider, but Victoria knew most of the guests from their visits to Crowsley.

"Don't try too hard. They depise it. And the Kingsley-Roes are morbidly insistent on getting everyone drunk."

Colin smirked. "I find that adverb odd."

"There was one particularly hellish evening when a girl tried to kill herself at the table."

"How?" said Colin immediately.

"She swallowed five tranquilizers with vodka."

"How you exaggerate," said Colin. "She was probably trying to get a good night's sleep."

"Why did she do that?" asked Victoria.

"She hadn't done very well intellectually. She hadn't been funny either. I took her pills away and drove her home. I suppose I saved her life."

"Spoilsport!" said Colin.

"Why are we going there if it's so unpleasant?" asked Victoria.

"Because the president of UCLA will be there. I've just told you. The Kingsley-Roes' parties sum up the academic world. I hate the competitiveness. You get there by who you know, not what you are."

"Well, you got there, honey," said Colin, "so don't knock it."

"It's different in the States," said Gerry. "There, it's what you do and how good you are doing it."

Colin turned from the sink contemptuously. "And you promised me you didn't have any illusions left."

"What do the Kingsley-Roes do?" asked Victoria.

"He's a foreign correspondent, the best in the field, and Sarah has rather a lot of children." He didn't like Sarah.

*   *   *

The Kingsley-Roes lived in Islington. Although their Victorian house was spacious, they did their entertaining in the dingy, depressing basement. It had been dubbed the "dungeon" by more than one acquaintance. Even if a guest managed to start off upstairs to the living room or study, he would soon be shepherded down the broken gray steps into the half-light. There was no choice. To make sure, they kept the drinks down there.

The light in the dungeon had nothing to do with lamps. It seeped out of the walls, a peculiar foggy green. Guests' voices, especially the weaker ones, echoed unattractively. Supercharged and witty in an ordinary room, they felt altogether different when they got down there. They blamed their poor performance on the threatening ceilings and the way Kingsley-Roe poured the drinks. Two inches of brandy snarled at the bottom of every glass of wine; wine on its own was only fit for children.

Dinner consisted of standing up and drinking nonstop. Food was never a noticeable constituent.

About forty men—newspaper editors, politicians, academics, television personalities—were talking loudly. There was a sprinkling of tough professional women. Wine circulated fiercely. There was a poky kitchen area with a long wooden table, a crucifix, a nineteenth-century overmantel, nowhere to sit. The dungeon wasn't meant to make people comfortable.

Lilly was used to making an entrance. Her dress was split intentionally, revealing golden summer legs. Her eyelids were sequined and brilliant. But if she was noticed at all, she was dismissed as just someone who dressed up. Gerry was surrounded immediately and became one of the centerpieces of the evening. Victoria pushed her way to a wall. Voices got louder, whining, braying. Her heart started, too noticeable, out of control. She closed her eyes. The only distinguishable word was "Gerry." It became the cry of jungle creatures.

Richard Holly, the literary agent, stood beside her. She'd known him since she was a girl. The fact that she was grown-up now didn't mean she liked him any better. He rocked to and fro on dainty handmade leather shoes. He was always packaged expensively. "Everyone feels overwhelmed at first. Nice to see you looking so well." He moved off to a more prosperous position, and a drunk Scottish journalist took his place.

"That's de Santos. He's always surrounded. Groupies, most of them." He squinted through the mist. "He's quite nice-looking. Gets all the prizes. Bright as hell. Only trouble is, he knows it."

A blunt, stocky woman crossed the room and almost magically a path was created in front of her. The way she divided the crowd made Victoria think of the Red Sea miracle. She gave a first impression of not taking much trouble with herself, but she had presence in spite of her clothes. An aged cardigan hung unevenly as far as her knees. It had long since passed the stage of having shape, even discernible color. She was in her early forties and durable. She stared at Victoria, her gray eyes steady.

"Who's that?" Victoria asked the Scotsman.

"Kingsley-Roe's wife."

The crowd swelled and Victoria and the journalist were separated. A soft-voiced member of Parliament backed into her and spilled wine on her shoes. The gossiping academic beside him stared at Victoria's legs.

The basement door had been left partly open and Victoria could see the untidy path leading to the street. It was dimly lit and dangerous. Toys, a sodden armchair, unexpected steps made an unharmed journey to the gate unlikely. Only drunks would be able to survive the obstacles, and drunks were what the hosts approved of. If a guest planned a sober departure, the path waited, promising punishment.

It was the first time Lilly, standing in a crowd of men, had not been the center of attention. She began to droop, a hothouse flower in the wrong climate. Even her hair flopped.

A small man in evening dress splashed punch into Victoria's glass. His bow tie was lodged near his ear and his startled eyes popped behind enormous glasses. Gerry put a hand over her glass.

"Watch it. Like all good punch, it tastes innocent."

"Come on," slurred the furry man. "Perfectly harmless."

"Wilmot Munro, the editor," murmured Gerry. "I can't think what's happened. He's usually comatose by this time of night."

Victoria looked for somewhere to sit. A painting covered one wall. It had long been forgotten and had about it the unmistakable whiff of neglect. In spite of its size, it seemed to be stuffed between the bar and the refrigerator, and over the years these valued tools of everyday life had impinged on its space. Through curls of smoke, Victoria could make out long, colorful figures.

"Sarah Kingsley-Roe did that," said Richard Holly, who had appeared at her side again. "She used to be good." His long, yellow-gray hair hung straight to his shoulders. Whatever the season, his face was always tanned from some exotic business trip.

The street door swung wide open and a boisterous woman pushed toward the bar. Richard looked eager. "Vron! That's Vron Gainsborough."

Victoria had never heard of her. A soft-voiced politician leaned across them. "I think our friend is using Hegelian concepts to elucidate what will surely become a Marxist confrontation."

Victoria could see the literary agent was having trouble with that one. He did his best not to appear baffled, but the politician was addressing not him but a writer to his left.

"I suppose I should get him to do a book." Richard Holly had good connections with politicians and the upper classes. "But would anyone understand it?"

Behind her, the conversation was about Gerry. "He was in Vietnam, you know."

"Whatever for?"

"To curry favor. Got him in at the White House. Then Jane Fonda turned him around. He liked that."

"What rot! He served as a medic briefly. Just so he could say he'd done what Gilbert Ricks did. Gilbert was a stretcher-bearer in the Second World War."

Through the gloom, Victoria could just make out Gerry. The lack of light suited his sensitive, indoor face. She was reminded of the man in the theater lobby. He was watching her. His eyes looked dark. She tried to look away from Gerry, found she couldn't. The noise was unbearable. She half fell to the door.

"What, walking out already?" said Vron Gainsborough, cattily.

"Running."

* * *

Gerry found her sitting out of sight by the trash cans. She'd taken her high-heeled shoes off to try and feel a bit more sane. "Watch the alcohol," he advised. "Always pour it yourself. From a bottle." He crouched beside her and put his arms around her.

"I don't know you," she told him.

"Too late. You've been at the punch. I did warn you."

"It was you in the theater in London, wasn't it?"

"If you want it to be," he said gently.

"But why didn't you say it wasn't you when we met in Oxford?"

"Because I fancied you. I could see you thought I was someone else."

"Were you there or not?"

He laughed.

"Who was the dark woman?"

"Why is it so important?"

"Don't tease me. It *is* important. Very."

"Why?"

"Because the man in the movie theater was Mr. Right."

"Oh, dear." He was very amused. "Do they exist? What did he say that was so compelling?"

"I never spoke to him."

"Well, then, how do you know if he was right or not?"

"Was it you?"

"Come on. Let's go and say something to Simon."

He squeezed her hand and they went back into the basement room.

An acid-haired, shrill woman in her late forties swayed up to Victoria and stared at her legs and towering pink shoes as though she hated them. "Who the hell are you?" She drank crookedly from a tumbler. Her young lover tried to take it away from her.

"Watch it. That's straight brandy."

"Gerry told me it's wine. He should know. He knows everything." She guarded the glass fiercely and turned back to Victoria's legs. "Where the hell did you get those shoes?"

"She's Gerry's girl so classical language would be more appropriate," said the lover.

"Do you think so, darling? Like fuck." She took a huge gulp of her drink and then passed out.

Victoria helped the young man place her in a chair. Sarah produced a cold, wet washcloth and smacked it on the woman's forehead, then straightened up and saw Gerry. "Really, he's ruthless." She laughed. "In both senses. Oh dear, have I made a pun? His boy gained a nice dowry with the American appointment but unfortunately, he also gained a bride. He's only twenty-five. Like his father, America suits him. The Great Opportunity Market, he used to call it."

"Why did you say 'unfortunately'?" Victoria asked. "Just now? About the bride."

"Well, you know who she is," said Sarah.

"Come on. That's just rumor," said the lover.

"Rumors are wonderful." Sarah giggled. "I find they're the only thing one can rely on these days."

Gerry approached with coffee for Victoria, and the conversation changed instantly. Victoria followed him back to the center of a circle where he continued a conversation. It was all over her head. Hegel came into it. Middle-aged professors swollen with drink wobbled uncertainly as the Kingsley-Roe children rushed around them. Glasses were broken. Dogs appeared and joined in the chase. A woman cracked her shin on the pedal of a bike left lying by the bathroom.

Wilmot Munro poured Victoria some more punch. "Drink up, young lady. Can't have you standing there watching my disintegration. No fun for either of us."

A woman cried, "Bring out your dead. Come on, Simon. There's a car outside for Wilmot. We may as well pile in the others with him."

They carried out the editor. A fat man waddled hurriedly after them. "Hang on. He seems to be wearing my glasses."

"Is everything all right?" James thought Victoria looked pale.

"What's going on? That's what I want to know." She caught sight of Gerry trying to disentangle himself from Vron Gainsborough, whom whiskey apparently made amorous as well as spiteful.

"He'll never be unfaithful to you, you know," said James. "Once he's found what he wants, he sticks. He should write his autobiography. Richard Holly's been urging him to all evening, and it's not such a bad idea. He can go over it all again. Sort it out. Rediscovery is very important for someone like my father."

The children and dogs had disappeared, and the guests who were still able to talk gathered around Sarah. Nursing her baby and smoking heavily, she quarreled with Gerry. She said America was a mistake, geographically and culturally.

A TV anchorwoman named Prunella nudged Victoria. "Don't you think your fiancé's avuncular?"

"He could be," said Victoria uncertainly.

"In the nicest sense."

"Yes," she agreed, not knowing what she'd condemned him to. She turned to James. "I bet they're death at Scrabble. What does 'avuncular' mean?"

"Does it matter? Everything means something different in this house."

"Oh, come on, Prunella. Surely you're not going." Sarah's voice rose in horror—a guest was leaving sober. "Have another one. Just a tiny one."

Simon uncorked a bottle of champagne. Gerry was staring at Victoria. All at once she felt shy, couldn't look at him. But she saw that Lilly could, her eyes full of light, excited.

"Oh, let's get out of here," said James angrily.

On the way back Lilly said, "It's the rudest house I've ever been in."

"I wish they'd had some music," said Victoria.

"Music!" shouted Gerry. "Talk's the thing. You have to be amusing or you don't get asked again."

Victoria hadn't been amusing. She'd hardly opened her mouth. But Sarah Kingsley-Roe called and invited her to lunch the following week.

* * *

Alice must have hardened over the years when she saw that life had nothing to offer. Her South London existence with George had made her thankless. She was spry, articulate, but dressed drably. She seemed able to make full use of her memory but she was more absorbed in the approach of death and not at all interested in the past. Alice had not been elevated and transformed by being the recipient of a great and moving love, and Victoria was disappointed.

Her jaundiced eyes shone, even in the hot, stark light of the hospital. Her body was thin and yellow and she looked like a stray from some Eastern tribe. She was worried about her color but she looked more impressive than if she'd been town-pale, touched up with Woolworth's face powder and rouge. She did not want to talk to Victoria and had no information about the mystery of the postcards. She'd stuck them in an album when she was a young woman. Life with Mr. Hunter after 1936 was such that there seemed no point in keeping a record and she'd given the book away. It must have turned up in some junk shop. She tied on a taffeta head scarf, a memento from Bognor-by-the-Sea, and was ready to leave.

Victoria tried to find something to say to engage her interest. She told her about Crowsley. No, Alice did not know Ruth de Santos or Colin Holt or Gerry, Lilly, or James.

Of course, she'd heard of Ruth Holt. Who hadn't? A wonderful pianist who'd died tragically. "What happened to her little boy?" she asked.

Victoria asked if she could visit Alice at home. Alice wasn't eager. She didn't trust Victoria, didn't trust any of it.

Preoccupied with her own problems, she got into the hospital van to return home. Victoria was forced to take the train back to hers. There had been just one glimmer of excitement. Alice was surprised by the mention of James Hamilton, surprised that he even existed.

As Victoria crossed Paddington Station to catch the train to Oxford, she saw Gerry coming out of the bar. She called out but he didn't stop. He crossed to an exit, casually unwrapping a package. Cigarettes? Candy?

But Gerry was in Oxford.

She called him again, started to run toward him. He turned and looked at her, or at something in her direction. The distance between them made positive identification impossible. Then he was gone. She went to the phone and called Crowsley. There was no answer.

Later, when she got Gerry alone, she said, "I saw you at Paddington Station, Gerry."

"I told you I went to the Didcot railway museum near Oxford with Ruthie."

Again she challenged him about the morning in the movie theater. He said the man in the lobby did not exist. She described the dark woman in detail. He promised her he knew nothing about any of it.

Stunned, she lay beside him. "Is it possible you've forgotten?"

"Ships that pass in the night, Victoria. That's what you're describing."

She couldn't remember the first meeting clearly anymore. Gerry de Santos was indistinguishable from Mr. Right.

"Sarah Kingsley-Roe telephoned. Have you known her long?"

"I don't know her at all, and you stay away from her. I don't find her a positive person."

"Did she know your wife?"

He answered decisively. "No."

She thought about him crossing the station unwrapping— it couldn't have been cigarettes. Gerry didn't smoke.

"I suppose I should have told you at the time we'd never met, but I liked you. I thought the movie-theater story was a ploy to pick me up."

"You pick up awfully easy."

"So do you, he replied."

Gerry said he was used to students trying to get him to bed. Her approach had certainly been unusual. Low on sex, high on depression. He'd looked her over, liked what he saw. The movie was okay as an excuse if that's what she wanted.

"So, it was my depression that interested you."

"I noticed it."

She explained about the right road and the wrong ones.

"Well, you shouldn't have picked me up. If you're on this right road, the right meeting will happen inevitably. You don't have to force it."

"Do you believe that?"

"No, but you do."

The next day, when she was talking to Sylvia about the theater again, it was obvious that Gerry de Santos could not have been in the lobby. He was one of the few people she knew who had not seen *The Godfather, Part One*. She'd gone off the road altogether.

Sylvia was amused. "Perhaps Mr. Right is sending the cards."

CHAPTER · 16

SHE FIRST HEARD ROBERT GITTES'S MILD VOICE COMING FROM the greenhouse. "Is that the white rose that used to be by the wall?" he asked Lilly.

"You're thinking of the Chinese climber. Yes, some people remember it, don't they? White petals, tinged with green. So pretty. But all that belongs to Ruth's time."

"So what's that one?"

"Iceberg. And the red is Superstar. Actually that sums up this season's happy couple."

"Really?" His voice revealed excitement. Lilly knew all about exciting men.

Although it wasn't the most flattering moment to introduce herself, Victoria entered the greenhouse and put a stop to Lilly's malice. Robert Gittes introduced himself as Gerry's "best man."

He was lightly built and fast-moving. His handsome face was thin and unaggressively tanned, his eyes black and challenging. He seemed composed and courteous, but Victoria felt it was a front for something far wilder. Although the day was hot, he was dressed impeccably. His soft, groomed voice could be heard from every part of the garden.

Robert was reticent unless he was alone with Gerry. Twice she saw him embrace his friend, not without passion. None of Gerry's descriptions of Robert Gittes fitted him. Victoria couldn't say what he was. Usually she had an instinct for what she saw and heard. This time it let her down. He'd worked at being elusive and knew all about exits. In her presence he did not mention his profitable business ventures. He said he was a professor of literature at Harvard.

When he thought she was absent, he talked about Ruth. "I dreamed about her last night. It was as though she were in the room." He'd slept on the sofa in Gerry's study. "I can't get her out of my mind today. That first concert at Carnegie Hall. What was it about that time? In many ways it was the best time, wasn't it? Everyone so young."

Victoria, out of sight, saw him touch the closed piano reverently. "Do you remember all those red roses from Sir Thomas—"

Gerry moved about restlessly.

"Red looked so good on her skin, she—"

"It was twenty-one years ago, for heaven's sake!"

"Does time make things forgettable then? Something I did twenty-one minutes ago can be forgotten forever. Other things, twenty, thirty years ago, are as reclaimable as if they'd just happened."

Gerry sighed and changed the subject.

Later Victoria roamed in the meadow on the other side of the garden and heard Robert speaking to Colin. "What does Gerry do these days?"

Colin chose not to answer.

"Does he ever talk about her?"

More silence.

"Of course he was wonderful to her when she was dying. I don't suppose you remember all that."

"I remember it." Colin resented the conversation.

Gerry joined them and the talk moved to the second-favorite dead person, Gilbert Ricks.

The roses were bobbing like Peeping Toms. If she had to have secondhand love she'd rather it was Alice's. To cheer herself up, she got out one of the postcards. A soldier standing at attention in a wood in France. In front of him an insubstantial woman stretched out her arms in welcome. He saw her, instead of the horror of war.

> From James to Alice from France, 1916.
> I suppose everybody's after you, Alice, like moths around the lamp. I'm not jealous. How can I be of something so natural—

Why can't I feel like that about Gerry? So generous. Oh, James Hamilton was a lovely man!

* * *

Lilly leaned on Gerry's shoulder, her breasts too visible in the silk dress. He shifted away out of range.

"My!" she said dramatically, trying to retrieve his good-will. "Is that a hybrid tea I see out there?"

"You know it is." James sighed.

"My father would never have one in his garden."

Gerry wouldn't look at her. She'd opposed him about the child so she was excommunicated from his affection. In the past several days he'd had as little as possible to do with her.

"My father's a rose snob, Gerry. You should see what he grows." When Gerry still didn't respond, she said, "You think you can put things right by helping the child. You can't."

Gerry got up, poured a glass of wine and went to his study. Lunch was something the rest of them got through. Robert tried to talk. Then the gloomy crow joined in.

The child needed Gerry. Every time he went out, she screamed. She refused to go to sleep unless he read her a story. She wanted his attention and had various antisocial ways of getting it. Victoria wasn't the only one counting the days till the wedding was over.

Victoria tracked Gerry down behind the ice-cream truck in the village. He was making an appointment with the child for the future. "You'll go to school." The word was enhanced by his pleasure as he cuddled her. "School." Cool, watery, pleasant. "You'd like to be with me, wouldn't you?" The child couldn't answer. "Of course you would. We'll go to the railway museum at Didcot. You liked that."

"Didcot," she echoed. Another much-loved word.

He straightened up when he saw Victoria. His manner was defensive. "I was just buying ice cream. Would you like some?"

"Does James know? About Lilly?"

He blinked, not understanding her.

"About what she did in the kitchen, unzipping your fly?"

"Oh." He was relieved. So there were still sides to Lilly she'd somehow managed to keep to herself. "Why? Have you told him about it?"

"Is she staying on? I mean, what's happening?"

He busied himself tying a handkerchief around the child's neck.

"If she stays, Gerry, I go."

He didn't like estrangement, unless he chose it. He jumped up and took Victoria's hands. "Just trust me. Please. I said I'd handle it."

"By the way, about that child. You can't have her, you know."

His arms opened wide; his smile was soothing, honest. "Did I say I wanted her?" The honesty spread to his eyes. They opened wide and very clear. Victoria should have been relieved. He waited for her to show relief. But she disappointed him.

"So James takes this job that's miraculously appeared in Oxford. And what do you know, Lilly and baby stay, too."

He stopped being charming and let his arms drop to his sides. "I spend my life trying to preserve the articulate, the worthwhile. There'd be something wrong if I didn't do the same for my own family. For example, if one of my roses doesn't thrive, I sometimes change its location."

"What does all that mean?"

"Forget about Lilly. I said I'd sort it out. She was drunk, that's all."

Victoria was amazed an hour later to see the married couple's trunk being carried from the barn. James followed with his business suits, which had been skillfully packed in plastic by Colin.

"Have to go, Vee. Something's come up at work." He mumbled about executive jobs, but his tone was bright— bright and false.

"What about the wedding?"

"Oh, I'm sure—well . . . where's my wife? We'll miss the plane." He ran to the front gate.

The child was already in the car. Everybody looked happy in an ordinary kind of way, but Victoria sensed another performance. Then she closed in to say good-bye. They all kissed her. Lilly was wearing too much perfume. James said something about coming to Boston. Then Colin did. Boston was mentioned at least six times.

"By the way, I have a little present for you." Lilly pulled Victoria to one side and gave her a lipstick. Victoria thanked her. The real gift was an outpouring of advice. In Lilly's opinion, marrying Gerry would ruin Victoria's life. "Surely you want to accomplish something, don't you?" She spoke quickly. "It's no good being a jack-of-all-trades. You need something under your belt when you mingle in that world, I can tell you."

Victoria thought that what she was saying was probably true. "What happened to the white rose, Lilly? You know, the climbing rose that was so beautiful and disappeared."

"I don't know anything about it." She got into the car.

"You did the other day when you were drunk."

James tried to kiss Victoria but she avoided him, put her head down close to Lilly's. "What did you mean?"

"Didn't mean anything." She sounded petulant.

"That's odd," said Victoria aggressively.

"Come on, Vee," said Gerry, not liking this secret, inflammatory dialogue with Lilly. "Or they'll miss their plane."

"Don't you say odd things when you're drunk? Poor Gerry." Lilly looked at him and laughed. "He's hoping the American slut will stay on the right side of discretion. I had such a crush on him. . . ."

James started the engine.

"Don't worry, I told you I was only a kid then."

"What about when you grew up?" said Victoria, angrily.

The child started to cry.

"No crush then, baby. I plain idolized him. But no love for Lilly. Some people say. . ."

The car started and her last words were drowned out by the child's screams.

Before the sound of the car had faded, Victoria grabbed Gerry's arm and shook it. "Were you involved with her? 'Involved' being the politest—" Her voice broke.

"Oh, Vee." He tried to comfort her.

"She said you think you can put things right by helping the child. That's a funny thing to say."

"Well, I suggest you take it up with her. She said it, not me." He removed her fingers from his jacket sleeve.

"How can I? You got rid of them. Didn't you?"

He went into his study, put on his glasses and prepared to work. She followed.

"How did you get them out so fast?"

"I thought that's what you wanted. She goes, or I go. Remember?" He did not sound friendly.

"Why are you so angry with her? You said she was just drunk. That's what you said."

He saw he wasn't going to get any peace so took off his glasses. "She had her hand on my cock. I hate to lose control to a woman. Women who do that. Feel me up. Sexually smug. I hate women like that. Lilly thinks she's so wonderful because she's got a pair of tits people look at. And I hate what she's doing to her child. That little girl is far too sexually aware. Lilly fucks in front of her. Too much goes on in front of her. That's why she doesn't speak."

Victoria had no comment to make about that. She had no idea if it was good for a child or bad. It all seemed to be a matter of luck, anyway, how you grew up.

"Did you tell James what she did?"

"No. After all—" For once he did not know how to continue. "You see, I've known her a long time and I feel partly responsible."

"You mean you encouraged her?"

"I mean she lived here. So I feel responsible for the way she is." He looked distressed. Was he aware, then, of Lilly's eavesdropping while he was occupied with his wife? Was it his love for Ruth that had made Lilly oversexed, kept her perpetually in adolescence, still needing him? Whatever he said, she thought he must have been excited by Lilly's erotic impulses.

"Anyway, let's shut up about her," Gerry continued, "she's gone and life's too short."

"Will it be all right then?" Incoherently she tried to tell him her fears. She almost got to Ruth, the noise of the dying, the lovemaking. She stumbled over the name Ruth, and then he got up, pulled her to him, his hands beautiful, caring, so thickly erotic she could not resist. There was something so irresistibly seductive about his excitement. That was his specialty in bed and out. He pushed her across the desk and lifted up her skirt. He undid his trousers; his hands burned through the cold silk of her blouse. He pressed hard against her breasts, and the nipples swelled. He asked her to perform the sexual acts he needed, and her body tightened involuntarily toward pleasure.

"Look at me. Go on. You're a naughty little girl, aren't you?"

But his eyes didn't look quite right. They pierced into hers, and the shuddery feeling she experienced suddenly had nothing to do with sex. Everything in her body went dry.

"I love the way you smell. How it excites me." Then the look was gone. So was Victoria's arousal. She'd seen that look before. After all, she remembered the snapshot. For a moment he'd looked at her out of his wife's eyes.

"It's nice, isn't it?"

His mouth made the words, but it was a woman's voice.

Terrified, she tried to break away. She didn't like the laugh. His? Hers? *It was in the room.* She cried out, distressed, and his excitement subsided enough to know she was in trouble. He straightened her clothes.

"Let's do it later if you don't feel like it now. Tonight." He licked her ear, bit it, and made her feel his erection. "You won't be disappointed, I promise you that."

* * *

Sylvia was lying in the dark in her famous father's Chelsea bathroom. Downstairs, the author was giving a crucial dinner party and she had been barred from the house.

"He caught me screwing Richard Holly on his desk. His new manuscript happened to be lying there. Perhaps I've put some passion into his work for a change. He says I've ruined the whole thing and he tore it up. That fooled nobody. He's got at least two carbon copies."

She sat up against the tub and hand-rolled a cigarette. "There's not much left of my father that he started off with. Certainly not his voice or his wife or his values. He's had his face lifted, his eyes done, his hair implanted. His prick, I suppose, has been left to luck. He's like a badly made movie star." Suddenly she squeezed Victoria's hand. "Go on. Have a cry. Let it all out."

But Victoria couldn't ever really cry. She shook noiselessly; there were hardly any tears. She'd absorbed the technique when she first went to the movies. She was three, maybe two. Her sister used to take her. Crying like that didn't embarrass people or mess up your face. It looked great on movie stars. Much of her emotional style had been dictated by Hollywood.

"I was making love with Gerry and his face changed. It became his wife's. He looked at me with her eyes. He—"

"That's happened to me."

Victoria fell silent, astounded.

"It's common. It's called guilt. You screw a married guy and as the passion builds, he sort of turns into his wife. Or you think of his wife. I mean, she comes into your mind at a rather inopportune moment. It's a bit scary. Usually the wife is alive and living with the guy. However, you're so obsessed by the dead one you're . . . Nothing to worry about." She waved a hand, nonchalantly.

"Are you sure?"

Sylvia was sure. "I can't understand why you don't speak openly to Gerry." A prestigious guest tried the bathroom door.

"Oh, piss off!" Sylvia growled. "What about this permanent position you're after? Not social work surely? Whatever gave you that idea? You're not serious."

"I want to do something worthwhile."

"Whatever for? Has someone upset you? Has Lilly been nasty again?"

"It doesn't have to be social work."

"Thank God for the depressed families of Oxford. The first bad case and you'd be on the floor with them." She got up, her coat pockets clinking with stolen bottles. "We'd better get out. That stuck-up bastard will have alerted my father. Go to Gerry. He's the one you should be talking to."

* * *

There were changes in the garden. It had become very still, ready to die. Some of the flowers were brown and curled at the edges. Gerry went around breaking off the dying bits.

"Yesterday when we made love in your study I—"

He tidied the roses, didn't want to hear.

"I think I ought to get a permanent job." The suggestion came out all by itself. It was one way to deal with his unwelcome mood. It perked the future up, too. She doubted if he'd even heard. In his presence she could not talk about his wife. Sylvia's interpretation seemed quite ludicrous, and the gravity of the house assured her all was not well.

She followed him into the bedroom and watched him put away his clothes. She thought that to find permanence, she must avoid all temporary areas: horses, modeling, reviewing. Perhaps she could be a personal assistant? She felt she could assist, but any talents in that direction were lacking in the bedroom with her fiancé. Every move, every breath she took, was wrong. He behaved as though it weren't she he wanted in the room at all. She started to leave. Even that was wrong.

"You said your mother wants us to plan the seating in the church, yet all you do is stand around doing nothing."

"But you're so deep in thought, darling." She wanted to sound sarcastic but was too upset to manage it.

"I've been thinking about Ricks. He had a bad war. I think it may have made him twisted and that's why he hated me." He reached for his shoes. "I hope so."

Colin had done a good job with the tape. The ripped photograph was back in place above the bed.

"I've never had much luck with those I've loved. I could have helped him, if he'd let me." His voice broke. "I had the charm, after all. I could have gotten him across to the faculty. But he didn't want me. I can—I even offered him money." He looked at his hands as though considering a manicure. She thought he was about to cry. Then he looked at her, his eyes filling with warmth. But it was all on the surface. It was then she realized what charm was. It was wonderful for other people, a chemical covering that had nothing to do with the inside of its possessor.

"But it's all in the past." She held him tight but he was controlled, on his own ground, in his space. He patted her arm. He put more into it when he patted the dogs.

"Well, come on, then. What's all this about the seating?" he asked.

"My mother wants a wedding rehearsal, Gerry. Two weeks before. August thirty-first. That's in a month. I can't get out of it." She spoke quickly. "I shouldn't be here in her house." Her hands were shaking. "And I've got to do something about it. Something's wrong. I can't go on being passive in this situation."

"D. H. Lawrence said a wise passivity is a very useful activity. Then that which is perfectly ourselves can take place within us."

He stood in front of her rocking to and fro, so their knees touched. The action wasn't altogether friendly. "I'm quite happy," he said.

"Frankly, I've had the feeling lately that all is not well and you're far from happy."

"I want peace." He whispered the noun. It sounded desperate, chilling, and put an end to any more discussion that night.

*　　*　　*

When she woke up, the morning sunlight was black. The previous day she'd thought she couldn't possibly feel worse.

They did the shopping together, walked by the river, had lunch in a pub. Colin kept out of the way; even the kitchen was free. Gerry talked about America, trying to cheer her up. He chopped the dog's food. "Do you like it here now?"

"You made love to me and for a moment you changed into your wife. Your eyes . . . I had to tell you."

"It's this royal wedding, isn't it?" He was gentle. "It's got on your nerves. It's your mother."

"I heard a woman laugh. It sounded like—'

"Why don't you do something really nice that you want to do. Something you like."

"I like the sea."

"The sea then."

"Will you come?"

"Of course." He was calm, unworried. Everything was all right.

"You heard what I just said. . . . I mean for a moment your eyes—"

He laughed. "Poor little girl. You're all muddled up. That's why you muddle everything else up. You'll be fine in America."

"Will I?'

"Of course."

America was the panacea for all his ills and always had been.

CHAPTER · 17

SARAH KINGSLEY-ROE'S BASEMENT WAS FULL OF CHILDREN. At first Victoria thought there must be a party, but it was just the household gathered together for a meal. Cats slithered away into corners, dogs nosed under the table for scraps. Sarah stood solidly in the middle of it all, smoking. Victoria thought she was just staring into space, but she was looking into a place where chaos did not exist. It was imaginary, of course. Sarah described it as "the patch of green inside me. Without it I would go mad."

She offered Victoria a cigarette. "Sorry, darling, I didn't realize you were Gerry's fiancée. No one tells me anything. Gerry might have introduced us."

The adult lunch had been cleared away and there were several empty wine bottles and the stubborn smell of cigar smoke. The tutors stood together drinking tea, and the air was full of five-syllable words Victoria had never dreamed of. Sarah put a plate of cookies beside them; if no one was greedy they'd get one each. Victoria would not have associated sun with the basement and was surprised to see a ray strike Sarah's hair.

"Have you just dropped in or are you meeting someone here?" Sarah had gone to the sink and began washing the dishes.

"You asked me to come to lunch."

"Did I say lunch? It's always at twelve, darling. Because of the tutors."

"You said one."

"I must stop doing that. Oh well, eating isn't everything, is it? Have some bread and cheese, and there's rather a nice pâté."

A child screamed, dogs barked, a tutor howled with laughter. Even the clock seemed loud. Victoria walked across to Sarah's big picture stuck between the refrigerator and the bar. It had about it a humility gleaned from all the eyes that had looked at it without seeing it. Sarah had ceased even to look at it herself. Yet its original vitality still struggled through the gray basement. Sarah collected another pile of plates and Victoria helped carry some glasses.

"But Rilke's dimension is inwardness," said a tutor.

"God, I hate obscurity," whispered Sarah savagely.

"I thought you'd be used to it."

Sarah turned off the water. "If only you knew how I hate it. All these compulsive ideas. They're dangerous. Feelings are never allowed. Oh, no." She sounded bitter. "But I found the way to survive. You have to be better at it than they are, darling. Rub their noses in their own ignorance. Beat them at their own game."

"I like your painting, Sarah."

"I'll show you the rest someday."

"Where are they?"

"Upstairs. Put away upstairs somewhere."

"Why did you stop?"

"Simon couldn't bear it. Men like to be fully supported night and day, darling. They don't like anything that takes you away from them." After a pause she said, "But you know all about that, coming from Crowsley." Her voice was silvery and innocent. "How they keep disturbing what you do if it doesn't relate to them. Also, you can't be better than they, of course. I expect you've discovered that."

"Well, I don't have much to take me away from Gerry. I mean, I haven't a career or anything like that. I wish I had."

"I'm surprised he's fallen for someone so uncommitted. He does seem to have changed." She muttered something about it not being her business and resumed washing the plates.

Victoria saw Professor Gully leaving by the front door. The phone rang and a tutor held it out for Sarah. She raised her eyes contemptuously and took the receiver. "Actually Simon's resigned from the 'War Is Hell' school of reporting. He's trying to revive the concept of 'War as Ennobling Experience.' Do you think it'll catch on?"

Victoria swept the floor and hoped Sarah thought she was trying to be helpful. The truth was, Victoria felt awkward and needed something to do. Colin had so deprived her of domestic duties she longed for the feel of a broom, a dustpan and brush.

Sarah hung up. "It's nice to meet someone like you, Victoria. A breath of fresh air. I can see why Gerry likes you. Oh yes, I can. I'm surrounded by these heavy, loveless men. How I hate them. You get the same ones at Crowsley, of course. Don't you find it a strain?"

"Not anymore. They've got nothing to do with me, what I am."

Sarah was frankly fascinated by anyone who could appear on the Crowsley scene and replace Ruth Holt.

"Did you know her?"

"She was my best friend," she said, simply.

So that's why she invited me. Now Victoria understood. She wants to have a look at Ruth's successor.

"Gerry doesn't like us. He only comes because our house is the place one goes to. He's caused immense trouble for Simon. He encouraged Simon's editor to think he'd made Simon a star. All done behind the scenes, of course. Gerry never comes out in the open about anything. He convinced the editor that Simon should be grateful and what's more, show it. After all, he gives Simon the space, the front-page headlines. He edits Simon's clumsy articles and sits anonymously in that small office being dull while Simon has all the excitement, the glory, and earns three times as much as the editor ever will. What business is it of Gerry's? His butting-in cost Simon a trip to New York. His expense account was halved. He couldn't take a taxi in the Middle East. Had to go everywhere by army jeep. It took three years for everything to settle down again."

"Why did Gerry do that?"

"Because Simon is a better scholar. At least Gilbert Ricks thought so."

Victoria turned the subject to Ruth, but now the older woman chose to be reticent. Victoria was there for her benefit. By the end of the visit, they'd decided to trade information. Sarah's brusque "What is he like in bed these days?" earned Victoria two questions about Crowsley in the early sixties.

"It was all academics. Gerry was frightfully keen on intellect and ideas. Poor Ruth. Only facts were valid and Ruth—" She stopped on the brink of indiscretion, her cheeks hotter than the teething baby's. "Let's go for a walk on Highbury Fields."

There was a lot of muddle and delay harnessing up the toddlers, changing the baby. The juvenile abundance was something Victoria could not appreciate. She felt she was standing in the middle of some grand mistake—Gerry had said the first baby was a modest mistake which Sarah thought she could turn into a success by having seven more. Today she tried to say the children were Simon's idea.

Victoria asked again about Ruth, but Sarah talked about her painting. "Simon wanted his lunch. Then he needed things typed. He couldn't find a shirt. And then there were the children. All that to do. That was before we had nannies and tutors and things. So I gave up trying to paint. As Simon kept saying, I could always go back to it."

After their walk, they went back to the basement and produced tea for four Kingsley-Roes under twelve and six friends. Then the tutors came down from upstairs studies and the library. It was after five before Victoria had a chance to speak to Sarah again. "Tell me something about Ruth."

"I'm never explicit, darling. You must read between the lines. It's funny you like that picture so much." She pointed to the big one and hummed a made-up tune. She was making a point. "I couldn't paint like that again if I tried. It's all dried up." She laughed, not humorously. "I don't see things in that way anymore. Not after living with him for twenty years. But that's quite common. That happens in marriage."

"But tell me about Ruth."

"Haven't I been trying, darling." She got up, disappointed in Victoria. "To thwart creativity is the worst thing, the most dangerous. Get it?"

"Who thwarted it?"

"Well, he did, of course. Didn't he? Thwarted love or ambition you can get over, but not creativity."

"Simon, you mean?"

Sarah gave up and did more chores in the kitchen. Victoria didn't believe it. Sarah had failed as a painter or was about to, so she used her husband's requirements as an excuse to stop.

"What sort of person was Ruth?"

"She got him where he is today. People don't realize that. She put everything into him. It was marvelous in a way. She made sacrifices. I remember—oh, years ago—when they used to have one meal a day. At least, he did. I think that's when she began the habit of not eating. It was before he started making that display of himself. They had no money, and he was holding out for the big job. She wanted him to. Not take just anything. She built up the clique, gave the dinner parties, sent the right invitations. She loved him so much she gave him her music. And he repaid her. How he did repay her!" Sarah lit another cigarette. Emotion on that scale was nearly more than she could deal with. "She showed him how to go deep and turn out really good work. Oh, she was lovely."

Victoria saw she was near to tears and changed the subject. "You've got such a lovely house. Why do you always stay in the basement?"

Sarah replied, "I like being near the earth." It didn't sound quite true. Nor did the little laugh that followed.

"Gerry says it's because the basement shows your guests up in a bad light."

"He should talk! He who knows better than anyone about lighting people to disadvantage."

"Sarah, I think it might be better if he didn't know I was here."

Sarah agreed to say nothing.

* * *

Before dinner, which they ate alone in the kitchen, Gerry showed her his father's collection of photographs of China. He was warm, enthusiastic. "They're marvelous, aren't they?" Produced by him, the word did sound marvelous. It had an infectious excitement. He was standing behind Victoria. Lightly he touched her leg and she could feel the effect in every part of her body. Her cheeks were hot. Head brushing hers, he leaned over, his body touching hers in a caress. Was that his hand pressing against her thigh? She looked down. It was only the edge of the chair.

"That's part of the Great Wall." His finger pointed innocently. "They've repaired it since my father's time." She could feel his shaky breath in her hair. They were behaving like adulterers. Why was the excitement so furtive? From whom were they hiding? He grabbed her hand, held on to it. He smiled right into her eyes until she was ready for anything. Then he caught sight of the rose garden. Victoria followed his gaze.

The scarlet Superstars were bobbing furiously, yet there was no wind. He stared at the flowers and straightened guiltily. He withdrew all his straying thoughts from sex, from Victoria.

"So tell me about your interview." He sounded weary. "You tried the *Sunday Times,* didn't you?"

"Do you want me to get a job?"

"Yes, I do," he said firmly. "I want you to do whatever you want. I want you, Victoria, to be free!"

The door squeaked open. Why didn't the person come in? She waited. Gerry refilled her glass. "There's someone—" She pointed to the door. "Out there."

"Just one of the dogs. Drink up."

But the dog didn't come in. She felt freezing cold. Death was like that. Numbing, silent, an anesthetic flowing through the body from its starting point. No stranger in this house. She did not feel real. Reality was somewhere else, along a different road. Sylvia was right. Victoria always saw her position in life geographically. Her early diaries were like maps. Main roads, minor streets, cul-de-sacs. Tonight she knew she'd gone off the road altogether. She stood up. Where was the exit?

"I hate this house. It's her fucking house, still!"

She got out before she became hysterical and ran into the meadow. The thing that hated her followed. The harming would come, she was sure of that. And she wasn't at her best anymore. Her instincts had grown soft.

He brought her back and put her to bed. He gave her hot milk and brandy, then sat by the bed reading a detective story, looking up to assure her she was all right. Whatever she did she could not get warm. Her lips were blue. Why was the air in the bedroom always so chilled?

"At least you didn't tell me to see a psychiatrist." Her mouth was trembling.

"I wouldn't wish that on anyone."

He got into bed and rubbed her arms and legs, then held her against him. The heat of his body eventually warmed hers. That night he shared his strength, his energy, his heartbeat with her, and she slept at last.

> *"Best trust the happy moments,*
> *What they give makes man less fearful*
> *Of the certain grave."*

Sarah Kingsley-Roe's voice undoubtedly.

Gerry lay beside her. "Are you sleepy?" Victoria asked.

"No."

She reached out and touched him and their hands gripped each other's in the dark.

"It's not a good thing," he said. But Victoria got on top of him as Sarah recited the same poem again.

Victoria made love to Gerry. "Don't worry," she said. "She won't know."

"I love the way you smell. Oh, how it excites me," he said, and his eyes didn't look right. They were piercing. "I'd quite made my mind up I'd got over you, Vee, but then I saw you in the coffee shop. We made a hell of a noise. Must have woken up the whole house." He sighed. "It can't go on."

"She doesn't have to know."

"Oh, she will." He was sure of that.

"Why should she? You're not the confessing type, are you?"

"She knows things like that. She'll smell it on me." He laughed, and it didn't sound like him.

"Send her some roses."

"Oh, she doesn't like roses."

She smiled at him. He wasn't right, but then exhaustion had its own fantasies. *"Have you ever been with anyone else?"*

"No. I love my wife."

"It was nice, though, wasn't it?"

"Yes, wasn't it." His mouth made the words, but it was his wife's voice. He was shocked. He tried to get up. *"Lovely, wasn't it, darling?"* Her voice again. Victoria, appalled, watched his terrified face change. Lips appeared, smiling, female; the cheeks softened. The breasts lay heavy. Ruth's large thighs squashed Victoria's. She could feel her sharp knees, the bristly pubic hair.

Victoria screamed. The woman reared up and stared into Victoria's face. Gerry was gone. *"Nice, wasn't it?"* she said viciously. *"You asked for it and you'll get this, and this!"* She clawed Victoria; the first gash took half her cheek off.

Victoria got up in the dark. She found Gerry in the rose garden.

*   *   *

The next morning, she supposed there were times in life when parts of you—in her case, her dreaming mind—turned against the rest. She'd fight. She'd survive. Only six weeks till the wedding.

It was Gerry who noticed the scratch on her cheek. "But it's really deep, darling. You must watch the roses."

CHAPTER · 18

Robert Gittes took Victoria to lunch at Claridge's. "I wanted to talk to you because I'd like to pick up the tab for the wedding. I know your mother's a widow."

She turned him down, as her mother would say, "naicely."

The talk turned to Gerry's first marriage because he'd been best man then, too. He remembered his duties.

"Why didn't Gerry remarry before?" she asked.

Robert tried to explain with long, bland sentences. The dead wife's memory had been too intrusive.

"After all these years?"

"They go past faster as you get older." Without pausing for a breath, he talked about the preparations for this occasion. She approved of his speeches, then turned the talk to Gerry's past. Robert kept it academic.

"He made himself indispensable. That's the way to survive. In at the top at UCLA. He asked for three times the salary they offered and got it. He knows how to ask for things. His father was a diplomat."

She could see by the way he handled the first bottle that he could hold his wine. She encouraged him. In her experience, drinking led to indiscretion.

"He was a midwife. He delivered the printed words of their meaning and presented it to the audience. There've been a few stillbirths, if the writer turned out to be weak or tacky, but if an image is there, real and kicking, he can handle it."

"How are they getting on in Boston?"

"Lilly's father's mostly in Atlantic City."

"I meant Lilly and James."

His eyes were very still. "Absolutely fine, as always. A lot of dons are performers. They pitch their piece dramatically. They love—no, *need*—praise. Gerry was more canny. He had a performer's talent, certainly. He made the audience feel the work needed them. By the end of his lecture you had the same joy of creation as the writer. Gerry was the greatest turn-on of all."

"Why put it in the past tense?"

Robert Gittes paused. "Everyone goes off with time. Scholars, athletes, actors—"

"Has he gone off?"

"You interest me. I hear you were immortalized by Alexander Galsworthy."

She poured him a huge drink. "What was Ruth like?"

But wine did not make him indiscreet; it just made him encourage other people's indiscretions. "I can't remember. As you said, it was years ago. Gerry said your portrait is hanging in New York. What's Alexander Galsworthy like? He seems to have a devastating effect on women. I run into the leftovers here and in Paris. He makes every girl feel she's the one who'll keep him. It must take a lot of energy to be that promiscuous."

That made her rather quiet and she took a large, comforting drink. It was after Alex's departure from her life that she'd turned to right roads and Mr. Wrongs. He made you aware of right, wrong. Was he good? Was he bad? She still didn't know.

"I've heard that women try to kill themselves when he leaves them. Does a man like that do it deliberately? Or is it subconscious aggression? What is it, Victoria? If he doesn't know he's doing it, he's not responsible. Would you agree?"

"It wouldn't bother Alex either way. He has no moral sense. He likes the edge. Three in the morning. Madhouses, whores, cancer, loneliness. He plays the artist stimulated by the gutter of life, yet he's never far from Claridge's or a shellfish lunch."

What would Alex think of Crowsley?

"As far as his work is concerned, he takes you over. His way of talking is catching. His admirers all want to be him." She realized that sounded familiar. Gerry came from a different social class, that was all. She poured Robert another glass of wine and asked urgent questions about Gerry. But he was not finished with Alex.

"What was he like with Ruth? Please tell me."

"Why do you want to know?"

"Nobody talks. It makes it sort of—important."

"Weren't you unhappy when you were a child?"

He was still unwilling to tell her what she wanted to know in spite of the alcohol.

"My mother was always sick so I was shuffled about. She had me too late. When I finally came home she was huge, unrecognizable. I thought I'd been played some terrible trick." She thought of her mother now, filling her days aimlessly, ashamed of her loneliness.

"That's what Gerry likes about you. Your sadness appealed to him when he first met you."

"But I wasn't sad." She remembered.

"Gerry was such a nice man when he was young. Ricks broke him. He was a bitter bastard. Everything black, white. Enemy list, friend list. It's no good for Gerry in Oxford anymore. I think that's why he's so depressed."

"Depressed. Does he get depressed?"

"He gets the blues. Ricks's death illustrates that. He was killed outright in an air crash. Gerry was in L.A. Nobody knew how to tell him, so we all gathered at the president's house at the university, trying to decide the best way and getting drunk at the same time. In the end, Lilly's father flew in from the East and broke the news. Gerry didn't break down as expected. He didn't do anything. Lilly's father assumed he was in shock, so he assured Gerry Ricks had died outright with no suffering. Then Gerry spoke. 'Some people have all the luck.' That's all he said. And you didn't know he got blue? That's funny."

She tried to know by asking questions. Her intuition would have been a better instrument. She didn't know Gerry. She fell for him the way she had for James Dean. What a time to decide that. Less than six weeks. He was a planet surrounded by highly colored, deceptive mists that were attractive and held the visitor's attention. Camouflage was his particular specialty.

Victoria tried to turn the talk to Ruth again. Her name was slipped in with the next brandy. This time Gittes rose to the bait. "She was born to play. It took Gerry de Santos to stop her." He went on as though he'd said nothing out of the ordinary. "Her Beethoven *Emperor* was magnificent. Then they got married." He sounded sad about that.

"What do you mean it took Gerry to stop her?"

"He meant more than her music. That's what I should have said. But after all, it was through him she became so successful. He found a sponsor for her, prestige, money. When he met her she was unknown. She'd had some little concert at Wigmore Hall."

"But I understand Gerry didn't have money to begin with."

Robert looked weary. "Did I say he did? I said he got her a sponsor. When they married he had nothing. He couldn't wait to marry her, although he didn't have a job. I remember she lay in bed in her impresario's house on the morning of the wedding and Gerry came in, and she looked so beautiful, so wonderful, he was so moved, he couldn't think of a gesture to do justice to what he felt. So he rushed into the garden and came back, his arms full of flowers. He covered her with them, from her feet to her head. Not roses. His passion for them began when she was ill. Before they married she used to wear a pink bud in her scarlet dress." Then he realized who he was talking to. "It's great with you, though. Much saner. Calmer.

"I don't think sex is so important to him anymore. I mean he's done it all. He can tell the decibel of a woman's orgasm just by looking at her. He's been satiated by women."

"What's he marrying one for?" she asked sharply.

"Something about you touched him. He has a true concern for people, you know. Once he takes you on, he'll look after you. I know Alexander's exciting, but I wouldn't have thought he's the stuff relationships are made of. I think you'll have a good life with Gerry. He's not jealous like he used to be, thank God."

"No, but I am," she whispered.

* * *

Because it was dark she was unsure which house was the Kingsley-Roes'. She peered through the high hedge trying to see what was going on in the basement. Shapes were visible, probably furniture. It had a gloomy, unwelcoming air. She couldn't see any people. The basements of other houses were lighted, ordinary.

She trod over a tangle of rusty bicycle and arrived at the back door. She pressed the bell and stood some moments, undecided. She called out and upset the dogs. Of course, the Kingsley-Roes wouldn't do anything normal like open a door. She gave up and went back to the street.

In the next house a dinner party was in progress. By chance she looked in and her attention was drawn to the festive atmosphere. She was reminded of the postcard of the beggar girl outside the restaurant: 1910. Some things hadn't changed.

Around the table, ten people were visible. Four of them were familiar: Professor Gully, Sarah Kingsley-Roe, James, Lilly.

She wasn't surprised.

She knew Gerry was behind the ruse. The offending members of his family were out of sight in a city called Boston, but available to him in a place called Islington. He wouldn't lose touch with the child. She should have known that. She had to admit he'd got them out fast, smoothly. What had he used? Bribery? Threats? How and why he had such power she did not know.

Of course, he admitted to nothing. They'd changed their minds on the way to the airport. Richard Holly had kindly put them up. At first he'd tried to act surprised. "In London? Are you sure?" The way she looked at him discouraged any more of that.

Now that she'd located them, there was no reason why they shouldn't visit. He suggested Victoria take the child out for an hour or two. "Lilly's in bad shape. She's depressed. You more than anyone should know the effects on a child of a disturbed mother. You could spend time with her and—"

She covered her ears.

He turned sensuously and she saw he was undressed beneath the sheet. "Come here." His eyes widened provocatively. Her body flared up and accepted but one part of her held back. He reached over, grabbed her leg. "Don't you want to?" He looked into her eyes. "You want to. Get on top of me." He threw off the sheet. He looked at her until she ached for him to touch her. Her hand, with desire of its own, tumbled toward his. He grabbed it, pulled her onto him, his hands firm and very alive. His breathing was fast, mouth over hers. "Don't hold back. Don't do this to me. You don't have to play games. You know that. I just said you could look after her sometimes. Something for you to do. You keep going on about getting a job."

The resisting part of her was talking, too. "He has to have his own way. He always gets his way."

Then the resistance was stripped off, an article of clothing, and that took care of what might have been a new thing in their life together. Some control for her.

By the time she got up from his bed she could see there were advantages in taking care of Ruthie. Making Gerry happy was one of them.

* * *

Victoria took Sylvia to Oxford to meet the family. Victoria didn't feel excluded anymore so she no longer needed to exclude her friend. Gerry took them to his favorite restaurant on the river. There was some light conversation about sickness for Sylvia's benefit. Everyone had a turn at that. Sylvia threw in a couple of medical horror stories which went down well anywhere. Then Gerry said, "There's no sickness. Just sick people."

"For chrissakes!" said Lilly, outraged. "Have you forgotten your wife? She was sick as a dog."

"She *got* sick, you mean."

"How can you say that after all you saw her go through? Oh, Jesus Christ. After all the help my father gave you. Taking her to Lourdes in a private plane. Flying in those new treatments from Russia." She held her head. "I just wish you hadn't said that." She looked as though one of the lights of her life had gone out.

Sylvia shooed away the whiskey and chose a mild cocktail. "Just a weak one." Victoria supposed she was trying to act demure. Also Sylvia had to be on duty first thing the next morning.

Sylvia was all right because she was used to her father's

evenings. She juggled brand-new gossip, failing careers and alcoholism without losing sight of the point of her evening. She'd promised herself Robert Gittes as her going-home present. She talked to him about contingency: Nothing was certain so you could do what you wanted. He got her message. Away from her father she flourished. Her hands were never far from Robert's body. She tried to look innocent but the "weak" cocktails—she'd had several—were catching up.

Lilly seemed dismayed. Gerry's statement, that the sick woman had brought it upon herself, had taken the sunlight from the Oxford vacation.

"Ruth did smoke a lot. Is that what you mean about making herself ill?"

Gerry ignored her.

Victoria left to go to the ladies' room. When she returned, Lilly was flushed, her eyes watery. "The Oxford job's not on. You can't have my little girl."

"Of course not." Everything about Gerry was honest, even his eyes.

"My father's a clever strategist," said James. "You must remember that, Lilly. His technique is one of sincerity. Gilbert Ricks said that." He turned to Gerry. "It suited you to have me sweating it out in the States. Then you see the kid and you decide you need to—protect her. Or cherish her or whatever it is. So we have the Oxford switch. It doesn't matter, you know. Only don't lie about it."

Smoked out, Gerry revealed his true motive. "I'd look after her, wouldn't I?"

"Perfectly," James whispered, upset.

"But she's my child as well!" Lilly cried.

"The old blood argument isn't that crucial," said Gerry simply. "Influences are more important. And we all know the influences around that child may not be for the best.

When I talked about pollution I didn't mean a certain city. I had in mind a certain family." He brought up the child's lack of speech. Even Victoria was convinced his wishes were all for the best.

Lilly looked at Sylvia, then at the other tables. "I think this is a conversation best held in private." Her tone was threatening.

"I won't see my flesh and blood in a spiritually unprosperous environment whatever the material benefit," said Gerry.

"You *have* changed. There was a time when spirit was just something you drank. In fact, I'd be very careful if I were you," Lilly warned.

Gerry snorted. "That's your father talking."

"My family did all right by you. They were there when you needed them." Lilly jabbed him with a fork, her eyes, everything about her, murderous. "My father won't like this."

"Don't start leaning on him, darling," said Gerry. "Or you'll disappoint me."

Sylvia was entranced. She whispered to Victoria, "What do you mean, they're hard to understand? I haven't had such fun at a dinner party for years."

"Better be sure you don't disappoint my father. He doesn't take well to that sort of thing. Now send me away again for bad behavior. Better make it farther than Richard Holly's this time. Your girlfriend's not altogether dumb."

Gerry cornered his son. "It's perhaps fortunate the child can't speak." He folded his napkin neatly. He was the only one not out of control. "She'll speak with me. Oh, yes."

Robert said coolly, "Start thinking about Oxford, Lilly. Okay?" He picked up the bill, ready to leave.

Lilly turned to Victoria. "Do remember what I said to you about having something to do. You'll be needing it. People change in this family. I think they have all the charm in the world, but they sure missed out on loyalty."

Sylvia missed the end of the quarrel because she was talking to Robert about a suicide attempt she claimed to have made. Victoria thought she should get Sylvia home.

"When I woke up still here, I thought I should try shooting myself. I got my father's gun and went into the garden. But I didn't do it," she explained.

"Why not?"

"The sun came out. Still another time. Don't tell anyone at the hospital," she told Victoria.

"You seem remarkably open about it," said Lilly. "I would have thought bungled suicide was a thing you kept to yourself."

"Life's a cage, said Sylvia. "Didn't you know? Attempted suicide? Just shaking the bars."

When they got home, Sylvia drank wildly. Victoria had never seen anyone so smashed, except Alexander. By midnight Sylvia was ablaze with drink but still standing. She could use words just enough to explain her immediate wants. Robert accepted responsibility for fulfilling them and took her back to London.

Before Robert drove her back, she told Gerry he was partly right. It wasn't sickness that made people sick. For example, in some cases suppressed hate caused cancer.

"Shut up!" he said, furious. "My wife had cancer. She was the sweetest, brightest person. There was no hate around her, I can promise you."

Sylvia said she was sorry and blamed the theory on a medical journal. When they next met, Sylvia showed Victoria the article: Repressed negative emotion can cause cancer.

CHAPTER · 19

Robert was right. Gerry did not let people down. On impulse, he took the family out on the river. They played poker, swam, picnicked. His enthusiasm increased toward dusk and they took a train to London. They saw a sex film, got stoned, got thrown out of a gambling club. A car was hired, a party gate-crashed. All the time, Gerry was smiling, loving, playing. Victoria had never seen anyone so unhappy.

"You didn't enjoy yourself, did you?" she said, when they got back.

"No. But I hope they did."

The bedroom, reflected in the window, had all the ebullience of a fairground. "Shall I draw the curtains?"

He didn't answer.

She turned toward the real room and realized what was different. Everything was new in the reflected room. The quilt was unused, the lampshade, especially, looked fresh. There was something white on the bed. Flowers? A wedding gown? Was this how the room had looked before the other ceremony? She didn't dare look at the reflection of Gerry but swung the curtains violently, and as they closed, they created a sound like jeering laughter.

"I hear you went to see Sarah Kingsley-Roe," he said.

"I was in the neighborhood, that's all." She told him what Sarah had said about her talent being thwarted. "I like the big painting, but I don't think her gift quite warranted all that suffering and deprivation."

"You're sure she was talking about herself?"

"Well, what was she talking about?"

"How do I know?' He sighed and poured a drink. "I'd like to get away from the self-obsessed world of the colleges and back into life. Lilly says academics are pathetic, over-qualified, inbred. She says we roll in relativism like pigs in shit. Do you know the worst thing you can do?"

"Kill someone," Victoria answered.

"Impose your will on another person. That is the real crime. Taking away another person's free will. There are people who are capable of that."

"Well, never mind about their problems. Get on with your own," Victoria countered.

She got into bed and he touched her hungrily. then he paused, cautious, and drew back his hands. "It's not a good thing." It was like the dream. She turned around wildly and tried to bury her head, her life. She must find reality again, the world she used to know, something she could rely on.

"What they're doing to that little girl . . ." he said. "You're so free, Victoria."

"Well, so are you."

He almost laughed.

*   *   *

Robert mowed the grass and said the Honorable Mrs. Brooke wanted to look him over.

"Yes, she would," said Victoria.

"Gerry's gone to the pub. He keeps talking about Gilbert Ricks and the past. You can't keep tilting at a ghost, so he might as well go into soft drinks."

"Soft drinks?"

"I understand there's a little leather-topped desk waiting for him."

"Where?"

"New York. He has a friend in the business. Be kind to him, won't you, Victoria. He's my dearest friend."

She wished she could burst into tears and let it all out, all the unexplained, distressing moments. The world had become schizophrenic. It wasn't she. She was sure it wasn't.

"Gerry used to be such an innocent person. He saw only the good in everything," Robert added.

Lilly came out wearing a white dress, startling against her tanned body. Robert bent low over her hand. "The way you look, you could have anything you wanted, Mrs. de Santos."

Victoria, having a pretty good idea of what she wanted, doubted it.

"James carried Lilly's shawl and said they were going for a walk. "Is my father actually serious about soft drinks?" he asked.

"Your father needs a challenge. He's been spoiled."

"It's such a jump," said Lilly. "Oxford. Orange soda."

"Will he be any good at business?" asked Victoria.

"His charm can exist anyplace: Oxford, New York, lecture halls, carbonated beverages, sales conferences. Charm is movable," said Robert.

James's silence was eloquent. In some lights he looked like his father. They showed disapproval in the same way.

"You don't seem convinced," said Victoria.

James turned on Robert. "I don't discern even a hint of reality in what you're saying. I'm sorry. The only tycoon that could be real for my father would be a character who appeared in a novel."

Victoria could never tell whose side James was on, if any.

"A very real person offered it to him," said Robert coldly. "He doesn't make offers lightly."

Several times during the following days she was aware of James looking at her, wanting to communicate without the danger of words. His expression was not without pity.

* * *

Mother asked, "Is the best man experienced?"

Gerry chuckled.

"I think we should talk about who pays for what," she said bluntly. "Traditionally the bride's family pays for the wedding."

He laughed. "Luckily, I'm a traditionalist."

Mother gave him a nasty look. "You haven't exactly been overextending yourself. In fact, you've done nothing."

"But you do it so well," he said soothingly. He took her hand. "Nowadays costs are shared, aren't they? So let me do half."

She disengaged her hand and helped herself to another portion of meat. Gerry tried to supply her with the remaining potatoes but she liked to do that sort of thing herself. "We could share the cost of the flowers with the couples who are going to use the chapel after you. That's worth thinking about."

"Don't get cheap, Mummy. Not in those ways. The Bonham-Hays will hear."

"Don't forget the rehearsal. Three weeks from now." She shoveled the rest of the potatoes onto her plate. As Gerry helped himself to meat she said, "You've got piano-playing fingers." He paused, fork held midair. Noting his discomfort, she said, "Isn't that what they call them?"

He looked at her thoroughly, her eyes, her bosom, her huge butcher's arms. He didn't trust her. About most things she knew nothing. About some, everything.

She was too full of food to let his hostility disturb her. "Summer halfway gone." She sighed. "Will we get to the end without a world war, I wonder? What with the Iranian students and now the Korean students. What's happening in the world?"

"Young people are sick and tired of American-backed, fascist governments, that's what's happening." There was a disapproving silence.

"More wine, Gerry?" said Victoria.

Mother, realizing the topic of conversation was at an end,

ate in silence. She disliked Gerry so much, she didn't bother hiding her greed. Only Victoria could disgrace the family so completely by marrying a Red.

They moved to her parlor for coffee and liqueurs. Mother stuck to port as a gesture to health. Someone had told her it contained less sugar. "I was going to get a new car but I think I should get a fallout shelter instead. The Sunday papers are full of advertisements."

"You'd better get one with an elevator," said Victoria. "With the trouble you have going upstairs, civilization will be over before you get the shelter door open."

"She didn't get on with her father, either." Mother yawned freely, letting all the boredom of the evening come out. "Mary was bottle-fed. I breast-fed Victoria and what a mess she is. It proves the books are all wrong."

Victoria shuddered.

"He's been after her for years. The psychiatrist next door."

"I'd be after her, too," said Gerry. "The man's got taste."

Mother, remembering the dictionary she'd glanced through in preparation for this visit, came out with a long, appalling word. Victoria thought it was time to take Gerry away. She suggested he visit her attic but instead he talked about roses, their soil and climate preferences.

"They taste nice," said Mother.

He supposed he'd misheard.

"Roses. Vee remembers when I was in the hospital the last time. They put me in for my glands. I thought hospitals were merciful places. Not at all. They stuck me in a room on my own and tried to starve me."

"They put you on a diet, Mummy."

"But in spite of their dollop of meat a day I didn't lose an ounce. They couldn't understand it. They thought someone was sneaking food in and started searching my visitors. My weight went up. I was the biggest medical mystery on the floor. Before I left, I thought I should tell them my little secret. I hadn't been eating extra food at all. I'd been eating my flowers. Roses tasted particularly good, I remember."

Gerry was speechless. Into what book would he fit that scene, thought Victoria.

"When you visit the Bonham-Hays, Gerry, I wouldn't mention your political preferences." Her voice was dry.

"If the subject arises they will be mentioned, never fear." Equally dry. "I served in Vietnam so I think I can say something on the subject."

"What on earth did you do that for?"

"At the time I didn't really care whether I lived or not so I did what more life-loving people would not. I flew in medical supplies to North Vietnam."

"Well, you seem to have got back your wish to go on living, so I suppose the communists can be thanked for something."

* * *

He climbed ahead of Victoria to the attic. He swung the loose tightrope she kept there. "So when will I see you on a tightrope again?"

"I wasn't a proper tightrope-walker or anything, you know. I didn't practice enough. I don't do anything enough. I mean I haven't a vocation."

"That's all right. I don't like women who are driven, who have to do things. I hate it."

"But what about Ruth? To be as good as she was, she must have been really—"

"Don't talk about my wife!" It was one of the few times he'd been angry with her, and he was immediately sorry.

Coldly, Victoria suggested he return to Oxford alone. She turned away, but he was reflected in the mirror.

She saw the pain then. Gerry flinched as though he'd been

physically hurt. It was stronger because it was private. Then he saw her looking at him and manufactured a smile.

She supposed what she did then was her instinctive way of trying to keep him. She pulled his head into her breasts and caressed him sexually at the same time.

"We can't. Not here. We make too much noise. Your mother—" He got control of her arms, then held her tenderly, beautifully. "I was so jaded when I met you. That's why you were so necessary. I quite lost my head over you, Victoria. I'd made up my mind, I'd got over—I'd—" He shook his head. "I'd never thought of marrying again, you see. Then I met you."

"Got over what?" Her voice could never be as cold as she felt.

"The desire to be on my own, of course." He'd pulled himself together.

In less than a month, the distress would be made permanent.

He prepared to leave. "By the way, get this rehearsal put off."

"Why?"

"Everyone will have forgotten what they're supposed to do." He kissed her, then stepped away to the door. "Let's do it in September. The tenth, perhaps."

"Do what?" she asked curtly.

"The rehearsal."

"Oh, I thought you meant make love."

CHAPTER · 20

MOTHER WOKE HER BEFORE SEVEN O'CLOCK. "YOU'RE TAKING him to the Bonham-Hays'. Don't let him do any of that Red talk."

"Mummy, I can't go ahead with it."

"Get up and get on. I don't think you're going to get married at all, and that's the truth."

She was pale and physically frightening. Victoria cowered away on good behavior, thanking people for wedding presents, talking to caterers. How could she cancel the Bonham-Hays and keep Mother out of it? She didn't believe in suicide.

Downstairs, two teenage bridesmaids were being scolded for overeating. Their dresses would have to be let out. Mother had no anxieties on that score; her dress contained enough material to drape a street. Bedrooms were being made ready for guests from abroad.

Victoria slunk back to the attic. She went on tidying things. She emptied her handbag and found a letter from Gerry written at the beginning of their affair. . . .

> Today you're full of light and lovely to be with. Such
> innocent things give you pleasure. It's a lovely
> quality. Never lose it. I have to manufacture my
> happiness these days.

He was referring to drinking. If the message weren't actually before her, she would never have believed he had once written it. She sat on the floor and tried to cry. It did nothing for the sadness. She vowed she would never, ever be loving and vulnerable to anyone again.

Sylvia phoned. She wanted to talk about Robert Gittes.

"I can't go back to Crowsley, Syl. It's over, washed up. I don't know how to tell my mother."

"What are you doing?"

"I'm all right. I'm washing sweaters and cleaning up the attic. Who would think that doing simple things like that could make you feel better." She sounded calm enough until she said, "I just wish it would get dark, that's all."

"It's funny you can't talk to him."

"Can't seem to do that. He's just the part of my life that's closed up. All that Mr. Right shit. I'll just have to find another way to be alive."

It wasn't true, she knew that as she said it. She hadn't given him up. It was just her pride saying the right things. Behind it she was longing for him to miss her and say he loved her, and then Ruth would shrink away back into the rose garden like a dying moth.

Downstairs, family and friends milled around in the drawing room assessing the wedding presents. The phone rang constantly. Victoria watched them briefly. Didn't they know it was doomed?

"The truth is, Mummy, I can't go through with it."

"Church reserved, cars rented, dresses for the brides-maids." She spat out the prices. "And the Bonham-Hays."

Victoria saw her mother was deeply agitated, the sort of mood her father used to counter by wearing "kid gloves at all times." If he'd used boxing gloves instead, Mother might have been well.

"Now Lord Bonham-Hay will lead the guests out of the church. . . ."

The Honorable Mrs. Brooke had killed her husband by a variety of means, all legal.

" . . . second Schubert song. We'll do away with 'The Wedding March.' That's only for people who don't know what they want."

The Bonham-Hays, every one of them, had had 'The Wedding March.'

Outside a crow was protesting. Had it followed her from Oxford? She wished it would be silent.

She'd believed that Gerry and she had nothing in common. Then she saw there was one bond. They'd been dominated by strong, obstructive people, both of them. His were dead.

Mother suddenly shook Victoria fiercely until her teeth ached. The attack was unexpected and reminded Victoria she was not dealing with a normal person.

"Where are you meeting him, girl? Come on! You're taking him to the Bonham-Hays'."

Victoria waved a hand with appalling nonchalance, couldn't think of a lie. Her mouth was dry. "It's all over, Mummy." She ran out and bumped into Mary.

"What's all this, Vee? Wedding nerves?" She was amused, until she went inside and talked to Mother.

When Victoria got back home, Mother was tramping through the house bellowing for her blood. Ornaments were knocked over, smashed. Victoria said all that kind of thing belonged in a field, among cows. She stood with her back to the stairs where she could make a hasty retreat, if necessary.

"Why did you not do as you were told and take him to your cousins?"

Mary tried to give Mother a Valium. Walter Guinea advanced from her other side with a handful of medical alternatives. Victoria hoped there was a tranquilizer strong enough so she could leave the house unscathed.

"How could you let the Bonham-Hays down?"

Mother was helped to the couch. Gerry called then and

Victoria spoke to him; otherwise Mother would be disturbed, more disturbed.

"Come home," he said.

"Home?"

"Crowsley. This is your home."

* * *

When she walked in everyone stopped talking. For a moment Gerry seemed unfriendly, then he turned to James. "I think one of the more attractive aspects of feminine thinking is to idolize a man without too definite an idea of what he really amounts to."

James made a loyal sound supposed to be laughter.

Victoria remembered when Gerry first brought her to Crowsley, how he'd taken her into the bedroom. She remembered the moment just before he gave himself up to making love. That moment linked up with all the other good things in her life. Now the memory could only hurt.

"The roses have gone from your cheeks," James told her.

Robert Gittes poured her a drink and the original conversation started up again and closed in against her.

Gerry said, "No, Victoria isn't musical."

Professor Gully undermined someone.

"Definitely no cake for me," said Colin. "I'm on a diet."

"But you're so thin," said Professor Gully.

"Honey, flesh is out." Behind a napkin he inserted two blue eyedrops.

Lilly sat silent, her face stony.

The conversation continued around Victoria. Amongst it, the other one, the happy one.

"You should always wear silk." Gerry's voice. Victoria hadn't expected it to be so young. And she could hear bees, just by the door. Summer then. Like now.

"You might turn on to it, Gerry." Ruth knew all about being playful.

"Only when you wear it."

"Promise me."

"Of course."

Her laugh was magical. Victoria could smell the happiness.

"Are you happy?" Ruth asked.

"Happiness all good and enough for a lifetime."

Lilly suddenly got up and tumbled out of the kitchen as though it were on fire, her face bright pink.

The men ignored her. "I'll tell you," Gerry was saying. "I want to—no, *need* to—surrender myself to something that's important, necessary."

"Soft drinks is an odd choice," said James.

"Well, I'm convinced that people don't want high standards in anything. All my youthful claptrap about the inspired man in the street was just optimism because I was high on—" He slid over "Ruth," changed it to "Ricks."

"Ricks was always destructive."

Gerry pushed away his food, uneaten. "He was closer to me than my father."

"But, of course. Solidarity is a better means of betrayal."

"Why don't you shut up, James," said Robert Gittes nastily.

"Because I'd like some honesty around here for a change." James's eyes stayed on Victoria.

Lilly returned. "I wish that crow would shut up," she said.

A choppy conversation about life followed. But the past kept interrupting. Ruth at Carnegie Hall, Ruth playing Chopin, meeting the president. She was still there, even in the silence.

* * *

The cricket game in the meadow was Gerry's idea but at the last minute he stayed behind. Lilly joined them.

"Poor Gerry. He has such a need to identify with something real that will give some meaning to his life. I doubt if soft drinks could give much meaning to anything."

"No, but I will," said Victoria.

Lilly laughed. "Well, we all hope so. You're not the obvious choice for Gerry de Santos. Still, times change."

"She's dead," said Victoria brutally.

"His memories aren't." Lilly walked away, pleased with herself.

Tea had hardly begun when the child started screaming. Victoria offered to take her home to Gerry.

He was lying in bed as they arrived unexpectedly. She smelled the familiar smell—he'd been making love. He'd made love to Ruth. She picked it up instantly, knew it to be true. The sheets were disarrayed. He did not have the appearance of someone taking an afternoon rest. When he got up to take the tired child, Victoria saw the photograph of Ruth in the bed.

She ran into the kitchen and splashed water onto her face. She felt too numb to speak. Only her eyes revealed her feelings.

"What's the matter? You're white." Colin had also found some excuse to come back to the house. "Is something wrong with Gerry?"

She could hardly tell him Gerry had been jerking off on the memory of his wife.

Colin rushed into the bedroom but was back immediately. "My, he's furious. Because we didn't stay at the game, I suppose."

She waited for Gerry's mood to be less dangerous before approaching him. She paused by the study sniffing the air for rivals. Thinking he was alone, she pushed open the door.

The rosebud child was sitting on his desk eating ice cream. "We're going to have to talk, Gerry." Victoria saw she didn't get what she wanted from people. Gerry got what he wanted. In this instance, it was silence. Victoria knew the child was aware of her discomfort. The adult eyes in the childish face watched the bride-to-be curiously. Then she turned and flirted with Gerry. The unspoken demands were direct. She knew all about getting pleasure.

"You write notes to your dead wife." Melting ice cream trickled onto Ruthie's knees. "You still love her," she accused him.

The tension gathered like air building for a storm. The explosion would come, she was sure of that. She wished it would happen quickly so she could get it over with. But he didn't want it now, and he only got what he wanted.

"Ruth had—"

"Don't tell me about my wife!"

"But James said—"

"I'm getting tired of this. Just change your thoughts. Make them positive. Replace a black one with a sunny one." He was open yet painfully detached. She'd lost him. Did it matter what she said?

"You make thoughts seem so important."

"Thoughts are the most important things that exist."

"Zen is in favor tonight, then. Why don't you offer me an orangeade slogan or a scene from a classical novel or one of Gilbert Ricks's utterances. Everything's so easy for you."

He chose not to answer that one.

The child's china-blue eyes watched Victoria intently.

"Can you say something positive, passionate?" Victoria asked.

His answer was surprising. "I feel passionately about Zen."

"But you don't feel passionately about me."

"I do, don't I?" He was insultingly smooth. The child laughed. When Victoria looked at her, the blue eyes filled with challenging innocence.

She knew there was no point talking to him. "You don't show it anymore."

"I expect that's because I like emotion recollected in tranquillity. I only like it that way."

"What does that mean? You can only get a hard-on about me in retrospect?"

He laughed, pretending it was all a joke.

"I'm sorry she died," she said, humbly.

The child giggled.

"Do you think of her much?"

"Never."

The "never" was terrible. It was said with such force. He sat very still and unapproachable.

She felt panic. She'd somehow lost the man she'd loved who had loved her in return. He'd slipped through her fingers. She felt a sickening sense of failure. He'd become remote from her in bed. There was also the question of her mother. Cancellation of the wedding could have terminal consequences.

"I didn't think you had to go through all this at twenty-two. You're supposed to have a good time."

"I don't like fuss, Victoria."

"Fuss!"

Outside, petals fell, a white rush of them.

Frantic, she held on to him. "I just want to be happy with you."

"What a strange person you are," he said icily, then pushed her away, not gently.

The child loved violence. She tossed the cone into the air, and it hit Victoria in the back.

"You want me depressed, colorless—"

"Well, you shouldn't pick up strange men in coffee houses. You'll get yourself a bad name. You've obviously been badly brought up in spite of everything." He wiped the ice cream off her back, then threw the cone away.

"I know you were very much in love with her."

"Shut up! You bitch! You bitch!" The storm had broken.

He was called to the phone and the child followed faithfully. Mother told him not to forget the marriage license. "And tell Vee she'll have to notify her bank and change her name on her credit cards."

The marriage must be stopped. Victoria imagined the effect of such a decision on the Honorable Mrs. Brooke. That great, breathless mass of indulgence and distress would turn pale green and die. Did it take big people longer to die than small people?

She must resist each and every attempt at bullying. Her father had had a similar code before mother dispatched him. He'd even pinned it up on the bulletin board in his office.

She thought about her father for the first time in months. They'd never been close, but he would not want her to be as unhappy as this.

Gerry came in and sat down, stewing in memory and unhappiness. He looked at his fiancée, one look, then turned away. She started to say, "The wedding's off."

There was a knock on the door and Johnny Pass from Atlantic City walked in.

"Well, well, well! The only happy couple left anywhere."

CHAPTER · 21

"A GUY WENT INTO A BAR IN DOWNTOWN NEW YORK AND TOLD a joke. One of the crowd chips in, 'Oh no, not another dumb Polack joke.' The guy nods and continues, and the barman, he's a big aggressive type, chimes in, 'Hey, wait a minute, Jack. You rat's ass! I'm Polish, don't forget.' And the joke-teller says, 'Don't worry. I'll tell it real slow.' "

Johnny Pass had the small, formless, greedy mouth of a baby. He was always sucking or chewing something, but unlike Victoria's mother, he didn't let the result settle any-where. He ran, boxed, worked out. He was tough, blunt and only felt good when he was dominating someone. At Crowsley, due to his educational deficiencies, he had to use jokes. His eyes were somber and had nothing to do with his constant smiles of goodwill, which Victoria at first was foolish enough to take for friendliness.

He offered her a cigarette from a heavy gold case. Everything about him was expensive. He was loud with women and children but almost too courteous with male strangers. She asked him what he did.

"Buying and selling."

Colin brought out a tray of food, and Johnny Pass eyed it malevolently. "Well, you only have one bad meal." He made a terminal gesture.

"Everything in my kitchen is fresh, Mr. Pass."

"Including you. You're very fresh, you are." He turned to Victoria. "But he's an unlucky son of a bitch. When his ship came in he was waiting at the airport."

Colin poured the wine sulkily.

"Who's the best man?"

"Robert Gittes," said Victoria.

Johnny spat. "He's not gonna chop down any trees. He looks like a tanned worm. Where is he?"

"Boston," said Gerry, brusquely.

"Oh, yeah. Someone is always somewhere in this house except they ain't."

Victoria was surprised. "When did he go?"

Gerry waved his hands about and didn't answer.

"So when's the stag party? Where's it gonna be held? The Turf Club again?" Johnny Pass got up and did a noisy tap dance. 'Who'll we have? Six tarts up the backstairs at midnight?" He winked at Victoria. Then she realized who he was. This was Softdrinks, Gerry's American friend.

"I'm too old for that," said Gerry.

"It's on me and I'm not too old for that."

"Why are you here, J.P.?" asked Gerry softly.

Johnny Pass tapped faster. Gerry smiled. "Having a good day, J.P.?"

"Never had a bad one, son."

Victoria looked at him in the light of the sun and realized he was much older than he looked. Money, health, could do a lot of things but you still grew old. When the tap dance ended, Johnny said, "You keep nudging me for a reason why I'm here. Should there be one except the real, heartfelt need to see you?"

"Yes, but why are you here?"

He sat beside Gerry and cuddled him. "You think you're in trouble, son? Is that it? You know when I mean trouble I never come personally. And what's more, I've brought you some rose cuttings. A prairie rose, to be exact. Now don't tell me that don't excite you some. You'll have to grow it real nice. When you come to me, do I ask why you're there? I assume the good Lord has seen fit to bless my house with your sweet presence."

Gerry looked at Victoria to see how she was taking it.

"You put moldy soil around the base after planting. It helps prevent it drying out. It's a delicate strain. When the root is well settled, give it manure, well rotted.

"Now you know what I want. I want to see the family. The little Ruth. Keep the soil acidic, Gerry."

Johnny Pass would only eat raw, home-produced foods, unadulterated with hormones or additives. He made dinner himself—a raw vegetable salad and lemon pancakes. When he had everyone's attention, he said, " 'O cruel intellect that chills/His natural warmth until it kills the roots of all togetherness.' Did Auden know old Killjoy Ricks, because that's who he was writing about?" Johnny threw open a window. "Let's have some light in here." The light he was referring to was not the kind that came through windows. Looking at Gerry he said, "He was manipulative, too. It makes people kind of unpopular in the end. They always get found out. In 'fifty-three he was so unpopular there was a move to find him a position as far away from Oxford as possible. Christmas Island was suggested. But Killjoy was not insulted. Why? He knew so little geography he had no idea where it was."

Gerry had never heard that story.

Gerry went to the phone and Johnny Pass lost no time. Swiftly he said to James, "I hear you been made an offer right here in the heart of Oxford. Gerry's devoted a ton of effort to make it appear spontaneous. It seems to have come out of the air like all good things. Don't be fooled."

James said he wasn't fooled.

That evening, Johnny Pass asked Victoria to accompany him to the local shop. They passed the run-down church singled out by the Brighton clairvoyant. Johnny told her its porch was two hundred years old. Damp and rain had loosened the gravestones.

She got the conversation around to Ruth. "Did you meet her?"

He looked at her cagily, and she saw he could be quite shy. "She spoke only when spoken to, trusted only those with true-blue accents like her own, and ignored everyone else. Gerry'll be great in soft drinks. I hope he'll consider my offer. I'll be glad to have him on board. Orange soda? Best thing that could happen. I like him, you see. He's got an instinctive understanding of people's unhappiness."

"Did you know her well?"

"I know you better. The houseboy showed me the stuff you write."

"Houseboy?"

"Colin Holt. Some of them reviews are great. How do you write something like that?" He sounded impressed.

"I use my head."

"And my brains," said Gerry, laughing. He was only steps behind them. Johnny Pass and Victoria Brooke. That was one pairing off he could not allow.

* * *

Gerry had trouble explaining Johnny Pass. It was made more difficult because the others explained him differently. "He's in real estate."

"In films."

"Gerry only recently met him."

"They've known each other twenty years."

Johnny did a lot of tap dancing and sang "Blue Skies." Little Ruth watched him derisively. The dancing slowed as he noticed the garden. "That pool needs attention. Color the water blue. Make it attractive. Nothing gets enough sun in this country. You're all coming over to live in the States, by the way."

He turned to Victoria. "I've got three houses in Beverly Hills, I've got another house down on the beach." He flung an arm around Gerry. "I don't want you getting anxious. You're getting anxious, boy, and that's the truth." Gerry looked anxious. "Now I won't hear no. The house is my wedding present, okay?"

Gerry murmured thanks. Within three minutes he had packed an overnight bag.

"Where are you going?" asked Victoria.

"We're going to the sea. That's what you said you wanted. Which seaside would you like?"

She chose Brighton. She wanted to ask the clairvoyant about ghosts.

On the drive she asked Gerry about Johnny Pass. "Who is he? Really?"

"He made a pile out of supermarkets and cheap restaurants. He took to politics in one of the southern cities. New Orleans, I think. The town was appalled. They viewed old Johnny's rise to power as an omen from God that civilization was ending.

"He's a study in ignorance. He's not a college dropout as his enemies like to make out. He never even got to college."

He noticed the mark left by the cut in her hand—the shallow scratch that had bled so profusely, the work of a rose. "That hasn't healed properly, has it? It's been weeks."

"Why is he so keen on you?"

"The university must have given him the high sign. Imagine Johnny as president? Honest Johnny, the poor white's friend. He'll make governor for sure. How can it happen in an enlightened age, one asks?" Gerry imitated Johnny Pass's drawl. " 'This is the South, lady; anything goes.' "

They stayed in the Grand Hotel, ate lunch in English's Oyster Bar. Gerry was talkative and good company. He dismissed any negative talk about the wedding as nerves. Everyone went through that. He clung to the idea of America, how good their life would be there. Crowsley was mentioned as little as possible.

The clairvoyant didn't remember Victoria, but she "saw" a ceremony in a country church. She described the one near Crowsley.

"The man you marry is in business."

"Well, he's a teacher," said Victoria.

"He must make money at it because I see money all around him. He has pale blue eyes."

"No, they're hazel. They can look blue but they're not pale."

"Well, I must be getting someone else, dear," said the woman.

"What about ghosts? Can a house be haunted?"

"Only if you let it. Be strong, dear, and there'll be no place for the departed ones."

"So they do exist. . . ."

"Come back and see me in a year. I promise you you'll be happy then." And with that she got Victoria to the door.

* * *

On the following evening, while she packed to leave, Gerry stood by the open hotel window looking out at the sea. Although his body was there, she knew he was absent. She asked a practical question about the journey home.

Coming back into the present to talk to a real woman seemed to exhaust him. "We'll eat on the way to Oxford." He turned back to the sea and the same brooding silence.

"I saw a note once. In your bedroom. 'To be conscious—' Are you listening?"

" 'To be conscious is not to be in time' ?" He sounded tired.

"What does it mean? It was by the bed one day."

He took a deep breath. "Consciousness is the opposite of the corporeal body. Over the years that thought has given me such comfort.

So he could believe that Ruth could continue to exist without her body. "Were you peaceful with her?"

He did not ask who. "Sometimes."

And passionate and sexually mad about her and jealous. She stopped going down the list. Too painful. Because Ruth was dead it was untouchable, the ecstasy. Everyday concerns could not dull it. That was something the dead wife had in common with James Hamilton.

"I have to decide if I can live without passion," Victoria said.

He didn't answer.

"She didn't play the piano much after she married you. I'm talking about your wife."

"I don't know who told you that. She did so many concerts in the first years of our life together, I hardly saw her."

"What about the last years? What did she do then?"

"She looked after me."

"Were you happy?"

He laughed.

"Did you quarrel?"

"Who doesn't?"

"We don't. What were the quarrels like?"

"Musical."

"You don't want me to compete with her. The trouble is, she's not really dead. Ruth is *in* reality but not *of* it. Being with her is still the most important thing, isn't it?"

"Ruth," he said, as though they were talking about a chance acquaintance.

He wanted to make love then, quickly, before they left. He wanted to be comforted. He needed escape. He loved being aroused sexually as long as it wasn't at Crowsley. He got on top of her and fucked her hard. He wanted her all over him, her performance just as big as she could make it. Away from home he was a different man.

He was too excited for it to go on for long. "Oh, I love it. Love it."

She was reminded of a quiet married man having a fling in a holiday hotel. There were no such flings when they got back to Crowsley.

CHAPTER · 22

COLIN CARRIED A TRIFLE TO THE TABLE AND JOHNNY PASS eyed it suspiciously. He waited till Gerry had eaten some, then he turned to Colin. "Keep the package in case we have to sue someone."

"You've seen too many movies," said Gerry.

"Yep. And people get dead in 'em." He smiled at Victoria. "If you like movie stars you should meet—" He paused. "Lilly's brother. You can't get a bigger star than that."

Lilly murmured something about him not coming to the house. The truth was, Gerry wouldn't invite him. "He's too famous for us," she said.

Something dark joined them at the table—even Johnny grew quiet. It was closing in, almost visible, a mere sound away. A rustle of silk alarmed Victoria but it was only Lilly getting up. Johnny Pass shifted awkwardly and forced himself to be the one to speak. "These sudden temperature changes don't suit me. You don't get them where I come from. Lilly's brother hasn't got education like she has, but he's good company."

The phone rang again. It rang constantly. Johnny's financial empire stretched as far as China. He hated Reds, but money, like children, was innocent.

Johnny Pass turned to Victoria. "Now, I know you are from the ruling classes, an aristocrat." Victoria started to object but he'd have none of it. "Compared with you, we're all red-necks. But I want to tell you about myself so you know who you're dealing with."

Lilly looked as though she were going to faint.

The American's voice boomed through the house. "I started with TB when I was nine. I had a crooked spine and blistered hands from working in the fields sixteen hours a day, every day. I got into the restaurant business. I had four dollars in my pocket, but through the great American free-enterprise system I increased my year's take nine times in two years."

Victoria was aware that this was the first time one of them had actually volunteered information. Why had the others so excluded her? Flaunting their love for each other, their enviable group intimacy, their superior education? Was it to keep her attention off other things?

"I was making a million bucks a year before the commie business reform under L.B.J.—"

"Be quiet!" said Gerry. "You're going to embarrass someone in a minute."

"L.B.J. had a bad case of Redbug. You can't be friends with Redbug. Wipe it out before it wipes you out. Redbug can look so nice."

James took Lilly outside for some air. She looked as though she needed it.

"Redbug is at its most lethal . . ."

Gerry, imitating him, said, "You've got a real cute way of getting rid of people."

"My parents came from Sicily, Victoria. They weren't work-shy but they never made a buck. I'm proud to have known them. I made my pile and while I was making it, I saw money was useless without education. Maybe you can do without it if you've got a title and know the top people. Maybe. I'm not sure. So with Lilly I was blessed because she got education and she ends up married to a professor's son. And she's even bright enough not to turn her back on her old dad."

195

Victoria managed to say something about not realizing they were related and how glad she was to meet him. She kept the speech brief.

"That's enough, J.P.," Gerry cautioned him.

"So the happy couple are out taking the sweet night air." He turned swiftly, his body, his mood. "What's this I hear about you taking my grandchild?"

Gerry cleared his throat. "How did you hear that?" He looked automatically at Colin, who shook his head.

"Lilly's a fully realized emancipated woman. You said that yourself. So what's all this? Taking a child away from its mother."

"Your daughter's depressed."

"Now we can't have that sort of talk." Johnny mashed his huge hands together.

"And the baby should be speaking by now. I'd like her to go to school in England. It's still a safe place."

"And you're gonna say it has the right atmosphere and influences."

"I wasn't. But you said it."

"So Lilly's not good enough all of a sudden. Well, I tell you, Gerry, I'm proud of my daughter, and it usually works out that when J.P. is proud of someone, the rest of the world is, too." He looked at Colin. "Ain't that right? Take my son. Take a lot of stars in the business. Take a bunch of politicians—"

"How did you hear I wanted the child?"

Johnny Pass got up, heavily. "A little rose told me."

* * *

Sarah Kingsley-Roe was giving a dinner party and wore long earrings. "Does Gerry know you're here?" She never sounded friendly in company.

Outsize professors tried to divide a skinny chicken without fighting over it.

"I wanted to ask—"

Sarah interrupted. "Simon, do you remember if the first performance of *I Vespri Siciliani* was in Paris?"

"Oh, I don't know, darling." He sounded tired.

The chicken was finished and the professors looked anxiously right and left for dessert. A cheese board? Fruit? Nothing. Simon refilled their glasses to the brim.

"If we infer things outside us from values and thoughts within us, then space and time are something real and actually existing outside us," one of them said.

Sarah said, "I'd love to have seen you take your clothes off." Everyone looked up. The men were relieved when they saw she was talking to Victoria. "Did you enjoy it? Do you need a lot of room to do it or can you do it anywhere?"

"She's not doing it here, if that's what you're suggesting," said Simon.

"Perhaps you need inspiration to do it, do you?"

Victoria didn't speak.

The baby lay in its basket, twitching like a dying chicken. Sarah swung it up fearlessly and changed its diaper before nursing it. "Tell me about it. The tightrope-walking."

Victoria told her the minimum. The professors were shifting about. Were they bored? One huge drunk had fallen asleep. He looked like a collapsed bison and it would take a crane to move him.

Victoria stood up.

"What are you doing?" said Sarah. She put the baby across her knees and flicked her breasts into her dress.

"Have another drink," said Simon, more out of habit than hospitality. Sarah winked at Victoria.

Now a professor turned to Victoria. "You're not like your predecessor."

"No," Victoria admitted.

"You don't smoke like she did. Gerry hated it. He used to

complain to Gully, 'She smokes because she's getting at me. She knows it's killing her.' He said to my mother, another heavy smoker, 'You must be very dissatisfied to smoke that much.' He was thinking of his wife, obviously. He used to come in—the ashtrays would be full, and he'd flare up."

"We're always hypothetical in this house, darling," Sarah cautioned him.

"Ruth and Gerry. They looked as though they had it all, didn't they? But the horn of plenty was undone."

"I've got something to show you." Sarah led Victoria to the stairs.

"The other way around, more like it. One of the men laughed.

"No tightrope-walking now," said another.

Out of sight, Victoria gave the men the finger, and Sarah laughed. She led the way to an upstairs room.

"Who told you about my tightrope-walking?"

"Gully, of course. I know you've got something urgent to ask, but never do it in public, darling. For example, the last time you came, you were spotted. Gully told Gerry. You never know when Gully's drunk and when he isn't.

Victoria described Johnny Pass.

"He's Mafia, of course. They all are. Gerry's obviously trying his best to keep the grandchild out of it. Quite sensible, really. Also, it's a repayment to Ruth if you like. She hated the Mafia. That's how James has done so well. Marrying into the Organization."

For a moment, Sarah disappeared behind the smoke from her latest cigarette. "Oh hell, I've lit the wrong end. I didn't tell you before, darling, because I think, in your situation, the less you know, the better. Innocence is the only possible protection in a climte of such violence."

"Why isn't Johnny Pass in prison?"

Sarah, highly amused, said "Johnny Pass is so bad he's

almost good. And he's so well defended. He's got sophisti-
cated bugging that follows him wherever he goes. That's
what James works in, of course. Laser detection."

"But Johnny Pass told me he had a poor childhood."

"The Sicilian bit was poor, but he got drawn into the
Organization in his teens. People die rather a lot in that
business, so he rose to the top before he was thirty."

"How did Gerry get mixed up in it?"

"He liked money rather a lot I seem to remember. His
friend Robert Gittes introduced him. They were at Oxford
together. Gerry wanted Pass to make Ruth famous, and he
did. In exchange Gerry educated Pass's daughter, Lilly.
She'd been farmed out to an academic at UCLA so she could
cram in some knowledge. It seems to me it just turned her
into a tart. And Gerry, of course, by promising to let his son
marry her, gave J.P.'s family education. The Organization is
rather keen on education these days. Good for the image.
But J.P. was wonderful to Ruth. He sponsored her career
and did everything possible to cure her of cancer."

"Where's Lilly's mother?"

"She was a prostitute, darling, in Naples. I'd love to come
to your wedding."

"Come."

"Gerry wouldn't like it. He always gets his way." Victoria
was alerted by her tone. "You'll find that."

The men were shouting downstairs, something about
ropes not being tight enough.

"We'd better go down, said Sarah. "This is how rumors
begin."

"But Gerry's not involved, is he? With the Mafia?"

"He's another kind of don."

*　　*　　*

When the local Oxford press interviewed Gerry about his
move to America, they invited the family to lunch at a

picturesque pub on the river. Johnny Pass hovered watch-
fully by the oak door. He had a way of making the most
pleasant doorway seem like an emergency exit.

Gerry called to him, "Why don't you say something?"

"I've been badly burned in interviews. Anyway, what's
the point? Anybody can get five wimps like these to print
anything. And get them to pay for their own lunch. 'Cause
I'm a millionaire gives 'em ideas." He tap-danced showily
while everyone looked on awkwardly.

"He's in a mood," said James.

"Oh, tell him a joke," replied Gerry scathingly. "One
thing he's learned since he's gone political is that the press is
his enemy, not the Left."

"People keep saying how far to the right he is," said Lilly.
"But he offered two leftist graduates jobs in his micro-
electronics firm."

"Which one?"

"Detroit!"

"Detroit!" Gerry sneered. "Your father doesn't care how
high a Leftie gets as long as he doesn't get close." He turned
to Victoria and explained some of the lighter sides of Johnny's business enterprises. The Mafia connection was left out.
Gerry found it very easy to leave things out.

When Gerry had finished, Victoria said, "I know who he
is."

Gerry stayed very still. When he spoke his tone was
matter-of-fact. "Don't tell your mother."

A journalist was unwise enough to ask Johnny Pass a
question. "What do you think of critics, Mr. Pass?"

"Give 'em some money and they'll approve of anything."
He turned to the journalist. "I'll give you something to put
in your paper, boy. This country's got apathy. And I don't
like apathy. I'd get rid of it for you. I'd start with the kids in

the schools. I'm not afraid of the word 'discipline.' His voice grew huge and Lilly cowered. "It would be brought back to the way it was in my pa's time. I'd start 'em thinking right because when they think wrong, they go wrong. I'd stop all this bullshit with welfare payments. You're not helping a man or his dependents by giving 'em handouts from the state or anywhere else. They should be encouraged to get on their feet, find their self-respect and do a day's work."

"What if they're sick?" Gerry asked, angry.

The Mafia boss opened his arms wide. "Nature supplies the answer. It's the survival of the fittest. Natural selection."

"Just like animals, eh, Johnny?"

"When a man shows eagerness to work and do right, reward him. I'd like to see higher wages in the university. I couldn't afford to be president of Oxford. A *black* couldn't live on what he gets."

Johnny Pass made a display of calling for the bill. He looked at it disapprovingly, then handed it to the nearest journalist. "Don't come here again. They've overcharged you."

The journalist looked around at his colleagues and they quickly dug into their pockets and came up with an assortment of money. It was shoveled into the middle of the table and counted.

"Now run along and have a wonderful day," said Johnny. He took Lilly's hand as he watched the departing newsmen. "Thank God you're in the world. There's so much shit around."

"So how's your wife?" asked Gerry, hoping to calm him.

He made a concise gesture that looked final.

"How did you meet her?" Victoria asked, interested, as always, in the first meeting of couples.

"I opened my wallet and she was there. I'm a family man;

that's why I respect and honor your forthcoming union and why I'm gonna be there, right in the front pew."

James raised his eyes to heaven.

Gerry stood up. "Let's go and have that wonderful day you're always talking about."

CHAPTER · 23

"DON'T WORRY, I'LL GET RID OF HIM," SAID GERRY.

"And just how are you going to manage that? asked Victoria. She watched him change his clothes, his movements, everything about him, quiet, unobtrusive these days. He was keeping himself to himself. "Why didn't you tell me?"

"I thought you wouldn't go ahead with our marriage. After all, you're clean. It was a long time ago, Victoria. Frankly, I didn't think you'd ever meet him. I had no idea he would come here."

"Why did he?"

"He found out about my intentions regarding a certain child. He's going to put a stop to them."

"Will he succeed?"

"Oh, no." Final, decisive.

"You could have told me about him. I'm not made of glass. You owed me that, surely."

"I owed Lilly something, too. I gave her my word I'd keep silent."

"You brought it all on yourself. You must have known who Lilly was when you let her play with James."

"I liked her. Of course I knew where she came from. It didn't matter. In fact, she resisted her family. She had an instinctive moral assurance and guts."

"And now?"

"There's some brutal side to her that was not there before." He sighed. "Maybe inherited traits work themselves to the surface in the end. Or maybe it's because J.P.'s insinuated himself in her life again."

"She can move away."

"He'll never let her go now. She's an attractive appendage. So is James. Good for his image. The educated man of business."

"Does he kill people?"

"Ssh!" He gestured playfully. "He's probably bugged the room."

"Why do you insist on taking the child?"

"Don't you know what surrounds a man like him? The low people, the tawdry pleasures. It's not just violence. James and Lilly can't shield her because they're not strong enough. They'll become like the others. The family influence is too strong."

"You let James marry into that family."

"I did it for someone else."

"Johnny sponsored your wife's music, you mean?"

"Yes. I went to him. In those days I thought money could get you anything. I wanted the best for Ruth. Whatever they say about me, I was not money-mad. I wanted to impress my wife, give her everything. I was young. But as your mother would say, all that glitters is not gold."

Johnny entered the room silently. Only his shadow gave him away. So far, no scientific development had overcome that. His shoes had two-inch-thick crepe soles. He knew he'd been spotted so spoke immediately. "I just been checking up. Apart from your son and yourself, my daughter is the best-educated person in this house. I was always hot on education. When Lilly was a girl I told her I could paper the walls with money for her but I couldn't fill that—" He pointed to Gerry's head.

Gerry laughed. "Except with lead."

Johnny Pass decided to laugh. "You're the only guy in the

world who could say that." He buried his face in a vase of violets. "I just can't get over the sweet God-given fragrance of a fresh violet."

"Why?" said Victoria curtly. "It's not real."

He looked up, alarmed.

"They're artificially produced in an incubator. They have to be sprayed with perfume before they go to market. They have no smell of their own."

Johnny's face fell.

Gerry laughed. "Wait till she gets going on Santa Claus."

"They call me Santa Claus back where I come from. I hope you remember to tell the lady the good things I do. You're not the only one that got rich, Gerry. The university did all right by me, too."

Outside, Colin swept the corridor, his eyes swollen and distressed. "Gerry's overweight tap dancer keeps insulting me. He just pulled my mouth, hard."

"You caught him on one of his nicer days," said Victoria.

Colin spread his fingers wide and stared at them, one of Gerry's gestures. "You've got to talk to your dressmaker. Your sister Mary keeps calling." He sounded depressed. "At least you've got something to look forward to."

"Well, you've got your career and—"

"I've got nothing, absolutely nothing."

Victoria tried cheering him up. "Why don't you start preparing another show? Everyone says—"

"You can't dance away your menopause. Although that's what Softdrinks' trying to do. All that phony tap dancing. He's grotesquely depressed underneath."

"I saw him doing his exercises this morning. He does hand-clenching." She demonstrated.

"What does he do that for?" Colin asked.

"So he has strong hands."

"What's the point of that?"

"Well, if one day he fell off the Empire State Building he might be able to cling on to something, mightn't he?" She laughed.

At the door, J.P. was telling someone to have a wonderful day.

* * *

The Mafia boss promised he'd be intrusive at the wedding. He wanted to meet the Bonham-Hays immediately and put some life into their marquee reception. His business associates would have to be invited and he wanted the Honorable Mrs. Brooke to do it personally. Gerry responded with glum silence.

"Okay, son, you hit it lucky. So share it. You're part of our family, don't you forget. It's not every day we get a look in at an aristocrat's wedding."

He threatened to keep the child on American soil. Roses flourished there, too. "I started growing roses as a tribute to Ruth. Did you know that? And have they done well? The kid will be okay."

Surprisingly, Gerry was calm as he sat in the twilight talking about Victoria's family. How different they were from everyone else. If Johnny was affected he wasn't showing it. Gerry had already shown him some Bonham-Hay press clippings.

When Gerry stopped talking, the American found the silence oppressive. "I never have liked this house. I can't seem to settle in it."

For a moment, Gerry looked delighted. Was Johnny thinking of returning home?

"I like you, Gerry, and I want you to have whatever you want, but you can't take the child from its mother's love. It's not Christian, you see. But then you have no concept of God-given family commitment. That's why you can afford to be so casual about my daughter."

"There are a couple of mother-love substitutes, by the way."

"Such as?"

"A title. The child could be brought up in an established upper-class structure, going to the right schools, meeting the right people, marrying into the aristocracy."

Victoria, eavesdropping in the bedroom, wondered just how Gerry was going to manage that.

"Just think, J.P., you could end up being proud of your grandchild. You could move the new part of your family away from the less savory parts you're stuck with. It's not as though you're fond of children. You haven't touched the little girl since you've been here. Not once."

"Any time I want a title, I can buy one." He spat on the ground.

"People will only laugh."

"It's only 'cause she looks like Ruth you're making such a fuss. If she turned out like me you wouldn't be so enthusiastic. The answer's no. Everybody stays where they are."

Both men relapsed into silence. Gerry, knowing such uneasiness could provoke unsocial responses in Johnny, started talking.

"It's been a bad day."

"Not for me, son. I never have a bad day. I don't allow a God-given day to go sour on me."

"How do you manage that?"

"I think positively. You are what you think. Didn't you tell me that?"

"I thought you are what you eat."

"All my food is fresh and natural. My chickens run around so much they die of good health. I don't drink, I don't snort coke. I get up at five every morning and do one hour's exercise. Then I run for five miles, never less. I wish the best for every man I come into contact with—"

"Unless he's a Red." Gerry couldn't resist it.

"I don't come into contact with negative elements." He got up and broke into a joyful tap dance.

"It sounds great."

"It should, Gerry. I got it from you. I looked upon you as an example of something that worked."

"But you'll spoil it when the sun goes down. I've seen you. Those ex-beauty queens are plain bad. Then all the exercises and good thinking come apart. You can't stay up playing all night. No man can have two at a time, not at your age, not every night, Johnny. Those two you had last summer at the Vineyard, they were a pair of snakes. They didn't leave till four. A quick shower and it was time for your five o'clock jog."

"I like 'em sweet, tender and two at a time. The blonde was a bit of a dog but she was twenty-two. That's old. But Little Miss California Orange was—" He tried to find the right word.

"Ripe?" suggested Gerry. "Full of juice?"

"She was a credit to the American System. You're awake all hours, too. You must be to know when my late show ended. What's eating you, Gerry? You're not happy. You haven't got over it. Time hasn't done it for you. I got everything in the world yet I couldn't make her well or make you happy."

*   *   *

In one of Gerry's father's books about China, she read:

> A man sometimes makes love to imaginary figures or ghosts. The pleasure derived from this kind of inter-course is much more intense than from normal coitus. Such a man might well enjoy these experiences, conceal the matter from everybody else and take his secret with him to the grave. The disorder is hard to treat and

arises from perverse energies in the soul. If it is not treated, the sufferer will die early.

When he came to bed Gerry said, "The old man's got such dreadful energy. It's ironic that the little girl doesn't speak because, as you know, the Mafia all take an oath of silence."

She didn't answer.

"I take the child and that's that." His tone was uncompromising and deadly.

"The way you were going on to him about the Bonham-Hays. Are you trying to sell something?"

"Maybe."

She laughed, not kindly. "You're not dissimilar from him, are you? You're both so possessive."

He replied lightly. "If you mix with shit it rubs off on you. I'm sure your mother's told you that."

CHAPTER · 24

"VICTORIA BROOKE, YOU ARE THE SLUT. ALL YOU WANT IS HIS cock. You can't stop thinking about it. But he's not going to give it to you."

What had woken her? She felt freezing, her mouth dry. The voice had come from some place nearby. She decided not to put the light on and find out where. Fear had something to do with that decision. The voice, a woman's, was one she'd not heard before. Gerry lay sleeping beside her. She spent time telling herself she was not afraid. Then she heard a rustle of silk and clung to Gerry, trembling.

The first light touched the room. "I'll get a blanket." He got out of bed and she watched his naked body moving toward her. As the woman had said, she did want it. How she did! Lust brought her to her knees and she pushed her face against his cock.

"You must. You have to, Gerry. You have to."

He lifted her back across the bed and started fucking her. Yes, she had heard the voice. Its being disembodied took nothing from its power.

A sound started up in the corner. She supposed something had gone wrong with one of Colin's kitchen appliances. Gerry was on top now, making love, wildly. She hadn't heard the noise before. It was ringing, jangling, a huge sound caused by something more than a mixer or coffeemaker.

"Come on, Victoria. Feel it. Tell me you like it. You said you wanted it."

A chaos of church bells, school bells, alarms, buzzers. The room vibrated.

"It's all right. Just trust it."

His hands, his voice, so attractive, she was drawn into the state where involuntary, pleasurable things happened. "Go on. Don't stop. Trust me." She had no resistance.

"Gerry, I can't stop shaking." The force of the noise rocked her as though she were on a factory floor. He held her protectively as she came.

"Well, that was worth waiting for, wasn't it?" He rolled onto his back.

"Yes, wasn't it?" said the woman, mocking. Had he heard it?

As soon as they lay apart, the noise came out of the corner. Deafening, it started toward Victoria. It scuttled up her body, rustling, a many-footed, vengeful spider. It settled on top of her head. Its harsh, tearing screams lifted Victoria's hair. The sound was poisonous.

"Resist her! Resist her!" Victoria shouted at Gerry. For all her panic she thought only of him. She held on to him as he slept. "Go back!" she cried to the creature. "You don't belong here anymore."

Ruth had chosen to appear as a huge spider. A mistake. Victoria was scared of a lot of things but not insects. A rose, now, that would have been different.

"I'm not frightened of you, Ruth!" Victoria shouted.

The woman showed herself then, her screaming mouth, full of blood. She was a gray-black imprint in the air. The jangling passed over as she was drawn up and off. Before leaving, she spat blood, and Victoria's face felt wet.

"It's over." Gerry was holding her. He said she was having another nightmare.

The terrible creature was silent in the corner of the room, wanting revenge. "I don't want to die," Victoria whispered.

A woman spoke distinctly, softly amused. *"No one likes change."*

"There's blood, Gerry. Spots of it on me."

"Darling, it's only shadow."

* * *

When Victoria got up, late the next morning, she knew all about the pianist. How female she was. She'd never have thought of that; no one had mentioned it. How sensual and yielding the woman was, how she needed Gerry. She had something else, too. She was charismatic, just as he was. Victoria didn't even consider the talent. Ruth was at heart a woman who had found a great deal of sensual happiness with one man and she didn't want to lose it. How did Victoria ever think she could compete with that? She thought it was ironic that Ruth, who was so musical in life, should be so jangling and discordant in death.

She opened Ruth Holt's tin chest before lunch while the others were in the pub. Colin had taken it from the barn and hidden it above the wooden box in the hall. A blanket covered everything, but Victoria could tell that the pile was higher. She still couldn't break the lock. She tried knives, a hammer, then a key that had been lying in the drawer of Gerry's desk.

The notes, hotel bills and letters that half filled the chest dated from the time of their meeting to a year after her death.

She opened Gerry's diary for 1953, the year he met Ruth. She'd just made her debut at Wigmore Hall and had had a small success. He described an acrimonious meeting he'd had with Gilbert Ricks. Then he called at Ruth's impresario's house, where she was being feted by a visiting conductor from New York. She wore a scarlet dress and a pink rose. He wanted to kiss her but didn't know if she already had a sweetheart. She came up to Gerry as he poured himself a drink and whispered that she loved him. He was too elated to speak.

"Are you happy?" she asked.

"Happiness all good and enough for a lifetime."

Victoria closed that diary.

Ruth had been worried about her lack of fame. What would happen after Wigmore Hall? Anything? She had nowhere to live. Gerry could see she was depressed. He wanted to help her—he would do anything for her.

Ruth wrote him a note, six years later.

> Dearest G,
> You never talk down to anybody. I feel I could ask you anything and it would be all right. They feel that too, the new boys. The way they come to you with their problems. I am quite jealous. You were born to teach.

When the cancer was diagnosed, the doctor sent a handwritten letter:

> You ask me for the impossible. How can I give you hope when she is obviously dying? She is filled with cancer. Of course I can't operate. All I can suggest is that you make her last weeks beautiful, as only you can.

She recognized Ruth's style. Dozens of notes passed between the two. A piece of thick writing paper was folded in half. One of them would write a note. The other replied underneath or up the side. Then there would be a reply to that in the middle of the folded sheet.

> R—
> I adore you! Absolutely adore you!
> Your exhausted husband

I can't stop thinking about it. I must do it again.
I'll come back between lectures. Be there for me. The
way I like you!!

She could feel the headiness of his sexual excitement as,
dressed for work, he stood by the bed, watching the sleeping
woman, remembering the ecstasy of the night.

Underneath, in pencil, Ruth had written: "So you adore
me? Whores get paid."

On the back, "The diamonds go around your neck. The
other, where you want it."

Ruth added, "Where you want it to be, you mean."

What did it mean? Who cared? It was undeniably erotic.
The other stuff was just too painful to read.

She wondered if in years to come, when they were all
dead, these love notes would be sent anonymously to some
wife-to-be. Turning up in a junk shop, would they be chosen
as the epitome of sexual love?

There was a sharp tap on the door. It opened. "I always
knock the first time. After that, anything goes." Gerry
mimicked J.P. exactly. Drink had put him in a playful mood.

Then he saw what she was doing. He kicked the chest so
hard the lid crashed down.

"I thought you were too well brought up for that." He
spoke in the detached tone she hated.

"You still write her notes."

"I could put flowers on her grave. The notes are instead of
flowers. So why do it? Well, you must have some idea."

"I've got nothing!"

"You've got nothing." He rounded on her. "Well, if I were
you, I wouldn't have come here. I'd sit at home by myself,
with all the lights out."

She laughed scornfully. She'd learned to laugh instead of
cry a long time ago.

She ran outside and stood at the side of the house. She wished she could be a whore. All that happy, perfect love recorded in the diaries and his letters made her want to do something drastic, destructive. Alex would understand that.

Gerry was a phantom who had only truly existed all those years ago. He'd been trying to reach back there ever since.

She looked along the empty alley lined with boxtrees. The unforgotten had won.

CHAPTER · 25

ON IMPULSE, SHE WENT BACK TO SOUTH LONDON AND SOUGHT out Alice. The high-rise complex, where Alice lived alone on the tenth floor, was shabby, its walls covered with graffiti. Alice didn't remember meeting Victoria at the hospital and kept the chain on the door.

"I'm Victoria Brooke and I've come to return your postcards."

The woman was puzzled.

"You remember? From your friends Lil and Mick and—"

The door was closing. "I don't want them."

"Please, Mrs. Hunter, what was James Hamilton like? I'd love to know."

The door didn't quite close.

"James Hamilton." She was amazed. "But that was years ago." Her hold on the door relaxed. "What do you want to know about him for?"

"I can tell he was somebody special."

"What do you want to know about our lives for? We were just ordinary people. Except for James. He was—" She stopped, suspicious. "Here, you're not one of Alan's friends in trouble again?"

"No."

"Well, if you'll excuse me . . ."

"Somebody's been sending your cards to me anonymously and I want to find out why."

"How did you know where I lived?"

"The hospital where—"

"They shouldn't give you my address. For all they know, you could be a bill collector."

Victoria kept asking questions but the door was closing again. Alice had had enough. Then she asked about Alice's illness, just one question, and the door swung open so fast, Victoria nearly fell on her face.

Everything was modern in the small apartment. Alice admitted she did not like being reminded of the past.

"Scaring visitors, that's the thing. Let them think you're dying. Make them guilty because they're well. Mine used to leave the ward, pale with worry. I'd turned their stomachs. They always came back for more."

"Have you had an operation yet?"

"Not yet." She looked gloomy. "You don't live around here?"

"Oxford."

"What on earth did you come all this way for?"

"To give you the cards."

"They're the past. I prefer to forget it."

Victoria drank tea at the dented metal-topped kitchen table. Every time anything was put down or lifted up, the table reacted noisily like thunder in a low-budget movie. She'd lost Alice's attention, so she tried another medical question.

"What they're going to do to me I wouldn't wish on a dog. They're talking of transferring me to Hackney."

"Why?"

"I don't know why. That's what I want to find out. I didn't know what was wrong with me till last month. I was all yellow, I knew that. They never tell you a thing. When you're in the hospital it gets so you don't want to see the outside world. Nothing bothers you. No bad news gets through. The nurses treat you like a kid. People get so they don't want to leave."

In spite of everything, Alice's dark eyes were young. Sometimes they had the soft, dewy expression of the women in the postcards.

"What about your husband?"

"George could have had better health. Life was harder in those days, but we enjoyed it. The whole Hunter family was consumptive. George's father was always in debt. He had so many burials he couldn't keep up with them. Every time one of them died, they had to have a collection up the street. I started going out with George the day after I got my first job."

"What was it?"

"At the lying-in hospital. I nursed for over forty years. ...George's father was a one. Spiteful with drink....I usually listen to the wireless at this time."

"What about James?" Victoria asked hungrily.

"George Hunter's father had a pushcart and worked as a fish-fryer at night. His mother was educated and tried to keep up appearances. What a mistake that was. You can't keep much up on what he brought back. Next to nothing, sometimes."

"How did they live on so little?"

"You didn't live on it. You died on it. When I started school my mother was twenty-six. She looked fifty. There were eleven kids; seven died before they reached their teens."

"Even so, I think you're very lucky to have had such a marvelous experience."

"And what was that?"

"James Hamilton."

"Oh, James. He was so bright the sunlight seemed to come out of him. I felt as though something lovely was happening every time he came into the room. He was different from other people." She leaned back. Her eyes closed, remembering.

"What did he do?"

"This and that. He wasn't in steady work."

"Have you any photographs of him, Mrs. Hunter?"

"Not anymore." She sat up, matter-of-fact. "He was going to be a doctor, that's right. His family was well-to-do. James Hamilton had an aunt who lived in Kensington. Fancy remembering that. The air was so good there it made a change from the stuffy basements I was used to. She had a bath with hot and cold water. I love James's aunt's house. You could sleep with the windows open. There was a lot of hardship in those days. People were more innocent. We did not know the things they know today."

"What did he look like?" She got the question in quickly. Alice was looking at the clock again.

"His face was delicate. The nearer you got, the younger he seemed. He was quick-thinking and you had to get up early to put one over on him. He couldn't abide slow people. He was tempestuous."

"Why was that?"

"It must have been all that red hair. Had he lived he'd have certainly become a professional man. He was that sort of person. He planned for the future." She paused. "Not what you're used to."

Victoria, taken aback, said, "What's that?"

"The furniture. I got it all from rummage sales. I used to have a lovely home but when George passed on, I came here. This'll see me out. I've lived past my time and that's the truth."

"What was so special about James Hamilton?"

"I've got to listen to my program."

Victoria gave in, stood up. "Well, thank you for talking to

me. You've certainly taken my mind off my own problems."
She touched Alice's hand briefly. "I think you're very lucky
to have had such an experience."

"In one way. It certainly made the rest look dull."

"What was it like with George?"

She didn't understand the question. At least she seemed
as if she didn't. Victoria tried again. "Well, where did you
go when you went out?"

"Kensington Park. There was never any air in those
basement rooms. Poor George was always sickly. But I
understood him. We were in the same trap."

"What were marriages like then, Alice?"

"Same as now. Love comes first in the house, and if it
doesn't you're in trouble."

"How did you meet James?"

"I went to a party with George, my young man, for the
boys going overseas. Although he was a casual worker, he
was very clever, James was. He was always the best whatever
he did. People looked twice at James Hamilton. He had some
quality in him that made him different. I held his hand. I
remember his eyes. He was watching me, so interested. I
tried to look away from him, but couldn't. I did feel silly.
And I knew what it was going to be. His eyes were
wonderful—I can still remember them. When he smiled they
heated up. I couldn't stop thinking how he looked at me.
How special it was, that look. People didn't look at me like
that often." She laughed. "They didn't look at anyone like
that often."

She got up and went quickly along a dark yellow hall that
smelled of oilcloth. The linoleum was stained. She opened a
closet and lifted down a suitcase. Victoria offered to help but
the woman didn't answer. Whatever she was looking for
wasn't there. Other closets were opened, a table moved, then
she came back with an old student's notebook. "I never was
able to throw it away."

It was James Hamilton's diary. The writing was hardly touched by the passing of time. It would be legible for a hundred years to come.

> Monday night.
> Alice, this is for you. I sit in the hut waiting for Charley to die. He's not in such pain now. I don't think he'll last long. I try and recall your face, your body. I get your eyes. Can't capture the mouth. Then you are there, wonderfully clear, smiling at me. I long for your hands. How they excite me, give pleasure. Charley's making a lot of noise now. I try and escape back to you. I've given him another injection. A terrible time, then he's gone. You're all blurred, your features, unsatisfactory. I must get them right. Oh, Alice . . ."

> Friday.
> Oh, I'd have met you, Alice. If I'd gone to the other end of the world, if I'd changed my name, if I'd married and had five children, I would still at 7:28 on that particular evening have held out my hand to you in that same way. Everything slowed down. Something lovely was happening. A glow came into the room. But we never touched. Then you said something and the resonance seemed to linger. You'd not taken your eyes from my face.
>   From James to Alice

"Yes," murmured Alice. "Meeting James Hamilton was predestined, I agree with that. I couldn't have avoided it. He was a wonderful lover."

"Did girls do it in those days generally?"

"You'd be a fool not to do it when a man like James Hamilton asks you. You're a bit old-fashioned, you are," she added wryly.

"How can you live without such passion?" murmured Victoria.

"You do. What's more, you forget, even the unforgettable. In the end, you forget." She sounded tired.

"There was one card from a church in Chester. Is that where he's buried?"

"Could be. His people came from there."

"One thing I never understood. Seeing he died in nineteen sixteen, why were the cards from your friends so cheerful?"

"They didn't know about it." She sounded shocked.

"Thank you, Alice. My friend Sylvia—she's a nurse, also—and I were very moved by your postcards. You had a real love affair. You're so lucky."

Alice was amused. "Have a happy marriage."

"And how does one do that?"

"Don't get into too much of a rut. Get up in the morning as though it's a new beginning. If I had my time again that's what I'd do. Don't let things get too dull. It doesn't do love any good."

As Victoria walked to the underground she believed she'd given James Hamilton back to Alice. She'd made her see how special her love affair was. After all, it could still kindle a response in other, modern women. James Hamilton was a jewel untouched by time, encapsulated in brightness, safe, not allowed to deteriorate by everyday habit. Ruth was like that, too. Safe in the past.

* * *

Sylvia lay along the edge of her father's bathtub like a shabby tiger. She was defeated, clawless, toothless, but she was still dangerous. The short spell at her father's house had been forced to an ending a second time, and she was desolate.

"I spoke to my analyst about Gerry. Not that it's the sort of love they approve of. Too straight."

"I don't want to hear it." Victoria would never let a medical man near her pain, twisting it to suit his expensive diagnosis. "Look, Gerry's all right to me. It's the house. That twisted arch leading to the garden, like a gibbet. Nothing about it wishes me well. I'm beginning to think I'm better with someone bad. I felt easy with Alex because I could tell him what I was thinking, wanting. It didn't matter because there was nothing to ruin. No perfection. I mean it was once perfect with Gerry. It really was. Alex made you feel okay about your bad side. The more black and mad a person's behavior, the more sense he could make of it."

"It's all that red hair," Alice had said. That was something James had in common with Alex.

"Perhaps you should see him again?" Sylvia tried to make the suggestion casual.

"He was too much for me, too. He made me feel I wasn't alive enough. My mother makes me frightened. You make me think I'm a prude. I'm the one who's always scared of taking the wrong road, embracing the wrong man. I turned a corner and ended up with Gerry."

"There are no right roads, wrong turnings, Mr. Rights, exhausting Mr. Wrongs. Find another relationship and get back your confidence."

"A relationship? What's that, Syl? A relationship for you could be anything slightly longer than twenty minutes."

"So what? I call one night with a loving, caring man a relationship."

"If it's that good, why does it have to be only one night?"

"They're invariably married, of course. There's a lot to be said for it. The married ones are especially therapeutic."

Victoria's expression hardened.

"Oh, don't go religious on me, Vee, please."

"I've always left them alone." Lies. Alexander was married. "I got that from my mother. She always said it's wrong to take a married man because you're taking something from his wife. You're having what he should be giving to her and you're inevitably paid back for it."

"Muck for an analyst. You don't take a man away from his wife. You couldn't unless he wanted to go. Sleep with someone else. Put yourself together. You come first."

Richard Holly, wearing a green smoking jacket, appeared without warning in the doorway to tell them they were to stay for dinner. In one hand he held a glass of whiskey made safe by a dozen ice cubes. In the other, some kind of herbal cigarette. He was always trying to make vice safe. He proposed plans for controlling the famous author's drinking. He really meant Sylvia's drinking.

"Stick to light white wine and nothing after dinner, Sylvia," Victoria said. "Professor Gully's coming."

Sylvia made an obscene gesture, and Richard Holly retreated. Victoria was sure he regretted everything about his involvement with the Jago family except the commission he got from the book sales.

"I can't face that house," Victoria said. "Ruth is just a thought away. Everything is a celebration of Ruth. What she did, what she wore—"

"If you didn't feel so inferior, if you weren't Miss Wrong all the time, there'd be no need for a Mr. Right. It's that same inferiority that's made a ghost of Ruth Holt."

"But she's in the fucking bedroom. She even has her own sound."

Sylvia looked infuriatingly blank. Unhealthy threesomes could get her excited, but an attack by a vengeful ghost didn't interest her at all.

"I dreamed this screaming, mad apparition because I feel inferior to Ruth Holt. Also, I feel guilty because he really belongs to her. That's what you're trying to say, isn't it?"

"I don't have to. You've just said it."

"You'd put your head in a bucket of shit if your analyst told you to."

"You're obsessed."

"At least I'm not obsessed with my father and boringly drunk all the time."

"You're going along the right road to getting yourself a new maid of honor."

Victoria ran down the stairs to the front door. Sylvia caught her on the step and held her tight. "The phantoms are your own, Vee. Get rid of these shadowy virtues that you believe direct life. Like signposts, they're supposed to point to the right road, but they're more like tombstones. They've led you into a hell of a mess. Right, wrong, they don't come from God. They come from your mother. Go and see Alex and get some sense into yourself. He's real."

"I might if I knew where he lived," said Victoria sulkily.

Sylvia wrote an address on the back of an envelope. "I didn't need any clairvoyant to tell me who was sending the postcards."

CHAPTER · 26

ALEXANDER WAS STAYING WITH A GROUP OF DELINQUENTS IN Kentish Town. Sylvia had got the address from his first wife, not the current one, whose ignorance of his whereabouts boded ill for the new marriage.

Once Victoria had found the house she didn't want to go in. She'd rather remember Alex as he had been than be confronted with another installment of change and super-charged excitement that would only make her miss him when it was time to leave, she told herself. She had more in common with Alice than she'd supposed. Alex was like James Hamilton. Safe in the past. He couldn't be spoiled. It's the ones that are with us now that are the trouble. She'd missed out. She'd been bobbed off. Gerry wants peace, not passion. Why didn't she bring out the passion in him? Lilly did. There was something lustful about them, even when they quarreled. Especially when they quarreled. But he didn't want intensity anymore, and he was a man who only got what he wanted.

She would have walked away from the Kentish Town house, but she wanted to know why he'd sent the postcards. The front door was unlatched, the hallway blackened from a recent fire. Alex was pretending to work but actually he was having his idea of a good time. His companions' main occupation was sniffing glue, which was cheaper and more available than drugs. Alex lived as one of them while working on a series of paintings of their lives. The glue worried him. "The thing is, I like a drink."

"Yes, I remember."

"They think I'm old-fashioned."

"You're so much older than they. Don't they distrust you? Isn't it dangerous?"

"Not all the time; I give them money for speed. I prefer hash myself, but they think that's passé, too." His smile, his carroty, spiky hair made him appear joyful. He wore an old black woolen sweater with holes in the elbows. "It's rather nice, isn't it?" he said. "The material. Feel. It belongs to Wild Hugh, who runs the house." The veins were big in his arms and throbbing with energy or high blood pressure. She thought the glue was probably a mistake. He slept on a pile of newspapers in the corner. It all looked sparse and admirable, but she suspected he ran off to one of his wives whenever he'd had enough. When he smiled, she was reminded how much she'd loved him. He touched her and she discovered the feeling was not altogether dead.

She looked away, said coolly, "I'm not visiting. I've come for the postcard album."

He got it out from under the pile of newspapers and didn't bother asking how she'd traced it to him. A few cards were still hanging from broken hinges. Nothing from James.

> 1936.
> Dear Alice,
>   Just a line to let you know we are having a gorgeous June. Lovely sunshine.

"What is it that makes Mrs. Hunter no longer Miss Murray?" asked Alex. "Is the change reflected in the sender of the card? Why does she choose weather and not fun?" He wiped his brushes and admired the houses across the street. Like Gerry, he could turn people on to what he liked.

Suddenly two young hoods kicked open the door and asked for money. They found Victoria's attractiveness threatening and said so with expletives. Alex pulled out a roll of ten-pound notes and gave them three. The sight of all the money made them jeer. They believed he got it from screwing women. They weren't altogether wrong.

"Is that enough? Do you want a twenty?" asked Alex, kindly.

"Fuck off, cunt." They taunted Victoria.

"Cunt!" The door slammed.

She could think of nothing to say about that, and it was too prosaic for Alex to comment on.

"How's the don?"

"He's all right."

He looked into her eyes, saw what he wanted. She supposed it was uncertainty. "How's your new wife?"

"She's fine. Let's have a drink."

"Why did you send them?"

"Let's talk about you. I want to know why you wrote to all those movie stars when you were a kid. Is that what you wanted to be? A star?" He laughed. "Is it?"

"You're after my dreams again. You want to take them over."

"So what? I've given you others."

"It's one way to take people over. Giving them dreams. So why did you send the cards?"

"Because those two knew a thing about love, about making it." There was a nasty pause, and she felt he was undermining her. "You make it like you make anything else. It should be a practical thing, like making pastry."

"I didn't know that," she said cynically.

"Then if you're lucky, the other little touches come in."

"Are you criticizing my performance then?"

"I took you to the fence but you always shied back like the horses you're so fond of. I'm not thinking only of the physical aspect. There are parts of yourself you just can't acknowledge, so other people get their hands on them and you end up at Ascot and Glyndebourne and—"

"Isn't that my business?"

"And mine. It means you're only half alive. Why be like that?"

"Perhaps it's the fear of jumping the fence and finding nothing on the other side."

"Oh, come on. You're brighter than that."

He rolled a cigarette from the butts on the floor; he had a lot to choose from. Even that action had something compelling about it. She always had to watch him, whatever he did.

"It's very dirty in here." She needed something to say. "So the postcards were meant to take me to the fence again?"

"What does your fiancée think? Doesn't he expose you? All those defensive—"

"This picture is marvelous, Alex."

"I wondered when you'd get around to that. You're the same. You go around the exterior disapproving of everything. Only then can you come to the center and approve."

"I wouldn't say that."

"I would."

In the past he'd challenged her. He'd wanted to burn her down, then reconstruct something better. Analysts, so Sylvia said, did that. He wasn't an analyst. That kind of thing was too slow and dreary for him. He was more an arsonist. When she was with him in Paris, she'd begun to hate her county mannerisms, her selfish small thoughts, her ordinariness. He'd forced her to live for the moment, dropping all preconceived ideas about how to get through the day. It was his idea that she take off her clothes and walk a tightrope in public. He exposed all defensive acts, especially in bed.

"Gerry de Santos doesn't question me, only soothes me. Thinking about you is all right from the safety of Haslemere."

"Or Oxford. That sounds like the same sort of thing."

"What right have you to say that?"

"I would take you further into yourself than you've been before. Surely you remember."

"You never left me alone, I remember that."

"Wasn't there anything you liked about it then?" He sounded irritated. He tried to find something to drink but all the bottles, even the hidden ones, were empty.

"You resent Gerry because he does what you do. It's funny. You can play God, but when he does it, it's not allowed. Still, you can only have one person in that part at a time."

"You're doing what you're about to do for the wrong reason."

"Why shouldn't I marry? You do it enough."

"Not that man. You need a man with more love and more threat. He's a deadly, manipulative bastard. All magnetic charm in public—"

"Well, it would take you to see that."

"But fuck the world in private!" He screwed the top on a tube of white paint. As always, he was meticulous about his tools. Whatever he did to himself he could not dull his energy or ruin his looks. Was it because he never settled down? He despised safety and was always after change.

"He's trouble undoubtedly, that man. You've chosen him so he can do your living for you. All you'll be in his life is an acquisition. That's safe. Get rid of safety!"

"Why do you care?" She needed to know if he still wanted her. In the midst of all the emotional chaos, that was suddenly important.

"Because once again you're not being yourself. You're not giving yourself a chance to be alive. When I read that engagement notice in the *Times* my heart sank."

"Since when have you read the *Times*?"

"I used it for a sheet on my bed."

"Why are you so interested in what happens to me?"

For once he didn't have an answer.

"Are you happy with your wife?"

"Very," he said warmly.

She felt disappointed. So she still cared what he thought about her. "But I don't see your wife here."

"She gives me space." He turned and smiled at her. His smile was always dazzling. It had nothing to do with what he was looking at and was radiant in the shabby room. His head, like a ragged sunflower, was the solitary thriving thing in a wasteland of modern litter. What did he absorb from these surroundings? What could he thrive on to be so exquisite? Such squalor would make other people ugly. His backgrounds always suited him, especially when they were disordered.

"I think my marriage to Gerry de Santos will be successful, too," she said with dignity. "Different from yours. I can't think of any reason why I'd need space from him."

"He'll answer all questions for you and keep you trapped in that academic life. You'll be dead in two years. Not officially, but in every other way. You'll get stuffy in the end. The professor's wife answering his letters, keeping people away. Still, you always had a strong streak of county to fall back on."

"What are you offering me?"

"I beg your pardon?"

"It's all very well people telling me to change my life, but what right have they if they aren't prepared to offer an alternative?"

He put his arms around her and her body, starved for love, drew him close.

"I just can't bear to see you go down the drain. Because you're scared, you'll settle for second best—though I hesitate to say what you'll get with him. Let yourself fall in love for once, trust it."

Stung, Victoria said, "It's better when I think about you, Alex. Seeing you is a mistake." She tried to let go of him but everything stayed where it was. She was parched, dying for love. So she spoke. "We had a good time."

Their bodies remembered. Hers flared up with a sharp appetite. His heart thumped against her. Passion was a caress away.

"A very nice, sweet little time, didn't we?" He was serious now.

Her body, expecting pleasure, would not retreat or respond to cautionary thoughts. Speech, too, was not on her side. He waited. It would have to be her decision. Like someone dying, she made a weak, incoherent gesture. He understood and let go of her. At least he was on her side. They moved about in silence.

"What I feel for you is too—well, it's too serious for a quick fuck, Victoria, but if that's what you want—"

She looked for her bag, her coat, and had trouble finding them. Her body was sulking.

"Do you want a drink? Alex asked. "We'll have to go to the pub."

"No, I must go. May I take the album?"

* * *

At lunchtime Victoria ate a watery curry in the usual dark red, gloomy Indian restaurant. Sylvia said, "I think Alex sent you the cards because he hates losing you."

"But he's got a new wife."

"He hates losing you in marriage to a well-established intellectual who can protect you with mature confidence. If it were someone like himself or a less attractive man . . . I've come around to thinking it's all a matter of how you look at a situation. You could say I've got my comeuppance, my father's contempt and rejection, because I screw every man in sight. On the other hand, it could be bad luck."

"You could say promiscuity is a mistake."

"You could. But the thing about mistakes is that you must go on making them. Gerry, for instance, doesn't make enough. There's nothing there, you know. He's had it. He's got nothing inside him anymore. In the beginning, you were dazzled, but it was just your love reflected back to you like the sun in windows. It's all reflection. Don't you see?"

Victoria did not like the mention of reflections. "You're beginning to sound like your analyst, darling. Soon you'll only be able to look at things from a prone position. If it's just needing someone to talk to twice a week, I'll listen willingly and for free."

"Forget the don."

"I was meant to meet him."

"It doesn't mean you were meant to marry him. Perhaps it's a testing time in your life, if there's any meaning to anything, which I doubt."

"If there's no meaning, Syl, you can do anything. Isn't that right?"

"If the fire burns you, don't go near it. Avoid pain. You can avoid pain."

"My, we are admitting limitations. The world is no longer the screwers' playground, I see."

They were too awkward and hostile with each other to calm down. Victoria called for the bill. "I bet you screwed Alex, too."

Sunlight streamed into the restaurant, giving life to the dreary windows. Everything was reflected—Victoria, Sylvia, the waiter, over and over, extending into eternity. She remembered Gerry staring at the glass door. What had he seen reflected there?

"You slept with Alex," Victoria repeated.

"He's got sense, Victoria. Real sense, and he's desperately fond of you. That's why he sent the cards. He did it for the most sensible reasons."

"How did you get the idea it was him?"

"Why not? Why shouldn't you have something in your past?"

"I'm furious with you for sleeping with him. Can't I have anything for myself?"

"Oh, dear. Possessive, are we? He's a funny choice for that sort of thing. He's the most promiscuous person I've ever met. He's worse than I am. Anyway, it's just your mother's women's-magazine beliefs objecting. You'll get over it."

CHAPTER · 27

As VICTORIA BRUSHED HER HAIR, SHE NOTICED THE ROSES. "There's something odd about them."

"Of course they're odd. They're bugged. J.P. had it done. That's how he knew I was trying to keep Ruthie."

"But why?"

"I suppose it's Lilly. She's important to him, his only daughter. He thinks people are always trying to get at her, so wherever she goes, he sees that the place is bugged in advance. I should have remembered that."

"Has anyone tried to kill her, then?"

"Not that I know of. Because he's been so destructive and evil he thinks other people are, too. I should have known he'd gotten to the roses when your hand bled so much."

"Oh, I don't think it was that." Victoria had a more sinister explanation.

"He has to use chemicals, you see. That could cause bleeding."

"Where is he? He's very quiet."

"He's gone."

"Just like that? How did you get rid of him?"

"I made him an offer."

She was impressed.

"I said if he stayed off my turf he could marry your mother."

Her hysterical laugh brought Colin to the door. "Gerry, come and be amusing out here. Our guests have arrived for dinner. No one's talking. Lilly's blue."

"Domestic hatred can become a habit-forming drug. Do you know that?" Gerry glared at her.

"No," she said.

Colin, whispering abuse, went away.

" 'Whose will to civil anarchy/Uses disease to disobey/ And makes our private bodies ill,' " Gerry quoted.

"No, I don't know it." She felt uneasy.

"So, you found out who sent the postcards?" Gerry asked.

"Alex sent them."

"I know."

"You know?"

"I guessed. I'm not the only one with a past. You only had to tell me you went to see him, not lie about Mummy buying a dress. How could she? That size?" His eyes weren't dark blue tonight or even gray, but slaty with displeasure.

Colin called angrily, something about more wine.

"Can we spend our wedding night somewhere else, Gerry. Not here?"

"Whatever you like." His movements were slower, he looked pale.

"It's closing in, isn't it, Gerry?"

He looked at her sharply.

"Only three weeks."

"Victoria, there's something I must—"

Lilly staggered in the doorway. Her heels were too high or she was drunk. Gerry ordered sharply, "Lay off the sauce."

"Your dinner party's on its ass." Her voice was slurred.

"When you see your father tell him I've put Ruth down for Bedales in 1990. And I advise a change of air for you. Oxford, for example. If your father goes near the child, he doesn't get what I promised him. That's called compromise, Lilly. He'll understand that. He needs a nice, plump comforter for his old age. And I'll let you take a rose back for him. A pink one. Tell him it's got bugs." He stroked her cheek, tauntingly. He was having his own way with a vengeance.

For a moment, Lilly looked so full of lust, it rose off her skin like pollen. She wanted to hold him, bite him, tie him up, cage him, if necessary. Then she spoke. She didn't approve of his plan for her daughter and used her father's style to tell him. It was thick with vulgar, well-worn threats.

"What else can I do?" he said simply, turning away. "Let's go and eat."

"About the little girl . . . It may all be for the best, but it's possessive, isn't it? And possessiveness is wrong," Victoria pronounced.

He didn't like hearing that.

"You want to keep the child. It's all to do with Ruth. it's all Ruth, anyway. That's why you won't sleep with me in this house," Lilly responded.

"You've reduced our relationship," he said, simply.

"How, exactly?"

"You've brought it down to whether I fuck you or not."

Colin waved desperately in the doorway. "Come and say it out here. Someone's got to say something."

"And you've reduced me, too," Victoria said. "So you can punish me because shc's been taken away from you."

"You're crazy."

"You want to accuse me of sleeping with Alex. You're so fucking perverse you make Richard Holly seem normal."

"You've been seeing him, too, have you? My, you've been busy for a bride-to-be."

She got hold of the first thing in reach and smashed it. He watched her warily out of the corner of his eye. He didn't like violence.

"If you're going to use these things you've trumped up

against me as a reason not to marry—"

With a slight gesture, he dismissed it all. "You'll feel better in America."

"Are we talking about the soft drinks business or—"

"UCLA." There was a long pause. She could hear the ventilating fan in the kitchen; its sound hypnotic. She wanted to fall asleep and just let it all be over.

"Gerry, we'll be all right if—"

"That's the first optimistic thing I've heard from you in a month."

"Well, this will cheer you up even more. You're off the hook, baby. You don't have to go ahead with it."

He laughed. "Let's go to our guest."

She wouldn't look at him but lay down and closed her eyes. To sleep would be dangerous. The roses . . .

* * *

At the table, Colin was describing Gerry's life using the grand "we." Victoria watched from outside, through the French windows. It was all temporary: Crowsley, the rose garden, the incomprehensible academic world, the pain of not being preferred. None of it went on forever. From that, she took comfort. Even the good things had to change.

Gerry waved to her to come in and she obeyed. She didn't believe in a right road anymore.

The conversation was centered now on Gerry's prize student. His looks, his truck driver's body, his ass-clinging trousers, his so-called girlfriend. If Victoria could read between the five-syllable adjectives, at least two of the men present had known him intimately.

Her neighbor said, "I have to drink because I've got a low blood-sugar level. Alcohol stops me from passing out."

"You'll have no medical problem tonight," she promised him.

"It helps reality, doesn't it? Booze?"

"Oh? What is reality?" she said scathingly. "You make your own. Someone else will always see a thing differently. Better, worse. It happens differently for them. That is the human specialty."

Gerry knew what she was talking about. When the guests had left, he took her hand, comforted her, and in spite of everything, she felt loved. He lifted her hair back from her eyes, his hands tender and caring. He was still the most beautiful, most magnetic man she'd ever seen.

"I'm going away, Victoria."

She assumed it was the drink distorting her perceptions. But she responded to what she thought she'd heard.

"Where?"

"America." So alcohol had nothing to do with it.

"Can I come?"

He didn't say no. There were so many variations on no. Silence was the cruelest.

"What about the church rehearsal then?"

"Put it off for now."

"Shall I put off the wedding, too?"

She drank a lot, quickly, to try and shut out the pain. She looked around the room, her throat aching with sadness. Breaking up. That sort of thing had to be his decision.

"Why are you going?"

"It may only be for a few days. Believe me, Victoria, I want only the best for you."

She covered her ears. Consciousness was too painful. Had T. S. Eliot touched upon that? It seemed more basic than "not being in time."

"You had such a marvelous marriage, didn't you, Gerry? Oh, yes . . . But was it really? You might be Gilbert Ricks now if you'd stood alone. And she'd have gone on playing."

"I don't want to talk about it."

Victoria closed her eyes, the room spinning. "I bet it

wasn't always summer days. I bet there were times when you wanted out."

"Oh, no. That isn't so. You don't just up and go as though it's a theater entertainment that doesn't please." He was humoring her. "You make it work. You put everything into it. Not a thought, a policy, a whim, but the lot."

"There were times when you wanted to sleep with someone else. Why don't you admit it?" She wanted the marriage broken up. The ghost was quiet now, but then it only approached when Victoria was getting something pleasant.

"My wife had integrity. Her values may seem old-fashioned to you, Victoria, but they'll still be here when sexual passion has worn thin."

"So, old values are better than new love? Is that what she thinks, your wife? She's wrong!"

Colin was enthralled. He stopped suffering and turned the taps off. He couldn't bear to miss a word. Victoria poured a glass of wine and spilled most of it.

"You're not being hypothetical," Lilly told her.

"Victoria has never been hypothetical," said Gerry. "A marriage is sharing. You share everything. I keep nothing from my wife. I should say, I *kept* nothing from her. It's the best way."

"Even fantasies?" said Colin.

"Especially fantasies." He turned to Victoria. "My wife is never wrong."

Victoria, bitterly hurt, stumbled to the door. She slipped away across the garden. These days Gerry belonged to the "waste sad time stretching before and after," to quote his favorite author. Whatever happened, she must belong to life.

All disjointed, she ran to the street, her shoes falling off as she went. She sobbed dryly. She was too bitter for tears, just as it could be too cold for snow.

CHAPTER · 28

RICHARD HOLLY CAME TO THE DOOR NEATLY PACKAGED IN A satin dressing gown and slippers. Even his hair was brushed. Middle-of-the-night callers didn't catch him unprepared.

"I can't pay for the cab. I left everything in Oxford. Where's Syl?"

"Out."

He had to rifle the author's secret money supply to give the cabdriver his return fare to Oxford. Then he took Victoria's arm and gave her a drink.

"It's the way they close ranks against me."

"Who?"

"Gerry and his wife."

"You're drunk."

"The barriers go up, hiding the secret physical things they do. He lifts up her silk dress and I'm an outsider, a nothing. He's been playing with me. I've been used. They've grown together, all over each other. I feel like some cheap marriage-breaker bitch."

"But she's dead. Ruth Holt's dead."

"She's spread herself over him, making him almost female. He is motherly, you must agree. It's hard to tell where one ends and the other begins. Still, I suppose that's what years of marriage do to you."

Richard turned professional. He had a lot in common with Sylvia. Don't let the sufferer see your shocked reaction. Textbook psychology is better than sympathy; also, it can be made to fit anything.

"Why do you want to separate them? Is it a parent thing you've got, Victoria?"

"I want to free him."

"An analyst would say it's an Electra complex." He wasn't quite sure of the "Electra." "It's something you should have gone through with your parents. Not that I have any time for analysts, you understand."

She was in no doubt he would be one himself if ripping off authors weren't more profitable. She drank out of his glass. Hers had been dropped into the long-haired, pedigreed rug.

"An education, wit, style. They make me aware I haven't got things like that."

"Bloody elitists."

"I don't normally think of what I haven't got. Sometimes I watch him hold the little girl and I wish I were she. The loving touches."

"You've had too much to drink. You should lie down." He took off her dress. "What is it you have to free? Is it something trapped in Gerry?" He swept his hands over her breasts.

"It's his longing for passion. He was taken over by her a long time ago. Something—sometimes he looks at me with her eyes."

"Guilt."

He pushed her down gently. She tried to make love but there was not one thing in him that resembled Gerry. She felt forlornly for the broad, silky back, the strong thighs. She knew whatever bad thing she did it wouldn't be enough. It wouldn't purge the unforgotten.

He had some kind of orgasm immediately, then lit a cigarette. "It wasn't much fun for you, poor one."

"Don't be silly. Forget it happened."

"I meant the de Santos dinner party."

At the end of the drinking bout, she felt sick and exhausted. She still loved Gerry and yearned for what he had given—still gave—to another woman.

* * *

Going out was the same as staying in. The things inside her head didn't change. She retreated into her imagination and made love with him. Every taunting caress, every possible seduction, all the things he had taught her could never be forgotten. She longed for his small, delicate hands—astonishing, the pleasure they gave. He seemed close and real. Perhaps because she needed someone to be close and real.

He'd gone to a place he called New York, leaving her to survive on fantasy, filled with longing that blotted out everything, even hunger for food, even thirst. The attic seemed unreal. Nothing was real except the heartache.

Mother was also waiting, hungry for news. Why was the bride continually upstairs when the wedding was less than three weeks away? Where was the groom these days? Victoria tried to think of a report that would cause the minimum of fuss.

"We'll have to postpone the rehearsal, Mummy. Gerry's been called to New York. Sudden business." Or "Everything's fine. He's got the flu."

She washed clothes, made meals, sat in front of a television set. She was closed off, a thick skin of silence forming between her and the outer world. Behind it, she talked to him in urgent whispers. She wanted to touch him with soft, enticing thoughts. The weekend was doubly painful—two dead days she could have spent with him. All that juice and desire wasted. She was a counting person now—days, hours. She was vulnerable to horoscopes. Would the wedding take place? Only time would give the answer.

Richard Holly brought her a bottle of wine and a jar of

caviar. They sat on the floor in the attic, and he told her he felt attracted to her. Her answer—"I wish Gerry did"— displeased him.

"But he's gone away."

"Only for a few days," she promised. She was so full of fantasy, her real life was gray nothingness.

Richard helped make dinner. He whisked the vinaigrette for the avocados while taunting Victoria with innocent references to Gerry's first marriage.

"You ought to have a good marriage with him. After all, Ruth did. Well, I went there enough and never saw a hint of discord."

"Her ashtrays," she said absently. "He used to be angry when they were full."

"How trivial."

After dinner he let her win at backgammon. "He pampered her physically. I once found him massaging her body with oil. They always took a bath together. Does he still do that?"

Ruth, Gerry, James, Alice. She was always getting love meant for someone else.

The literary agent didn't bother trying to make love to her again. As a parting shot, he said, "You might be young and exciting, but don't fool around in there. You're not in their league. Ruth Holt, even dead, is too strong for you. Whatever you offer him in bed won't compete with fifteen years of fantasy. She can't be replaced."

*   *   *

The glorious evening had passed and with it the guilt about not going out. It was dark and Victoria felt as though it were the middle of the night, but she felt like that most of the time anyway recently. For three days she hadn't gone out. She wished there would be some sign he still cared for her, some word, even someone else's word.

She thought of his delicate, caring hands. If only he would heal the longing with a few sweet words. . . .

By morning, the depression had gone into her body, making it heavy and sick. Compared with her, even Mother seemed lively. Hope had kept her going. Without it, she might have given up, gone in another direction. Friday passed, and she knew he was back. Her life was waiting, waiting. Is it because I'm meant to learn patience? What is it I have to learn? If you take away hope, what is there? What if there's just this—the attic, the wintry summer day, no love, just sadness, aging, death?

As Gerry had said, to survive you had to be self-determining. She started looking for a job. If she got full-time permanent work, perhaps the transitory, dangerous people would leave her alone. She wrote letters applying for staff positions on London newspapers and magazines.

Richard Holly, dressed in a soft, innocent-green suit, stopped by with a proposal. "Marcia Montgomery, who handles the British side of a well-known American theatrical agency, is looking for some help. The office is in Belgravia. It could be interesting."

"What sort of help? Personal assistant?"

"Not quite. You answer the phone and look at films and shows she can't get to. It's a start. But you have to be permanent. You might get some experience in the distribution office."

"Where's that?"

"Near Paddington Station."

She thanked him and said she'd think about it. He tried to kiss her before she shut the door.

"By the way, I saw de Santos the other night."

She knew he was setting a trap to get a reaction. If he had his way, she'd be in his arms half the night, crying. Still, she rushed toward it.

"Where?" Color crept into her cheeks.

"He was crossing the street near Worcester College, in Oxford."

"Which day?"

"Monday."

"Not possible. He was in New York." She tried to resist his watery green, aquarium eyes looking at her with contempt because she'd deteriorated so.

"Break it off, Vee. If it's your mother you're worried about, I'll handle that for you."

She lay on the bed and felt deeply ashamed. She'd failed to get love. Because she was so needful of affection she'd misread the light in Gerry's eyes. It was no more than a mirage experienced by a dehydrated person stumbling across a desert. He had left her.

In her wishworld she'd made love to him in trains, in lavatories, in cars. They'd done it in foreign hotels. He'd covered her with flowers. Then she remembered he still loved his wife.

* * *

Because her thoughts were elsewhere, she found herself unexpectedly in Mother's company.

"He's gone, hasn't he? Just buggered off?"

Victoria disliked the calm tone. In the past it had heralded tremendous madness and upset.

Mary got up from the sofa and said quietly, "What have you done with your fiancé, Vee? You're making Mummy ill."

"You hang around waiting all day for that middle-aged Red." No description did the don justice. "You're the laughingstock of the Bonham-Hays. So where is he?" she screamed.

Victoria ran out of the house and across the town. In the afternoon, she found a deserted park. Weak sun filled the well-behaved space with lemon light.

She thought about the first black Sunday at Crowsley. There was something she should have taken notice of. The rose garden, the don, the family, all that opulence. It was warning me, whatever it was. Sometimes it almost comes into my mind. Something half learned, half remembered.

For one evening she tried to live with Richard Holly and found there were worse things than staying in her room on her own. After two hours, they both admitted the domestic effort was a mistake. He left the room while she prepared dinner. She was making moaning noises, deep, painful sighing so horribly reminiscent of her mother. It occurred to her that Mother was rising up to her surface. It was like one of the magic painting books where a design was printed on the page. Wet it and another, the true one, seeped through, obliterating the original.

She didn't spend the night. Neither of them saw any point poisoning the hours of darkness with their hopeless incompatibility.

The wedding, a huge scaffold, had been added to every day for months. Overnight, the building supporting it had been taken away. The vast construction stood alone for one short hour, then it swayed, only slightly, before crashing to the ground. Mother was left with hundreds of guests, wedding presents, an orchestra, photographers, royal visitors.

"He's in Oxford. I know he's in Oxford!" Mother was demented.

If he was in Oxford, Victoria had lost him. That was what the silence meant.

She remembered her favorite aunt disappearing. Up to heaven, they said. It always sounded a train ride away, like Brighton. She thought other losses should be handled in the same way. You got on with things out of a sense of duty. Death hadn't taken him away, life had.

She phoned the theatrical agency and made an appointment to see Marcia Montgomery, then she crouched down and put her head in her hands.

"Oh, Gerry!" She got up and wrote thank-you notes to her cousins, the Bonham-Hays. "Yes, everything is marvelous. Yes, I am so happy. In ten days I will be Mrs. de Santos."

Even the wishworld was evaporating. The daydreams had worn thin. No safety anymore. No life she could control.

"You'll have to do something about Mummy," said Mary. "It's not fair. Can't you find someone who could talk to him? Influence him?"

The influential people in his life were both dead.

Downstairs, her mother lay bloated with depression. Victoria made her some soup but the fat woman refused to eat.

"Who's going to tell the Bonham-Hays? Tell me that."

Victoria tried to spoon the soup into her mouth. She felt deeply sorry for the distress she'd caused but was unsure how to put it into words.

* * *

Colin flapped a dish towel at the professors, herding them toward the garden.

"You should have rung, Victoria, and saved yourself the trip. I could have told you he wasn't here."

"What's going to happen, Colin?"

He looked upset and banged some saucepans about.

"It's making my mother ill."

"I'm sure it is, Victoria, but it isn't your fault. It's not the first time in history a man has left a woman at the altar. Well, we can't have everything we want."

"Why not? I think we should have everything we want."

"Oh no, Vee. Life isn't like that." He stood in the fog of boiling vegetables, his voice unfriendly.

"I'm trying to get work on a paper. I'm sure if I keep trying—"

"You have to make do with what you've got."

"What if you need other things?" Victoria asked.

"Need? *Need?* Life isn't supposed to give you what you need. If you haven't got it, do without it. Go on a diet."

The professors, like a flock of startled birds, swooped up and off with dry, multisyllable cries. The dogs slipped away. Colin smacked the kettle onto the stove.

"I read some of your reviews, the ones you did before Gerry started interfering. You've got a voice. Oh yes, you have. The trouble is, it'll be your voice but his songs."

"But he's helping me. It's very good of—"

"Good? Gerry *good!*" he shrieked. "From good men good things happen. Think what happens around him. That's why he's so deeply distressed." Colin pretended the soup was doing something dangerous and turned off the stove.

"Is he distressed?"

"Was, not is."

"Why do you stay, Col?"

"I'm just hung up on him, as I know you've pointed out countless times behind my back. I sort of got sucked into what he was doing. It's a family weakness." He stopped abruptly. "I want to stay on the right side of things here. Gerry makes me feel safe. I'm not confronted with anything in this kitchen. When I was in school I was given the wrong impression about a lot of things. Homosexuality, for instance. We were simply told that sort of thing did not exist except among dogs. I've never heard of a homosexual dog. So, if I want to wear an apron, it's fine with Gerry. Lilly's a gunman's daughter, but that's okay, too. He's very accepting about some things."

"And others?"

"He's good at getting everybody doing what he thinks they should. My sister didn't perform after four years of marriage to him. And music was—well, breathing came first."

"He's really not here, is he?"

She felt like a would-be mistress in hot pursuit, rather than bride-to-be.

"No, he's not in. He's in New York, honey." The "honey" was hostile and showed her she was an outsider again. She got up and left.

He was there. She'd never been so sure of anything.

The rose garden looked ordinary. Even tawdry. It looked like a showing of faded cloth flags. How could she have been frightened? It was a vegetable existence in her control, in anyone's control. Had it backed off, become something innocent and humble, now that she was defeated?

She sat down by the pond. It had belittled her because she was a nothing. "Yes, I'm ordinary. Not even talented. No one will notice my dying. I'm not a rose. A weed is more like it."

Birds sang, happy.

Professor Gully pushed open the gate. When he saw Victoria, he got on his bike and sped away.

CHAPTER · 29

WHY HAD GERRY STOPPED HIS WIFE FROM PERFORMING IN public? Because he wanted her available only for himself?

When Victoria had asked about Ruth Holt, Sarah Kingsley-Roe would only talk about her own problems.

"Every time I started to paint, Simon would come into the room. He wanted to know something, or someone was on the phone, or a baby wouldn't stop crying, or he wanted his lunch."

Was she a monstrous egoist or was she just trying to say something without being explicit? "I'm never explicit, darling. Gets one into trouble." Her husband was a journalist, mostly out of the house. He didn't stop her from painting.

She had been talking about Ruth.

It had been more than a week since Victoria had seen Gerry, and it had taken that time for the love she felt to harden into obsession. The juices of insecurity and sexual tension kept it going. Obsession was a gobbling black hole. The way to conquer it was to regain ground. No more fantasies about screwing. Do more in the day—housework, talking to people, walking, reading. There were other men in the world. The thing was when she was depressed, there only seemed to be one.

She was washed out from waiting. Even if he did call, her words were now too prepared, the salacious speeches past their prime.

Her old cat waited for its food and looked at her with the

same greenish, reproachful expression as Richard Holly. Her life was poisoned by absence.

If I could just understand him. You nearly always forgive once you understand.

Someone had persuaded Mother to sit up on the sofa. She sat at the very end, her eyes staring into some hellish place where the Bonham-Hays were putting on their best, expecting a wedding. No, she was sadder than that. All the unhappiness of her life was in her face.

Victoria said, "The earl mustn't be upset. I appreciate that."

"I wish I were dead, out of it," Mother whimpered behind closed eyes. Her chilled skin went blue. For a moment she looked as though she'd get her wish.

Victoria felt the way she had at six, when Mother had had a breakdown. Age hadn't made any difference in the reaction. It was still panic. Shaking, Victoria called for the chef.

She knew she'd have to come to terms with her mother. She would have to get near enough to say what she loved about her, how sorry she was it had gone wrong between them. Even if she only accused her of being a bad mother, the past would have to be put right, before it was too late. If she could not make this statement, she would be bound forever in hopeless, tangled ambiguity with every woman she met.

She tried to hold her mother's hand. What have I done? Reduced this glutton to the point where she's so sad she's even off her food? All because I took a wrong turning . . .

The chef rushed in with Walter Guinea close behind, and Mother tried to stand up.

"I must get something down me. I must get something down me."

"Don't let any of this be known outside the house," said Walter Guinea.

Victoria crept to the door. Mother called her back. Quite distinctly, she said, "I understand about being the least favored. I had a successful sister, too, don't forget. She could have had anybody. She was so pretty. That's why I wanted you to have the better wedding. Why should your sister have everything? You're hard to love, Victoria, but I do love you."

"Oh, Mummy!" She couldn't bear it. She must say something about the past. "You sent me away, don't forget. You kept sending me away."

"I wasn't well enough to look after you. You were a mistake."

Sunlight filled the doorway. It had the same haunting quality as it had that first Sunday in Crowsley. Is that what sunshine became when it entered a sad house?

Victoria phoned Richard Holly. Even mistakes could fight back.

"About Gerry's first marriage. You said that whatever I offered in bed could not compete with fifteen years of fantasy. That's a strange thing to say."

" 'Fidelity'—you misheard."

"What do you mean?" She knew she hadn't misheard.

"Exactly what I said. He's always been faithful to Ruth. Death didn't make any difference. Some people are like that."

The professors had hinted at existences she'd never dreamed of with their indecipherable conversation. Crowsley was constantly full of references to possible solar systems and behavior beyond the limitations of time and space. In one of these spheres, Ruth waited.

* * *

Robert Gittes came to visit Mother. He was already talking about Ruth so all Victoria had to do was find a chance to speak with him privately.

"She dismissed the Grieg as cheap stuff."

Mother fingered a dozen expensive presents. "I understood she had to play what her sponsors favored. I gather her sponsors were quite intrusive. But then Sicilians are musical." Mother was no fool. Robert was glad to be out of her presence.

"So this is the funny little attic Gerry likes so much."

"And this is the funny little bride who's going to be left at the altar."

"Don't be silly. He's having to give a little thought to the future, that's all."

"The future will all be used up if he stays away much longer. Nine days."

"He's a serious person. If you want the truth, he's dealing with the urgent problem of self-disgust." He made a gesture of washing his hands. Confession time was over, as far as he was concerned.

"Where have you been?" Victoria asked.

"I'm sorry?"

"You disappeared."

"I went to Atlantic City."

"Oh, I thought it was Boston."

He sighed.

"I bet you haven't been farther than the Randolph Hotel in Oxford."

"Oh, I don't want to get into it, Victoria. It's Gerry's business."

"I want to know why people say his marriage was so happy."

"It was."

"Tell me the unhappy part."

"The roses blooming made her depressed. . . . I'll see you on the big day. Have a good rehearsal—have it the day he gets back."

"I talked to Ruth Holt's best friend, Sarah. It seems Gerry stopped her career."

"Yeah, well . . . I didn't know you knew Sarah. I'm surprised she'd say a thing like that."

"She felt it only right to talk to me."

Encouraged by Sarah's revelations, he added some of his own. "Poor Ruth. Well, what can I say? She put everything into him, that's right. And what thanks did she get? When she was successful he smothered her. He threw a blanket over her as though he were putting out a fire."

"Why?"

"How could he expect her to live without her music? That's what I want to know."

"She didn't."

"Gerry should tell you all this."

"He should, but he doesn't."

"I like you, Victoria, and I'll tell you something that happened at Crowsley. It will sound a little fantastic. I didn't feel easy there because I went into his bedroom on the first night after she died, and he was lying on the bed. There was a woman there. I saw her quite clearly, taking off a white dress. Do you know—it was Ruth. He was watching her. But he wouldn't talk about it. 'Don't be silly,' he said. 'It's only a reflection in the mirror. Just turn the light off.' The next day he denied the whole thing. Just paranoia.

"He stopped her music. It's as simple as that."

So someone else had seen the ghost. But her relief was hardly noticeable. She no longer needed proof. Now she was more interested in Gerry. She asked Gittes why he had stopped Ruth's music.

"He couldn't bear her to have a life apart from his. Something died in that lady even before she died. It started off innocently enough. He said she couldn't leave James, she mustn't do any more foreign concerts. Then she mustn't play in London. He only wanted her to play for him."

"But he doesn't like music."

"He did then."

"But why was he so possessive?"

"I've thought about it. Perhaps he couldn't bear the applause because it wasn't for him."

"It's such a long time ago."

"Yes, isn't it. But it's not every day of your life that you can silence music."

Then she knew that the marriage had not been happy whatever anyone said. Why had the wife's smoking made him angry? Because he believed she was flaunting her dissatisfaction. A bedroom full of smoke, a million unshed tears. The smoking was the tip of the iceberg. It drew her back to Crowsley. Gave her hope again. About happiness, she could do nothing. But if he was haunted by remorse, Gerry could be rescued.

*　*　*

James was walking in the garden. A book, a drink, letters to be answered on the table were ignored. He seemed at loose ends. He wasn't sure where Lilly was. The child, too, was absent.

"Are you accepting the Oxford job?" Victoria asked.

He didn't answer.

"So, your father will bring up Ruthie? Is that really going to happen?"

"Really? Real? He doesn't know what, if anything, is real inside himself, let alone outside. He avoids reality."

"Where is he now?" she asked sharply.

"New York."

"That's about as real as the rest of it, James."

He sighed. "Oh, look, I don't want to get into it. I'm not taking the Oxford job. I'm staying in Boston. Lilly and my child come with me. Dad will just have to make the best of it.

I'm not giving up. I may not be the best administrator in the world, but I'm not going to be manipulated."

"But Johnny Pass? The Mafia? It's not good for a child." She was using Gerry's point of view because she believed it was right.

"He should have thought of that twenty years ago."

When she told him his father had stopped his mother from performing, he was surprised. The surprise caused indiscretions.

"Look, Vee, I hated my mother, if you want to know. She was constantly unfaithful to Dad. She went with anybody."

Victoria shook her head. "I don't believe it."

"I know it as surely as I'm looking at that prairie rose J.P. brought over. Why do they make such a thing of roses? My mother hated them. She destroyed the white Chinese climbing rose. She got out of her bed and around to the wall somehow. She tore it down, into pieces. She mashed up the petals. Her poor hands were all cut. And she was so ill. How did she get the strength? She was so full of hate, she actually uprooted it. No one knows how she even got out the back door. She must have dragged herself along the floor. She used to cry out, 'I hate those stinking roses. Shut the window!' My father cleared up the mess of that climbing rose and hid it in the compost heap, but Lilly noticed it was gone. That's why she keeps on about it now. She's jealous. Because he's getting married."

"Why did your mother turn against him?"

"I expect she liked screwing around. She did it enough."

She saw Colin pretending he wasn't there. He was crouching below the level of the stove so he could turn the kettle off the instant it whistled. She pushed open the back door, and he acted as though he was just picking something up off the floor.

"Just in time for tea." He tried to smile.

"Where's Gerry?" She sat down. "I expect he's in the part of Oxford called New York."

She told him what she'd just learned from James. One person's indiscretion caused other revelations, effortlessly.

"My sister never screwed around, honey. No, I won't have that. James, poor boy, hasn't understood, and why should he? If you want a true picture, you must talk to Gittes."

"You could tell me."

"He has an independent view. I can't trust myself to be impartial. He's Gerry's best friend. That's what best friends are for."

Jealousy had driven Gerry to the music room to interrupt with what seemed rational requests at the time. They paid a price for their marriage and he was still paying it. "Then you came along," Colin said. "You satisfied his middle-aged desire for company and at the same time, you were not strong enough to change the status quo. Another girl might change things. You were meek. It was beautiful the way you retreated to the edges of the house, disturbing nothing."

"Do you think the house is haunted, Colin?"

"Of course not. But there was so much hatred and deception when Ruth was alive. Where could it all go? It had no conclusion. She died before—"

"But what was this hatred? Whose?"

Victoria wasn't aware that Gerry had come into the room. Colin looked faint and sat down suddenly. She thought it was the effort of remembering.

"Whose hatred?"

"Well . . . hers, I suppose. Is that what you want me to say?" He watched Gerry coming up behind Victoria.

"You say what you want," she said, realizing something more serious was wrong.

Gerry said, "He's never said what he wanted to in his life."

Colin burst into tears.

She couldn't turn around. She couldn't think of one thing to say. Colin sobbed noisily.

Gerry touched her shoulder and was about to make some kind of greeting. She turned then and hit him hard in the face.

Colin ran out braying with fear. She hit Gerry again with all her strength. And again. She didn't stop until she was exhausted. Then she asked questions, dozens of them.

He just stared at her, his nose bleeding. In the end she said, "What are you?"

He didn't like that one either.

"Well, you can say what you are, can't you?"

"A widower."

CHAPTER · 30

Gerry made Victoria a cup of tea, then told her a joke. She joined in the laughter, hers more shallow. Was she really here or was this one of her daydreams?

"How is your mother?"

"Not at her best. We haven't had the rehearsal and—" Two lone tears splashed onto her hand.

"Well, then, let's do it," he said simply.

"So, is that the conclusion you came to in New York?"

"I didn't go to New York." He had nothing else to say.

It was a relief after the huge fantasies to have the object of them stand opposite her, to find he was just flesh and blood. The reality of it soothed her. The afternoon light revealed all the secrets of his face. Everything was clear and at her disposal.

"Is that what you really want, Gerry?"

"I don't want to hurt you. That's what I really want."

Victoria thought, in spite of everything, he could be a nice man.

"So you will do this rehearsal and go through with this wedding ceremony?"

He nodded.

Why did he suddenly allow her to dominate him? Guilt. Guilt because he was secretly still loving his wife. The others knew, without knowing. Because something was secret did not mean it didn't exist. It could be nosed out, sensed, then responded to, without the simplicity of confession. Events set vibrations going which could be experienced. Then they led to an awareness of the event itself. He was a man having a passionate, forbidden affair with the specter of his dead wife. He made love to her regularly. People responded to that.

He went to bed first and she stood near the window, wondering whether to lie beside him. How best to touch him? His eyes were shut, his face sensitive and very pale. In spite of everything, she was dying to touch him. She moved toward the bed.

"Come to bed, darling. You're tired. Try and sleep." He touched her hand in friendship.

When he was asleep, she reopened the tin chest and looked at the photographs of Gerry and Ruth together. Couples always looked so complete, so engrossed in their pleasure. Seeing two people close together still caused her an involuntary stab of pain which no amount of experience could quite dull.

One of Ruth's letters described her feelings the day after they'd first made love. "Happiness made me do things I would never have thought of. The wind would have lifted me if I'd found the right way to let go. With you, that high, joyful morning in the garden, even gravity could be defied. After all, in my dreams I fly. You'll be the last thing I see as I lie dying, the last memory I let go of. You are the one sunny thing in me."

And yet she had died full of hate! If they were so happy, what went wrong? Ruth and Gerry, the happy diners in the old postcard—and Victoria, the beggar girl on the outside, looking in. What happened when they got up from the table? What turning did they weakly pursue in the snow, mistaking it for the main road?

Victoria shut the tin chest. Of course, hope was deceptive. She'd discovered that. Promise was better.

Before going home in the morning, she was tempted to

leave a note: "If you want me, the rose garden will have to go."

* * *

He wasn't there when she got back to Crowsley in the evening. He had been there, so she supposed he was avoiding her. His suit was laid out ready for the rehearsal the next day. His new shoes were brightly polished.

The child was mashing up a worm by the back door. She pretended not to remember Victoria. She was pale and very silent and going back to Boston.

"I don't think he's coming home, hon," said Colin. "You'd better go now while it's still light. You've got a lot to do to be ready for tomorrow."

Before she left, Victoria sat in the rose garden. "I feel sorry for you, Ruth. I almost know you now. I don't want to take your place. I want to keep you alive for him." She talked to the garden as though it were the first wife. She assured it she was a generous person, prepared to share. As she didn't feel any better after the speech, she assumed the deal was not on. But there was a discernible pressure in the air that had not been there before. She felt low, uneasy, realizing that the presence was not a benign one. What was left of Ruth hung around at the edge of death, waiting for her husband.

* * *

As she stood beside Gerry in the church, Victoria knew he hated her. She was alive and Ruth wasn't. He did not once look her in the eyes. He did plenty of deep sighing.

Sylvia assured her it was nerves. She knew about those. She'd had the worst hangover of her life and had been sighing for a week. Sylvia told the minister she did not believe in God. Mother sat down and said Sylvia had been born that way.

While the minister talked to Gerry, Mother gave Victoria

the correct order for guests to be presented to the royal visitors.

"The first ones arrive at three-fifteen and join the formal receiving line. Why does Gerry look so distant? Is he part of this or not?"

Victoria joined him at the altar and the minister went through the ceremony, explaining the meaning of the vows. Victoria spoke softly to her fiancé.

"Why are you marrying me? I mean, I'm in love with you. Is that enough?"

Gerry didn't answer.

"Do you, Victoria Jane, take this man . . ."

"I do."

" . . . love, honor and obey . . ."

As she said "I will" she thought of the Brighton clairvoyant. Well, I said it. I said "I will."

Then Gerry said it.

"Now the choir is joined by the congregation . . ."

"You may kiss the bride." Gerry smiled at her instead. He still wasn't looking into her eyes. She remembered how she once wanted to hear from him, hold him, lie with him, die in his arms before she died in him. She remembered good things, the jokes, the seaside days. She thought about the way he had sat reading to her when she was ill. Not a lot of good things, but she could make one good thing go a long way.

"Now, Victoria, you take his arm and lead the procession down the aisle."

If she could concentrate on the good things she might find the way to make everything all right. If she could be strong, stronger than he, she could do it. The trouble was, she'd thought he was perfect. Now she'd come to believe there were no good people, just some good in everyone. The secret of success was finding that good.

She decided to talk to him after the rehearsal, but as soon as it was over, he waved a small good-bye and left. He had a college meeting in Oxford.

Was it seeing his rude departure that made Mother collapse? All at once, Sylvia came into her own. She moved the bridesmaids away and helped Mother back to herself. As she came around, Mother said, "I never thought we'd actually do it. Get those two in church."

"I think we should get you to the hospital. Let them have a look at you. We want you all right on the big day."

* * *

There was considerable delay when they arrived at the hospital entrance because no one could find a wheelchair that would fit Mother. It took five people to carry her into the emergency room. Several doctors had a look at her, more through curiosity than need. How could such a mountain of greed survive when more frugal people did not? She lied about her eating habits and got the attending doctor to agree with her that three meals a day was hardly abnormal.

When they got outside, Mother was quite cheered up. "Well, at least that doctor proved something. I'm not a compulsive eater."

Because she was late getting home, Victoria missed two calls from the theatrical agency. Marcia Montgomery would not be available to see Victoria as arranged. Could she come this afternoon at five-thirty?

Victoria took the train to London. She couldn't get her mind off Gerry. It was always the same picture. He was by himself, it was cold, and he was being pushed farther and farther into the snow. All around were howling wolves. Everything in him was finished. There was nothing alive in him anymore. His last breath was only a matter of time.

The dark, rangy brunette from the movie-theater lobby walked into the agency waiting room and introduced herself as Marcia, friend of Richard Holly and personal assistant to the president of the company, Patrick Williams. She did not remember Victoria.

She showed her the office, outlined the duties. She was worried about Victoria starting so soon if she was just about to get married.

"You have to be full-time so I'd sleep on that one." Her voice was low and American. "Anyway, you'll have to meet with the president. He's usually in the L.A. office or New York, but he's in this week. However, he's in conference right now. You could come by to say hello toward the end of the week when he gets back from Paris. He has to okay all new personnel. When he's in London he's usually in the distribution office near Paddington Station. You could see him there."

Before she left, Victoria asked Marcia if she remembered the retrospective of *The Godfather* two years previously. Did she remember standing in the theater lobby with a man slightly shorter than she, with streaked hair?

"Oh, I go to so many previews. I meet more people in a year than the average human being sees in his entire lifetime."

"The man had blue eyes—"

"You sure you want to be full-time?"

"The man looked like Gerry de Santos and—"

"Streaky hair? Blue eyes? I can't place him."

Both elevators were in use so Victoria walked down. Would she come back to this place? Could she be permanent?

She started down the last flight. That's when the excitement began. She turned the final curve of the stairs in full view of the revolving door.

He was there. The original Mr. Right. Two years had not changed him.

He stood with three men waiting for his turn to enter the building. Too many home-bound secretaries had squeezed in together and the door was jammed. There was a lot of giggling while one got out. He was deeply interested in what the men were telling him and did not notice the women. He was still talking as he crossed the hall.

He was bigger than Gerry. His eyes were not gray; they were pale blue. He was older. He didn't move like Gerry. He didn't have death around him, either. As he had on Paddington Station, he unwrapped a pack of cigarettes.

As he approached the elevator, he turned and saw her. He stopped talking and stared at her with some surprise. Intrigued, he looked again before the sliding doors shut him away. She thought he smiled.

She knew he was Patrick Williams, the agency president, but still she asked the receptionist his name. She decided to be permanent.

CHAPTER · 31

SHE WENT BACK TO GERRY BECAUSE SHE'D FOUND THE WAY TO make everything right. If he could face the reality of his past, Ruth would be exorcised. Gerry was innocent. He had not foreseen the consequences of his actions.

He was lying on the bed when she came in. Colin was somewhere in Oxford with James, packing trunks. James was flying his family back to Boston the next day; he thought it best not to wait the five days for the wedding.

Gerry was not exactly pleased to see her. He couldn't deal with anything anymore. He looked at his watch.

"Eight o'clock."

There was another note propped on the bedside table. He didn't try to stop her from reading it. " 'Lady I take record of God/in thee I have had mine earthly joy.' "

"Who wrote that?"

"Thomas Malory." He sighed.

In spite of her new intentions, she was angry.

"James Hamilton made love better than you. At least his words were his own."

He got up slowly. "Do you want something to eat? Have you eaten at all today?"

She took a deep breath. "I have to make a decision. It's about a job and being permanent. First I must ask you something about Ruth. Colin said you stopped her being—"

He turned on her savagely. "Don't tell me what I did to my wife. I loved her. I knew my wife."

"But Ruth thought—"

"Don't you dare tell me what she thought!" Furious, he rushed from the room.

She found him by the back door feeding the dogs. She couldn't get what she wanted from him—in this case, healing revelations about his original love. She didn't have the confidence or the power to make him talk. She didn't even have the nerve. It was not much fun being cut off from him either, as Lilly had found.

"Shall I just leave then? Shall I just fuck off? There's a job I can get. I'll take the job." She was in a losing position again and tried to locate her newfound strength.

"It was lovely at first, wasn't it, Victoria. Especially in bed."

"Then you had to make sure I was no good. I must not take her place."

"But I did not know you could not take her place. What I'm trying to say is that when it all began with you I had no idea the other thing was still there. I've tried my best to work it out, Vee. That's why I needed time alone. I don't see why I shouldn't be happy with someone else, but I do belong to her and that's the truth."

"She's dead!" Victoria said angrily. "And I know all about the rose garden. Your guilt produced those flowers. They're evil. That's why they turn . . . Guilt keeps you alive. You shouldn't be alive. You only like the dead. And I know you had a terrible marriage."

"Wrong! The first years were exquisite."

"Then why did you make her stop playing?"

"Because I couldn't share in her world. There was no place for me. I felt left out, very much in the cold. I was unnecessary and had to be dealt with, humored. I can never forget that feeling. The terrible feeling of being left out. You wouldn't know about that."

"I know all about that. I have felt it here so many times. But you have to come in out of the cold. You must do it yourself. No one is going to invite you in."

"Why on earth didn't you say more about it?"

"It's not a position that makes you talkative. I felt ashamed."

He held her gently.

"Is that why you're guilty? Because you stopped her music? I mean, she wouldn't have gone off for long. How many weeks were involved with these concert tours?"

"I was sexually mad about her. That's the truth."

Out of all the hurt of the spring and summer, that moment was the worst. However bad the marriage had been, there was a lot of passion in it. She'd always known that.

"Weren't you shocked when she died?"

"Furious. Fury that she could be taken away. Someone so perfect. And yet there's so much mediocrity still around. We had an ecstatic marriage. Whoever told you otherwise should not be trusted."

"You think about her when you make love, don't you?"

"I try and keep that private. Something that's just for me. I don't choose to think about her. She comes to me. . . ."

Jealousy made Victoria say, "I heard that you smothered her and in revenge, she went off with other men. It doesn't sound that ecstatic to me."

"She wanted to get back at me. That was where I was vulnerable. She had nine men a day, then locked me out of the bedroom. I hated her then. But those were the last years."

"If only you'd face it, Gerry."

"Face it? What do you think I do every day of my life? Suppressed hatred causes cancer. Didn't you know? All right, I did break her career, so she broke my heart. I'm telling you all this, and it is the truth, because I owe it to you. I couldn't bear the musical world taking her away, so she didn't play anymore. She paid me back, though. Oh, yes. The sleeping around was very hard to live with. I did not know, I had no idea that stopping someone gifted from practicing that gift was harmful."

"Why do you say you made her ill? Couldn't she just have had a weakness? You did what you could. The rose garden—"

"They said in the seventeenth century that an exhalation of the earth caused the plague. There seemed no other explanation for it. She was so young. There was no other reason why she should get cancer and be taken from me. In the plague years, they believed that if you could surround yourself with a different air you could combat infection. And they weren't altogether wrong. You have to change something to get something. That's why I made the air sweet around her."

"I understand she destroyed the white rose."

"She got that one because it was outside her window. She tore it into pieces. She was so sick and I don't know how she got the strength. Poor little James was badly frightened. She hated roses by then, she hated me."

He veered between the time when she hated him and the time when he loved her the most. Nothing was said about the years in between.

"I must say, Victoria, that if I'd known what I know now, I would not have asked you to be my wife. I went into it wholeheartedly, believe me."

"So, we can't marry then?" Her voice was small.

"I was most aware of her that night when you were made ill by the roses. So I tried for a simpler wedding. I felt if everything was reduced, she'd go away, be at peace. I did what I could. But she started competing with you, ridiculing you. I changed the time of our making love. Night was when she got to me, particularly when we'd made love well. That happened with other women, too. Once or twice over the years I brought one here, and if it was good, she was there. I was obsessed by her when she was alive. After her death I supposed I was free, naturally. I've come to realize that I'm bound forever."

"But she's gone." Not true. Hadn't she seen the wife in the bedroom?

"She's very good at ridicule. She ran off with Robert, good old Robert. Then she got sick and had to come back. But now, when she comes to my bed, it's the way it was at the beginning. We got all the good things back in the end. Ruth isn't quite dead. That's the trouble."

The darkness thickened. The windows were opaque. He told her about the first time he realized Ruth was still around him.

"I had to meet a woman outside Wigmore Hall. It was raining, so I went inside. I hadn't been there for years. It was the smell that brought it all back. I forgot about my date and left. I felt Ruth's presence, at the same time her absence, in every street I walked, every corner I turned. Like a forgotten friend, all the love and anguish I'd felt with her seemed to greet me and cling to me. Every piece of it. The fact that I'd aged twenty years didn't make it any more bearable. When I first met Ruth, every moment was glorious. They all mattered. I had her. Then I didn't have her. I can never be free. There is too much feeling . . ."

She realized he was crying, quite silently, and she longed to go over and hold him, comfort him. He sat at the corner of the table, head in his hands, forlorn. But she couldn't go near him. She'd started to believe, too, that he was not hers. The comforting was not up to her.

"And now I want to see her more than anything in this world. If I could just go and take a train or plane and go to her. Do you know, she was the first warm person I ever met, and I will never get over her." He suddenly remembered who he was talking to. "You have to pay for everything. Now I have to pay for hurting her. She died before I could put it all right."

"Let's go away from this stinking garden. She mustn't hold on to you like this. I've seen her. I've heard the awful sound." She described the woman's mouth, full of blood.

"Poor Ruth. Ruth in hell, longing for a body. She had such a lovely one when she was alive."

"Is that how you see her, then? Her mouth full of blood?"

"No," he said, very quietly. "I don't see her like that." She waited but he didn't say anything more.

"All the time she hangs on to your every thought—of course, you'll never be happy."

"It's not her holding on to me. That's what you don't understand. I hold on to her. At the end I made her promise—"

"What?"

"I shouldn't marry you, Victoria. It would not be right. I'm sorry. I'll do everything I can to help you get over it."

She tried to see out of the gleaming black windows. Almost gently, she said, "Yes, the rose garden won after all."

She asked him to call a taxi, but he wouldn't let her go. He held her hand—she must see it wasn't her fault. She was a marvelous companion and would have great happiness. She deserved passion. A lot of what she felt was right. "Of course, I'm still possessive and of course, it's wrong. I try not to be with little Ruth but—you see, I wanted my wife to love just me. I didn't want her near other people because she had some quality that attracted men. I couldn't bear it. Not deliberately—it was the way she—"

"But it's all in the past," she said savagely. "It's all to do with things that happened years ago. Nothing has happened to you in fifteen years. I don't know if she really is around you. I never did believe in ghosts or Santa Claus. She could be in your mind, and I've caught her from you. You said you wanted a new way of being alive. Why don't we just go out into the real world, take off our shoes and walk in the mud. I can't make you feel alive but I can maybe help you see things differently. I'll spend my time with you. I promise I won't take up the piano."

He almost laughed.

"I'll try if you will. We like each other. That's on our side."

He walked about the kitchen, touching things.

"I know you think my beliefs come from a women's magazine, but I know that what you're doing is wrong. Because you're stuck in the past, you're not living in the present." She was full of purpose and strength, and he reacted to that more than to her words.

"I don't know anymore, Victoria." He sighed, gave up. "Not St. Margaret's."

"Well, where?"

"The one up the road. The fortune-teller picked that one, didn't she? And the ceremony must mean something. People are gathering together for an occasion that is, after all, joyful. I haven't seen any of that in Haslemere." He held her very tight. "Oh, you're so young."

She felt light-headed and slightly elated as though she'd been through a war. He said he felt all right now. He put the kettle on and made some tea. Ten to three. She wanted to go to bed but didn't feel she should leave him.

"What would you do, Gerry, if you didn't marry me?"

"I'd go on as I am."

"In this house?"

"It's all right. When I'm alone."

"We'll make something together, you'll see," she said brightly. She felt stronger than she ever had. It was that new strength, not anything she'd said, that had influenced him.

"Do you want to eat something? I'm not as good as Colin." He put a plate of crackers and cheese on the table. She poured the tea. Suddenly, he didn't feel well and went out to get some air.

She watched him walk off to the rose garden. No, not walk, he was drawn there. She drank the tea and thought of the picture of the beggar girl. She found it touching that Gerry had once felt as she had. She thought about that first sunny day again. How left out she had felt by the glories of the weather and Gerry's love.

Advantage had not been taken that day. That day was the path they never took, into the rose garden. Something they never did, couldn't find. And because the day was not used properly, it became just a setting for another scene, a reminder of something else. A scene from some film. She almost remembered—roses, opulence. Suddenly, she was scared.

Barefoot, she ran across the grass. A scanty dew had made it moist. She could see someone in the rose garden, near the pool. She thought it was Gerry bending over. Then she saw it was a woman.

"Lilly!"

She could see the splendid breasts. As she watched, the figure disappeared. It didn't move; it switched off, pinged out like a spent light bulb. For some seconds she could still see the faint radiance where it had been etched against the bushes. There was no sign of Gerry so she approached the place where the woman had stood.

He was lying on his back and as he'd fallen, he'd pulled

down part of a rosebush. A creeper was tangled in his hair, another tore at his legs. It seemed he'd had a heart attack. His expression was one in which surprise, welcome, horror, were mixed evenly.

* * *

The ambulance attendant closed Gerry's eyes. Most of the horror disappeared. After a while he looked quite peaceful, which was, after all, what he'd always wanted.

Victoria said she'd wait in the house for James and Colin. The theme she couldn't remember was the death of the don in the garden in *The Godfather*. It had been present every day of that summer.

Out of habit, she went into the bedroom and stopped between the door and the bed at a certain angle, the one in which James had stood as his mother died. The grandchild had stood there, too, looking at the bed. Victoria watched a scene unfold, quite clearly.

She saw Ruth as she lay dying and Gerry crouched over her. The figures were distinct, yet insubstantial, like those on the negative of a photograph. It was a trick of looking, to see clearly. Gerry said, "There will never be anyone else, ever."

Ruth whispered, "Do you promise?"

"There couldn't be. In the end, we've got it back, all the love. How did it get so spoiled? It was there, wasn't it, all the time? Why were we so silly?" He sounded pleased and calm. Then he cried out, "Stay close to me, Ruth! Don't go!" The dying noise increased, and he held her hands up and tried to lift her. "I need you, Ruth."

Ruth tried to speak.

Victoria watched as the bed cleared. Every hair on her body was standing on end and her legs were stiff and trembling. She thought that that was one scene she was meant to see, had been privileged to witness.

There was still something there. She moved closer. In the

morning light she saw red rose petals lying on the bed-spread. For a moment, they'd looked like blood. She supposed they must have blown in through the window.

She walked out of the house onto the main road.

*   *   *

Johnny Pass buried Gerry in the run-down church in the village. He said, "We look after our own."